"Do you know who I am, Lord Ashwhite?"

He grinned at her, showcasing a spectacular set of ivory teeth. "I see a lady in need of a dance. They say exercise can relieve many ailments, including a corset that has been overly starched."

She tucked back a gasp at his outrageous comment and focused on the most pertinent point. "My lord, I do not dance, and since you are not aware of my status in the ton, let me inform you that I am most firmly on the shelf."

"This means you may not dance?"

"A lady always knows her place," she repeated, feeling an unnerving heat creep through her. Who was this man, and what right did he have to question her? "If you'll excuse me, I must check on my cousin."

"Not so fast."

Jessica Nelson believes romance happens every day and thinks the greatest, most intense romance comes from a God who woos people to himself with passionate tenderness. When Jessica is not chasing her three beautiful, wild little boys around the living room, she can be found staring into space as she plots her next story, daydreams about raspberry mochas or plans chocolate for dinner.

Books by Jessica Nelson

Love Inspired Historical

Love on the Range
Family on the Range
The Matchmaker's Match

JESSICA NELSON

The Matchmaker's Match

HARLEQUIN® LOVE INSPIRED® HISTORICAL

Recycling programs
for this product may
not exist in your area.

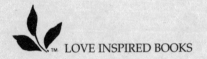 LOVE INSPIRED BOOKS

ISBN-13: 978-0-373-28329-3

The Matchmaker's Match

www.Harlequin.com

Printed in U.S.A.

We love Him, because He first loved us.
—*1 John* 4:19

Acknowledgments

Thank you, Grandma Charlene Schwirtz, for
supporting me in both word and action. Though you've
experienced terrible heartache in your life, you choose
to laugh and to love. You're a blessing!

During one of my darkest times, Someone Special
told me to surrender to God…best advice ever
(for both myself and Amelia).

A giant thank-you goes out to Robert Lee Edwards Jr.,
because he showed me the beauty of companionship.

Many thanks to my editor Emily Rodmell,
whose openness has given me a new book in print!
Plus, she makes my stories better.
Dear readers, please trust me on this.

And, of course, my heart is filled with gratitude
to God. His gentleness never ends.

Chapter One

London, England
1815

Lady Amelia Baxley admired the male species. The way they looked, their scent, the way they walked as though they owned the world—which everyone but man himself knows is a fabrication of the highest order. Yes, they were intriguing creatures to hunt.

Take this one. The new Lord Dudley looked positively dazed in Lady Havern's ballroom. His thick brown locks framed a sweet, innocent face. If only Amelia could redirect his odd interest in her, he'd be perfect for Cousin Lydia.

Straightening her gown, which kept twisting due to her maid's unfortunate antics with the needle, Amelia lifted her shoulders and tugged Lydia's arm. She strode toward the gentleman in question with Lydia in tow. An easy quarry this time. She smiled to herself as she adjusted her spectacles against the ridge of what she'd been told was quite an extraordinary nose.

"My lord," she said above the noise of the Beau Monde. "Have you been introduced to Miss Lydia Stanley?"

"Madam." He bowed, and Cousin Lydia responded with a lovely curtsy.

Things were going quite to plan. Smiling, Amelia pointed to Lydia's dance card. "I believe Miss Lydia has a spot open for the next dance. A quadrille, I presume?"

"You are indeed correct." Lydia giggled and proceeded to fan herself in a vigorous fashion. Amelia cleared her throat, and Lydia stopped. Thankfully.

A blush rose to Lord Dudley's face. Naturally he realized the prime position he was in as the new master of a prosperous earldom. Many hopeful misses would set their caps for him this Season. But Amelia was determined he give her impoverished cousin a chance. Yes, Lydia could be opinionated, but her looks were outstanding and her manner charming, if at times not quite impeccable. She deserved a good husband, one who would take care of her and her family.

Amelia gave the young earl a pointed look. His face reddened even more before he stuttered out an invitation. The music started, and the two made for the floor.

Satisfied with the outcome thus far, Amelia headed toward the balcony for a respite. Though she loved matchmaking and needed the funds to supplement her income, spending hours in a throng of overly dressed, heavily perfumed *haut ton* made her temples pound and her skin itch. How much better to curl up in a soft chair with a great book. Particularly *Sense and Sensibility*.

The author, referenced as "A Lady," inspired Amelia. Who could not help but feel moved by the sisters' plight in the story? Furthermore, she appreciated how the author emphasized the silliness of giving in to impulse. Nefarious emotions were for those without good sense.

She stepped onto the balcony and inhaled the warm, sweetly scented air. A lovely night for the Season, to be sure. Stars glittered above her and creative lanterns of varying colors had been hung within the trees, lighting a walking path for those seeking to escape the press of the ballroom.

She rested her head on her arms and let her eyes drift shut. A giggle flavored the night, followed by the low tones of a masculine voice. She listened to the variance of sound, her ear tuned to the lovely cadence of the gentleman's voice. It was soothing and deep.

She smiled to herself, then startled at the shriek that pierced the calm night. The distinct sound of a slap followed. Cringing, Amelia straightened and debated whether to run back to the ballroom or to investigate.

A rather choked version of weeping reached her. Rather than the lady striking a gentleman for behaving like a bounder, *he* must have slapped *her*! Well, that most certainly made up her mind. Amelia squared her shoulders and marched toward the sound. She rounded a jutting corner of the house and happened upon a tall, well-fashioned man who stood in front of a woman wearing an alarming number of jewels.

Indeed, they were almost blinding.

Amelia stifled her disapproval of such vanity and tapped the gentleman on the shoulder with her fan. There was simply no excuse for hitting a woman. Not even if she'd spent the last of the family funds on extravagance.

"Excuse me," she said crisply before he'd even turned around. "My breath of fresh air has been disturbed by your callous behavior. I suggest you move to the ballroom before I irreversibly damage your reputation."

She would never do such a thing, but this rogue must not know that.

In a lithe movement, the gentleman faced her. She took in the mark on his cheek and the blush on the other woman's. Obviously Amelia had been mistaken at first—the woman had slapped *him*. Had she interrupted a spat? Her eyes narrowed. The woman was…familiar somehow.

"May I introduce myself? Spencer, Lord Ashwhite." He reached for her hand. Unwilling to embarrass herself any further, or give in to bad etiquette, she allowed him to take her fingers and perform his bow.

"Lady Amelia Baxley." She pulled her hand back and offered a perfunctory curtsy. "And I do apologize for interrupting. I had thought something foul was afoot."

The woman's jewels clinked as she pointed a finger at Lord Ashwhite. "He is a cad."

"Did he harm you?" Amelia peered at the woman.

"He only has forever broken my heart," the lady declared in a decibel-shattering voice.

Her heart?

"Miss Winston is upset because I did not write to her while I was in the Americas." His wry tone held no humor.

This was quite obviously an emotional quarrel. In which case, Amelia had more productive ways to spend her time. She took in Lord Ashwhite's appearance, the way his notable green eyes appeared to flash in the moonlight. He had strong features. A firm jaw and handsome face. Thick hair of the deepest brown. At first look, he'd make a good prospect for one of her customers. Of course, she'd need to examine his character first.

Some tidbit of information niggled at her consciousness. Something she should remember about his name…

"There is nothing afoot, my lady, but an evening of dance and merriment. Please accept my apologies for disrupting your evening. Miss Winston was just leaving."

A sound that might have been outrage strangled from the woman, but after leveling a severe glare at Lord Ashwhite, she brushed past in a flurry of silk and gemstones. Amelia suppressed a shudder and wondered again why the woman struck such a discord within.

"My lady." Lord Ashwhite commanded Amelia's attention. "May I steal a dance from you later this evening? To atone for my atrocious behavior?"

Was she supposed to laugh at that? Perhaps it was a trick of the glittering stars overhead, but there seemed to be a definite flash of mischief about this gentleman. She narrowed her eyes at him, wondering if he could see past her spectacles. She'd been told she had an assertive gaze and she tried often to put it to good use.

"Do you know who I am, Lord Ashwhite?"

He grinned at her, showcasing a spectacular set of ivory teeth. "I see a lady in need of a dance. They say exercise can relieve many ailments, including a corset that has been overly starched."

She tucked back a gasp at his outrageous comment and focused on the most pertinent point. "My lord, I do not dance, and since you are not aware of my status in the *ton*, let me inform you that I am most firmly on the shelf."

"This means you may not dance?"

"A lady always knows her place," she said, feeling an unnerving heat creep through her. Who was this man, and what right did he have to question her? "If you'll excuse me, I must check on my cousin."

Indeed, the strains of music undulating from the ballroom had slowed. A new dance might begin at any moment, and she needed to find Lydia before then to ascertain the merit of Lord Dudley's courtship. She must also not let matters progress too far until she heard from her Bow Street runner on Dudley's background. Though he appeared innocent, she'd learned the hard way how deeply deceiving appearances could be.

"Not so fast." Lord Ashwhite moved toward her. His tall stature made her feel at a disadvantage. She drew herself up and met his arresting look with a firm one of her own.

"Sir, do you dare detain me?"

"I dare." He grinned. "You see, your name is familiar for some unknown reason, yet it is only now that I meet you. My curiosity has been roused. A dance might put it to rest."

"You speak in circles," she said lightly, feeling an unusual breathlessness creep into her voice.

"Surely you jest, my lady, for I have been quite clear in what I want from you." Again that roguish smile crossed his face. His eyes crinkled at the corners.

Warmth suffused Amelia, for she had not danced in years. Not since The Great Disappointment... No, she did not wish to think of that. Swallowing against myriad feelings she had no name for, she offered the gentleman before her a slight smile, preparing to reject him. She had little patience for men who went around breaking hearts. Indeed, she had little patience for men at all.

And then she spotted the enamored Lord Dudley heading toward her. She did not think she could endure another conversation with him. He simply did not take a hint.

Oh, dear. She met Lord Ashwhite's impertinent look.

"I will allow one dance with the understanding that it is probable I will step on your toes."

Was it possible for his smile to widen? For that was what his lips appeared to do, easing upward in a most disconcerting, charming way. He swept her a bow and then offered his arm. "We shall dance, then, and see if a few rounds about the floor might clear my head. Perhaps I shall realize you're not quite as fascinating as I fear."

Despite herself, Amelia chuckled. His arm felt warm and sturdy, and the merriment in his voice was catching. "Fear not. You can rest assured that by the end of our dance, you will find me both dreadfully boring and an awkward partner."

"Do not disappoint me, my lady," he warned, his tone teasing.

She patted his arm. "You, sir, will soon realize that Lady Amelia Baxley never disappoints."

The marquis of Ashwhite could not take his eyes from his dance partner. She had disappointed him terribly. Not once had her toes flattened his. In fact, as they performed the steps to the quadrille, he admired her flawless dancing. She had misled him.

What was it about this lady that provoked his attention? Not her dress, certainly, for while she wore the height of fashion, and the colors seemed acceptable enough, the dress did not stand out in any way. And the lady herself was not extraordinary.

She stood an average height with an average girth. Her hair, tucked into a respectable hairstyle for which he knew not the name, was a tame brown. She hid her eyes behind overly large spectacles.

Perhaps it had been that strident, no-nonsense tone as she'd rushed around the corner and hit him with her fan. Or maybe it was her skin, which looked like luminous velvet beneath the gentle glow of moonlight. He shook his head. Ridiculous musings.

Still, Lady Amelia had captured his respect for running to the aid of another, though misdirected. Such heroism was uncommon.

He watched her now, the graceful movements of her arms, the slender line of her neck as they completed the steps required. Yes, she had distracted him from the difficult problems that faced him. Because of a bizarre clause in his father's will, after he finished this dance, he must scan the ballroom for prospective wives. This Season had produced a mass of simpering misses whose young faces looked fresh from the schoolroom.

The music slowed and as he crossed the floor with Lady Amelia on his arm, he noticed the way a smile teased the corners of her surprisingly full lips. Her gaze flickered over to him and—was that laughter he saw in her eyes?

A most intriguing lady.

The song ended and he escorted her to the edge of the floor.

"Lord Ashwhite, I must thank you for the dance." She fanned herself, but still a blush stained her skin, turning it rose-petal soft. A beguiling creature, to be sure. "It has been much too long since I had such a delightful partner."

He inclined his head, unwilling to take his eyes off her. "Truly, it was my pleasure."

She gave him a broad smile, and then her expression stuttered as she looked past him. "Oh, dear. If you'll excuse me, I must rescue my cousin." Her features slid back into that commanding expression she'd pointed his way earlier. "Miss Stanley has no head where suitors are concerned. I have told her repeatedly not to speak with known *rakes*." She drew the last word out with a heavy distaste.

Spencer winced. So here was the downfall. Lady Amelia might make a delightful dance partner, but in the end she would prove to be as stubborn and stiff-necked as any dowager of the *ton*. And just as judgmental. With a rueful shake of his head, he turned away while she glided off to rescue her cousin.

He knew the young man with whom Miss Stanley spoke, and though his reputation might not be spotless, he certainly was no rake. A self-deprecating smile tugged at Spencer's mouth. What would the straitlaced Lady Amelia think if she found out with whom she'd danced?

It had been surprising that she hadn't recognized him by name or Miss Winston by looks. The actress was well-known amongst those who enjoyed the theater.

"Ashwhite!" Lord Liveston, Earl of Waverly, clapped him on the back, ending his ruminations. "You've arrived from the Americas, I see? How was the trip, old chap?"

"Enlightening."

"And?" Waverly's mustache twitched with mirth. "No special young ladies over there? I thought you might return with an American miss. Or at least some adventurous stories." His best friend snickered and chucked him on the shoulder again.

Spencer threw him a stern look. "I'm done with philandering."

"With what? Oh, yes, yes, I received your letter. A bunch of rubbish. Tent meetings? Yelling preachers and people repenting publicly of their sins? Why, I can't imagine such a thing happening in England. Those Americans are an untamed lot." Waverly squinted at the procession of dancers moving across the floor. "Eversham and I are about to leave for more exciting places. Care to join us?"

"I think I'll stay here," Spencer murmured. His stare centered on Lady Amelia only a few feet away, whose fan kept time with her mouth.

"You really have changed…but for how long?" Waverly followed his gaze. "She's a fine-looking lady. If I was in the mood for a wife, I'd take that one."

"Yes, she's intriguing."

"Who needs intriguing when you have beauty like that?" Waverly grinned. "Those blond curls are artfully designed to trap a man, along with his fortune."

Spencer's chin snapped up. His friend obviously had focused on Lady Amelia's cousin.

"The plain one is Eversham's twin sister, you know."

"Indeed?" Spencer tried to keep the shock from his voice. "Our friend Eversham? She's the one…"

"Yes, she's *that* one. Difficult and independent. Refuses to do anything he says. A bluestocking of the spinster sort, if you ask me."

She sounded like Spencer's mother, and he had no patience for women like that. His mother was gallivanting on the Continent at this very moment, and who knew when she'd decide to return to her home.

"The lady appears benign." His eyes narrowed on the subject of their conversation. Perhaps not so benign after all. There was a purposeful air to her as she scanned the ballroom. Like a hound nosing for a fox. He'd seen that look on his mother far too often for comfort.

"Ha, that's not what Eversham says. Though he doesn't talk much of her, apparently there was a small ruckus last week, and when we met at White's for coffee, he acted distraught." Waverly pulled out his pocket watch. "Time for a bit of sport. You're sure you won't come?"

Spencer shook his head. "I'll meet you at White's tomorrow. I need your and Eversham's help with something."

"That sounds alarming."

"Quite." He felt a glower tugging at his brow. "I met with the family lawyer today. I'll give you details tomorrow, but in the meantime, keep an ear open for eligible ladies in need of a husband."

"Don't tell me you've decided to get leg shackled?" Poor Waverly sounded distressed.

"Indeed," Spencer answered grimly. "And I've less than three months to do it."

Chapter Two

"Do you suppose I shall ever have a waltz?" Cousin Lydia swirled around the morning room, her dress fluttering precariously close to the sideboard.

"It is an impractical dance and frowned upon for a young miss fresh in her first Season." Amelia plucked a piece of bacon for her plate and tried to dismiss the sudden memory of Lord Ashwhite's hand upon her sleeve last night. She'd realized why his name prodded her conscious. He was an old friend of her brother's but had just now come into his title, hence the change of names. She knew him as Mr. Broyhill.

She eyed Lydia. "Why are you daydreaming about such a thing when we've other goals to pursue?"

"Oh, I don't know…" Lydia shrugged. "I suppose I feel like an ox on the market. Picked at and looked over. It is all decidedly unromantic."

"Which is why we will find you the perfect gentleman for your nature. He will bring you flowers in the morning and write verses devoted to your fair beauty every day." Amelia smothered her smile as she sat at the small table to read *The Morning Gazette*. She took out the gossip column and set it to the side. Sunlight bathed the simple furniture in a lovely hue perfect for a painting. Perhaps today she would have time to take out her easel and paints.

"You aren't going to read this?" Lydia flipped up the gossip column. "Why, Lord Ca—"

"Stop at once." Amelia held up her hand. "I do not partake in gossip."

"Why, Amelia, are you serious? Never?"

"Never," she pronounced, careful to add stiffness to her tone. If there was one thing that rankled her more than anything, it was the idle chatter of busybodies. She'd much rather gather the hard facts, not emotional speculations.

"But how do you find husbands? How will you know their worth?"

"Certainly their worth won't be determined by what others say about them. Would you please sit down? You're making me quite dizzy."

Lydia flounced into the chair beside her, a pout upon her pretty features. "I am not sure I want to be married, Amelia."

"Then, why do you partake of my services?" She took a bite of her bacon. Perfectly crisp and delicious. She must find a way to give a bonus to Martha for being such a wonderful cook. Perhaps if she could sell a painting soon…

"It seemed a promising idea. After my dreadful mistake, I thought perhaps I'd need help on the marriage mart. Father and Mother agreed."

"Your *mistake* was minor and quickly forgotten. Just do not take any more moonlit walks without a chaperone and mind your tongue."

"He deserved a dressing-down for taking liberties with my person." Lydia's eyes flashed with pique.

"A good swat with your fan works wonders. A true lady does not lose her temper in public and call a suitor ungentlemanly names."

Lydia uttered an amazingly loud sigh.

Ignoring the melodramatic response, Amelia continued, "In the meantime, we shall work with what we have. My particular specialty is providing young ladies with a love match." Amelia met Lydia's gaze. Her eyes were a delightful cornflower blue most men would adore gawping at. "You will not have a problem attracting admirers, but to find a man who sees past your outer beauty…that is our challenge."

"There may not be much beyond my face." A glum note entered Lydia's tone.

"Come, now." Amelia touched her hand. "You are intelligent and lively. A good man appreciates those qualities."

"And why are you not married? You possess those qualities in abundance."

Amelia tried not to groan. She finished her bacon and patted her mouth with a delicate napkin. "This is a conversation about you and not about my marital status. I am perfectly happy with the shelf I have set myself upon."

"Is that so?" A mischievous spark glinted in Lydia's eyes. She leaned across the table. "Then, why did I see you dancing last night? And with an eligible marquis, no less?" A smirk hovered across her face.

"That was nothing," Amelia said firmly, though her nerves felt afire. "I saw an overzealous suitor practically running toward me and needed an escape route. Lord Ashwhite is an old friend of my brother's. Dancing was a deviance from the norm, I assure you."

"I have never seen you dance before. You were lovely.

So very graceful. The gentleman looked quite enraptured with you."

"Oh, stuff and nonsense." Amelia stood quickly, unsure why she felt so skittish. "We have much to accomplish today. A new gown for next week's ball and then the theatre tonight. I am hoping you shall see Lord Dudley there. What did you think of him, cousin?"

Lydia stood as well and rounded the table.

"He is nice enough, but I think we should keep our options open," she said as they walked to the small library on the other side of Amelia's modest townhome.

She was fortunate the stipend her brother gave her covered the cost of maintaining her own house. The home was located at the edge of Mayfair, a distinguished and safe neighborhood, and whilst small, suited her purposes most admirably. She enjoyed the privacy and location, not to mention the salon boasting huge windows that let in a good deal of light, perfect for her paintings.

Her allowance also provided for a cook, a butler and a housemaid. She needed her side career of matchmaking only for paints, canvases and good deeds. And once in a while, a new gown. She'd started her business two years prior and had no plans to end it.

She and Lydia spent the rest of the morning practicing an assortment of fine arts every lady must know. As the oldest child of a country baron, Lydia lacked some of the refinement a lady of the *ton* demonstrated, but Amelia was confident she'd learn quickly. She'd begun her lessons last week. Her *mistake* was the reason she'd been pulled out of finishing school. Her parents had decided a personal tutor would work better. Thanks to a successful matchmaking assignment, Amelia's services had been recommended to them.

Unbeknownst to Lydia, Amelia was not charging her

parents. She was family after all. This put her in a bit of a bind, but she hoped a sold painting might put her in a more comfortable spot until a new client came along.

After discussing subject matter a lady should and should not indulge in while conversing, Cousin Lydia left with her parents to go back to the townhome they rented during the Season.

Amelia exhaled with relief when the lessons ended. She detested how ladies must be bound by proprieties men did not observe, but it was the society in which she lived, and if Lydia wished to flourish in this society, she'd have to know the rules before she could break them.

Pursing her lips, Amelia went to her writing desk situated near a window. Speaking of rules, she had a few complaints to send to the House of Lords. Not that anyone there would take her seriously, but she meant to irritate them. Then she'd plant a few nuggets in their wives' ears.

Perhaps next week at Almack's. She'd finally gotten the invitation for Lydia, and she did not intend to miss such a prodigious opportunity. If Lydia did not wish to know Lord Dudley better, then Almack's might present a whole new round of young men for her perusal.

Love blossomed when least expected. It could not be forced, though. How she wished it could. Her thoughts wandered to the past, to the man whom she tried so very hard not to remember. Their last dance…

Dipping her quill, she forced herself to concentrate on her letters. What was past was past. There was nothing to fill that broken space within.

As she finished her final letter—more a rant, really—her butler, Dukes, poked his head into her study.

"My lady," he said softly, his voice as old as his age. "Lord Dudley left his card."

"You may dispose of it, Dukes. I shan't be seeing him."

The man could not take a hint, it seemed. She did not wish to be cruel, but considering her plans for Lydia, she certainly could not encourage the avid tendencies of Lord Dudley.

She rummaged on her desk until she found the letter she'd written requesting a Bow Street runner. Some investigations were better handled by professionals. She held it out to Dukes. "See that this is delivered immediately, please."

He took it. "Very well, my lady." He cleared his throat. "Also, Lord Eversham is here to see you."

"Oh, bother." She dropped the quill into its holder and spun around. "You don't suppose you could direct him to come back later?"

"No, my lady. He is insisting he see you at once."

"What is the delay?" Her brother's voice grew louder and then he was at the door, sliding past Dukes with a scowl upon his handsome face. She'd never understood how he could have inherited all the looks, but to be fair, she considered herself to possess the bulk of the brains.

"Good morning, brother. How do you fare this fine and bright day?" She plastered on a sweet smile, smothering the laugh that threatened to escape as his scowl deepened.

"A moment, Dukes." He waved off the butler, who flashed Amelia an apologetic look before closing the door.

Amelia folded her letter to the House of Lords before taking her stick of sealing wax and heating it above the flame of her candle. She pressed the stick against the paper and sealed the letter closed. She placed it on the teetering stack of her correspondence and returned the sealing wax to its place on her desk. "Do calm yourself,

Eversham, or you shall pace a hole in my already faded rug," she said mildly.

"You…you…" He could not finish but rather continued his erratic pacing, his breathing ragged.

Why, he was really at the end of his tether! She frowned. Though her brother often proved to be a bossy irritant, she loved him dearly and had no wish to cause him undue pain.

She cleared her throat and rose from her seat but did not approach him. "Dear Ev, please take a breath and explain what I have done to upset you so."

He stopped abruptly and faced her. Though they shared the same nose, the same eyes and the same hair, on him those features became suave and handsome. He'd always been popular with the ladies. At this moment, though, his eyes were dark with anger, his lips pressed tight.

She grimaced. It took much to put her brother into a rage. What had she done this time?

He crossed his arms as he glared at her. "It has come to my attention that you are running a business."

She felt her face go slack.

"Aha!" He pointed at her. "I knew it must be true. Amelia, how can you do such a thing? You will never find a husband like this. Dillydallying in politics, serving food at Newgate with that…that woman."

"Her name is Mrs. Elizabeth Fry, and she is quite respectable. She is thinking of starting a school for the female prisoners."

"I care not one whit about her name. You are creating a reputation for yourself, and it's not a good one."

"And why would an earl with the fortune you have be concerned with reputation?" she countered.

"You know why." He stalked toward her and then

dropped into her desk chair. "I am being nagged night and day—"

"Perhaps you should have married for love rather than money," Amelia said pertly, though inside her stomach twisted. "I do not wish to cause you stress, Eversham. But I must paint. I must keep myself busy. And I am quite positive I shall never marry."

His head dropped into his hands, and her heart grew heavier.

"I am sorry to be such a burden to you," she said quietly.

"It's not that," he muttered.

"My business is proceeding nicely." She walked to her desk and picked up her last invoice. "Do you remember Lady Goddard? She and her husband are on a trip to the Continent right now, but I earned a good bit from training her and helping her find him. They are immensely compatible."

Eversham sighed and lifted his head. "I do not understand you, Amelia. You spout nonsense about love, but you are the most pragmatic individual I have ever met."

Relieved to see him calmer, Amelia settled on the edge of her desk. "Perhaps our definitions of love are different. It is not some silly feeling or a fainting spell but rather an action toward an individual. It is the most practical of all emotions and the most helpful."

Her brother's lips almost tilted but then chose to settle in a firm line. "Nevertheless, I have come here to demand that you cease your business at once. You are a peer, the daughter of an earl. You're comfortable here. Why do you need extra finances?"

"I cannot quit my painting, Eversham. Canvases, brushes... They cost money."

He let out a large, overdramatic sigh. "Very well. I will enlarge your stipend."

"Your wife will not allow that."

Eversham winced. He could say nothing to that. He'd married a woman who tightly controlled the purse strings. Amelia wasn't sure how, as her brother had never been a pushover, but for some reason he regularly gave in to the whims of his wife, a woman whom Amelia studiously tried to avoid at all times.

Eversham rose from his seat, so Amelia followed suit. A familiar bulldoggish expression crossed his face, which did not bode well for her.

"I am insisting you quit this nonsense," he said. "Find another way to buy your supplies, but your business ends today."

"Do not think that because you were born three minutes before me you have the right to order me about. I shall not end my profitable venture." She lifted her chin, daring him to defy her.

His eyes narrowed. "I'll not have you upsetting my wife. If I hear anything more of this…" He trailed off ominously.

A slither of fear snaked through Amelia. Was he contemplating what she thought? She rubbed her arms, which suddenly felt cold. "What, Eversham? Do say it."

"Harriet and I have discussed the problem in depth." His tone turned serious. "If you continue this preposterous business, we are prepared to leave off renting this town house, and you will come to live with us." His brow lowered. "Forever."

Leg shackled, indeed.

The last thing on earth Lord Spencer Ashwhite wanted was a wife.

He winced as Eversham's spouse hit a particularly high note with her words. They were in Eversham's curricle on the way to Drury Lane, and Lady Eversham had not stopped jabbering the entire way. Her conversation consisted of frippery. Lots of comments about fashion and the Prince Regent.

Spencer tried to tune her out as Eversham seemed absorbed in her opinions and hadn't bothered to involve Spencer in conversation. Thankfully they were almost to the theater. Though Spencer hoped to avoid Miss Winston, who was likely to be here tonight. If not starring in the show, then watching it with her friends.

Their relationship had been short-lived, but she did not like that he'd left for the Americas. He grimaced as he remembered the crack of her palm against his cheek. Over nothing but his refusal to continue their relationship when he returned to England.

She'd felt slighted, not seeming to understand that his priorities—nay, his very heart—had been changed.

At least this afternoon's jaunt had provided a solution as well as comfort. The clergyman had listened well to Spencer. In fact, Spencer had been surprised by the cleric's attentiveness. He'd even pulled out a Bible and shared scripture with Spencer. His advice had been sound, and Spencer had decided to go with his recommendations about pursuing marriage.

Though at this very moment, with his ears ringing and his patience sorely taxed, he was tempted to lose his estate rather than find a spouse.

The curricle pulled to the curb. Spencer exited and then watched as Eversham helped his wife out. He appeared deeply devoted to Lady Eversham, though Spencer knew for a fact that her money had initially snared Eversham's interest.

He followed them into the theater, contemplating his friend's change of actions. He must ask him about it, especially since he'd be imitating Eversham's choices. Once ensconced in Eversham's box, he turned to his friend.

"Before our show begins, I have an inquiry."

"One moment." Eversham turned to help Lady Eversham with her dress, which had snagged on a chair. She flashed him a grateful smile, and Spencer watched in surprise as the back of Eversham's neck burned red.

Quite interesting.

Finally his friend faced him. "What can I help you with?"

"It's of a personal note." He glanced at Lady Eversham, noting with relief that she was conversing with a woman in a nearby box. "Your marriage appears to be flourishing, and yet it did not do so at first."

Eversham squinted at Spencer. "Is this about your goals for marriage? Because I told you at breakfast that I don't want any part of the sham."

His friend had been vehement, actually.

"It won't be a sham. I'm just trying to figure out the best way to go about things in order to fulfill the terms of the will," Spencer said smoothly. "The chaplain said—"

"You spoke to a clergyman?"

"I'm a new man," he said, voice stiff, feeling embarrassed when he shouldn't be. "God is a part of my life now, and I am being careful to act in a way of which He'd approve."

Eversham rolled his eyes. "Surely it's not that difficult. Find a woman who suits you and marry her. No one is going to reject a rich marquis."

"That's a cold way to look at life."

"Ash, what has gotten into you? See here, if you're that concerned about right and wrong, hold your tongue until my sister arrives. Her notions are firm and unalterable. She won't hesitate to tell you what she thinks, and most often, she's right."

"Your sister is coming? Tonight?" Unaccountably his gut tightened as he remembered how distastefully she'd said the word *rakes*.

"She'll be here shortly. I'm forcing her to be social but, even more, to keep company with my wife." Eversham's smile was strangely tight. "Amelia's actions of late have been unseemly, and it is past time she accepted her lot in life."

Spencer drummed his fingers against his legs. He didn't much care for bluestockings, either. His mother's unconventional ways had ruined his parents' marriage. "You sound perturbed."

"My sister is creating a mess that I do not care to clean up." His gaze cut to his chatting wife. "And I surely do not mean to put up with her shenanigans."

"She's a bluestocking, correct?"

"A political one, but that is the least of my worries." Eversham leaned forward, cupping his mouth. "It has come to my attention that she is running a business."

"Really?" That would not settle well with the dowager set. "Do tell."

Eversham nodded sagely, keeping his voice low. "I will concede she's an innovative sort. She has found a way to earn money by finding husbands for young misses in their first Season. Apparently she's been wildly successful in supplementing her meager income."

"A hardly shocking venture, Eversham," Spencer said drily. He'd been expecting something a little more ludicrous. Perhaps hoping for it, fact. Hoping she was less than what she appeared—less than proper, even. Then he could dispense with the doubts about his own character and how she might judge him for past deeds...

Eversham gave a priggish sniff. "Shocking, perhaps not. But most decidedly unacceptable. She is the daughter of an earl, the sister of an earl. I'll not have it, Ash." His friend straightened, a frown upon his lips.

"I've never known her actions to bother you before. In fact, you've hardly mentioned her, and when I met her last night, I didn't realize she was your sister." Spencer narrowed his gaze on his friend. "We danced, and I found her to be a most interesting woman."

"Interesting?" Eversham scoffed. "If you find women who are covered in paint half the time and write weekly letters of complaint to the House of Lords attractive, then you are daft. Her opinions never cease, and they are centered on matters no woman needs to have knowledge of." His expression changed. "Did you say you danced with her?"

"Quite enjoyably," Spencer drawled, grinning at how Eversham's face darkened.

"My sister doesn't dance."

"She did with me."

"She must not have realized who you were." His friend's countenance grew serious. "For all my talk, I love Amelia deeply. Do not treat her as a pet lady. I plan to marry her off."

Spencer's chest tightened at his friend's implication. "Do you mean to say I am not good enough for your sister?"

"Let's just say your past has not enamored me of your husbandly qualities. Either way, Amelia would never have you, but we can make a wager if you'd like?" Eversham let out an annoying chuckle that made Spencer's knuckles itch.

"Those days are behind me." He scowled. "And it is not I who is treating her as a dispensable item, now, is it?"

"Trust me, she is not your type." Eversham inclined his head, his gaze shifting past Spencer. "But be the judge of that yourself, for here she comes, and knowing my twin and that particular expression upon her face, she is not in the best of moods."

Indeed, Spencer turned to see Lady Amelia walking toward their box, the striking blonde from Lady Havern's party trailing behind her. Lady Amelia's appeared to be quite a reluctant walk, and though he could not read her eyes behind her enormous spectacles, he knew the exact moment she recognized him.

Her walk stuttered. A delightful curve graced her mouth. He admired her lips for a moment before looking away. He'd always had an affinity for a smile. There was nothing worse than a woman with a pinched mouth. Thin lips that knew only how to frown.

But Lady Amelia did not seem to suffer such a malady. She entered their box regally, her mouth tipped into a sincere smile. The scent of rosewater filled the air. When he stood for the ladies, all his senses engaged until, for that moment, he saw nothing but the lovely woman beside him.

Chapter Three

Amelia's pulse pounded in her ears. Her mouth felt dry and her palms sweaty. Every nerve tingled and all her senses seemed heightened, for beside her stood the very man she'd danced with the other night. A man she thought never to meet again despite his friendship with her brother.

Lord Ashwhite.

She felt his regard intensely, for he had not stopped staring since she'd entered the box. Perhaps her spectacles sat askew? But no, she'd have noticed that. Her hat, mayhap, crooked upon her head? Self-consciously she touched its brim and noted that it remained straight.

"Ah, sister, you've made it." Eversham's voice sounded overly bright. "Allow me to introduce you to Lord Ashwhite."

"We've met." She frowned at the sound of her voice. Breathy and quite unlike her normal self.

"I have not had the pleasure," piped up Lydia. She hadn't yet sat and dropped a perfect curtsy.

"This is Miss Lydia Stanley, a cousin who hails from Sussex for her first Season," Amelia said.

"A pleasure to meet you." Lord Ashwhite offered his own bow.

Amelia watched the marquis carefully to see if he showed any interest, but his attention to Lydia was perfunctory at best. An odd relief filtered through her.

Then Lord Ashwhite turned to her and bowed. As he rose, the smile that graced his face caught Amelia's breath. A strange fluttering danced through her stomach. Feeling uncertain, she returned his manners with an inclination of her head.

"Why don't you sit by me," she said to Cousin Lydia, forcing her gaze to leave Lord Ashwhite's and hoping desperately the strange feelings spreading through her would disappear. She must have eaten something bad earlier. Or perhaps the stress of having to be in Lady Eversham's company was giving her the jitters?

Amelia spotted a familiar face in another box. She nudged Lydia. "Lord Dudley is present tonight. Shall we bump into him later?"

Lydia wrinkled her nose. "If we must."

"Really, cousin. Do not do that with your nose."

"Did I hear Lord Dudley's name?" Lord Ashwhite interrupted them, his deep voice sending a pleasant shiver down Amelia's spine. "He is a cousin of mine."

She could not forget how his voice had sounded the night she met him, how it held a musical cadence that thrilled her each time she heard it.

"Why, yes, he is our acquaintance," said Lydia.

And a possible marriage prospect, Amelia wanted to put in, but she restrained herself. She hadn't met with her runner yet. Besides, there was no need for Eversham to know she refused to give up this business. Not until she'd sold a painting. Then perhaps she'd consider his ridiculous demand.

"We shall go speak with him during intermission," said Amelia, feeling the graze of Lord Ashwhite's stare upon her cheek. "It is quite hot in here tonight, is it not?" She pulled out her fan and used it diligently, but the heat in her cheeks did not recede.

"I am feeling a touch cold," said Lydia.

"Lady Amelia," Lord Ashwhite said, "your brother tells me you are interested in politics."

"Is that how he termed it?" She smiled.

"Not quite," Lord Ashwhite amended. Those adorable crinkles appeared at his eyes as he grinned. Yes, he would make quite the husband for some fortunate lady.

"I thought not." Amelia flashed him a knowing look. "But yes, I do make my opinions known. Especially on the state of Newgate. There are prisoners who are quite literally starving to death. Others have been locked up for years over a piece of stolen bread. Children living in filth with their criminal mothers, who are treated horribly. The men have families waiting for them. They've very often learned their lesson, and yet they're given few options to redeem themselves." She knew indignation was making her voice rise and tried to lower her pitch. "Their children resort to begging while the mothers are forced into more horrific careers."

"You sound knowledgeable about these matters." Lord Ashwhite's eyes held hers with regard, very serious, as though he'd absorbed everything she said and cared.

His eyes were quite a marvelous green, as bright as emeralds. How she'd love to find an oil in such a shade. She blinked. *Focus on the subject at hand. Inhale.* She was not a young miss prone to a fit of the vapors.

"Yes," she breathed. "I have written numerous letters to the House of Lords on the subject."

"Lady Amelia, do tone it down." Harriet's voice cut

through anything she planned to say next. "I apologize for my sister-in-law's enthusiasms. Come, tell us if you've seen this play before, my lord?"

He directed his attention to Lady Eversham, and Amelia all but melted into her chair. Her limbs felt as soft as wax. It was her sister-in-law's doing, no doubt. Just being in her presence caused Amelia's heart rate to rise. She dragged in a deep breath and willed some strength into her body.

Lydia was watching her, a curious quirk to her brows.

"What?" asked Amelia.

"Do not sound so cross. I am simply flummoxed."

It was Amelia's turn to raise a brow.

"I believe it was only this morning that you specifically told me to disregard politics as a conversational tool."

"He asked me first," Amelia pointed out. "Furthermore, *I* am not on the marriage mart. *I* have no need to curtail my tongue in those matters."

"I see."

"Good." Amelia frowned. She did not like the satisfied look upon Lydia's face. It was almost as if she was suggesting…something. Amelia did not quite know what her cousin implied, but she felt that it was threatening somehow.

While Lydia thumbed through the evening's schedule, Amelia snuck a glance at Lord Ashwhite. His profile was exceedingly handsome. As she looked, she felt those butterflies again, and that was when the knowledge came upon her.

She was attracted to Lord Ashwhite.

An honest-to-goodness affinity for the marquis.

She pressed a palm against her stomach and looked away. Surely it could not be so. Why, she had not felt a passing interest for any man in years. Not since Lord Markham, who'd teased her and danced with her, his dimpled smile charming her into believing he held more regard for her than he really did.

She'd told him all about her dreams. Her aspirations to change society, to make life better for others, and he'd listened. He'd listened so well she thought he actually loved her.

The remembrance of his attentiveness brought a sour feeling to her stomach.

No, attraction was deceptive. True love did not involve the senses but rather actions. She nodded. She would not respond to this absurd feeling burgeoning within. Her goals for life did not include a husband.

Home involved paintings and letters and books. Not a husband. Why, did she want to end up like Eversham? A man who'd always been strong-minded and progressive? Now look at him. A poor sot chained to his wife's side, doing her bidding, forcing his sister, *his very own twin*, into drastic measures just to preserve her way of life?

She thought not. And that was why she wouldn't gawk at Lord Ashwhite, let alone engage in conversation with him. At this time her emotions could not be trusted, and she certainly did not want them to interfere with her plans.

The lights lowered, and the play began. Something about one of the actresses niggled at her memory, but she couldn't place her. Eventually the story line pulled her in, and the night passed with laughter, temporarily relieving her from the worry that had gnawed at her since her brother's visit.

Despite her interest in the play, she never forgot who sat beside her. His laugh was low and contagious, and she discovered that they invariably laughed at the same lines.

Finally the play ended. As they rose from their seats, she felt a tap upon her shoulder. She turned and found Lord Ashwhite studying her closely.

"My lady," he said, voice serious, "I would have a word with you."

"Privately?" Her gaze shifted to where Eversham was busy helping his wife.

"Yes."

She blinked. Oh, dear, this was not going as planned. She could feel those exuberant butterflies waltzing within. Heart pounding, and despite her better judgment, she nodded.

His hand pressed gently against her back as he guided her toward the box's exit. She shot Lydia a glance, but her cousin had become entangled in a conversation with Lady Eversham.

Slipping out, she gave Lord Ashwhite a bland look. Best to keep her voice modulated, as well. She did not want to give away her nerves in his presence. They were jangling wildly and affecting her ability to think clearly.

"How may I help you, my lord?"

He moved closer and glanced furtively about the theater before meeting her gaze square on. "I am in need of your services."

Baffled, she couldn't help squinting at him through her spectacles.

He chuckled. "You heard me correctly. At the present moment, I find myself in a quandary that I think only you will be able to help me out of. My lady—" his grin faded "—how much would it cost for you to find me a wife?"

Spencer repressed a smirk at the stunned expression crossing Lady Amelia's face. Indeed, her lovely mouth rounded as if she'd forgotten those manners she seemed to pride herself on. Then she drew herself up, and her eyes flashed beneath the lowered lights of the theater.

"Sir, you are mistaken." Her nose lifted, though she couldn't possibly look down at him from her spectacles because he towered over her. He had the feeling she wished he would shrink. "I am not for hire."

He allowed his lips to tilt in a mocking smile. From experience, he knew women tended to be partial to his smiles. Lady Amelia would be no exception. "Come, now, my lady, that is an untruth."

"I beg your pardon?" She had the audacity to look shocked. The fan she'd been gripping tightly waved about her face, which was turning an attractive shade of pink.

There was something about her movements as she fanned herself, something both hurried and graceful. His gaze rested upon her fingers. Discoloration marked the tips of her nail beds. Oil paint residue? It must be costly to paint...

"I believe you heard me quite clearly and are being deliberately obtuse," he said.

She gasped, and her fan picked up its pace.

"In fact, if I were a wagering man, which I'm not, I'd say you are most definitely for hire, but the fact you wish to conceal this is intriguing." The purse of her lips was distracting him. Her eyes were indignant behind the spectacles, but even more, there seemed to be a spark of curiosity there.

"My lord." Her gaze darted past him to the opening of her brother's box. "I am not in the habit of finding wives." She pinned him with a severe look that made him want to laugh. "I beg you to forget this conversation and leave me be."

Noise filled the space as Eversham, Harriet and Miss Stanley joined them.

"The play was ever so lovely. Do you not agree, my lord?" Miss Stanley batted her eyelashes at him, amusement playing about the corners of her mouth.

"It was," he said, though he found his stare returning to Lady Amelia. Said lady appeared to be communicating with her brother via glares. Tension filled the air as the group fell silent.

"Well, I believe we shall be going. We have an early-morning stroll planned for tomorrow." Miss Stanley linked her arm through Lady Amelia's and flashed an even row of teeth. "I do hope we'll see you again, Lord Ashwhite. Perhaps at Almack's next week? We shall be there often, and I shall reserve a place on my card—" Her voice cut off suddenly, and then Lady Amelia bestowed a syrupy smile upon the group.

"Good evening, everyone."

Was he mistaken or did Lady Amelia just forcibly nudge Miss Stanley to turn and leave? Unable to stop his grin, he watched the two depart.

"I do not understand why you invited her," said Lady Eversham beneath her breath.

"You must get used to her presence." Eversham's voice held a stern note.

Lady Eversham's eyes cut to Spencer then back to Eversham as if warning him to keep their personal matters out of public hearing. A mischievous streak prompted Spencer to speak.

"I quite enjoyed their company. Will Lady Amelia be living with you? Seeing her more often would boost my mood immensely."

Eversham growled and stalked toward the theater's exit. Lady Eversham kept quiet, confirming Spencer's suspicions.

So the lady might have to move in with her brother

and his difficult wife. What a dilemma. His mind raced as he followed them to their waiting curricle.

A dilemma for her, but for him, quite possibly the opportunity he needed to keep his estate.

Chapter Four

"There has to be a way out of this." Spencer flexed his fingers and watched the lawyer carefully. After realizing the dearth of suitable ladies on the marriage mart and being subjected to Lady Amelia's forceful refusal to help in his search for a wife, Spencer decided to call on the lawyer again. Perchance he'd misunderstood him on the first visit. Early-morning light slanted against the elderly man's wig and outlined the offensive papers upon his desk.

"No, my lord. The will is airtight. You must find a wife within three months' time or your entailed property will pass to your cousin, Lord Dudley."

"He already has an earldom." An earldom that was mismanaged, to say the least. "I will not lose Ashwhite to him. My father… I don't know what he was thinking." He ground his teeth. As always, his father had gone too far in meddling with his life. Even after death, the old man insisted on controlling things. "I will fight this."

"Perhaps you should marry and be done with it." The lawyer adjusted his spectacles, reminding Spencer of Lady Amelia's refusal last night to help him.

He wondered what she might think of this clause in

his father's will. He focused on the lawyer. "When was this updated? Might it be said my father's mental faculties were impaired when he wrote it?"

"When did you last see your father, if I may ask such a thing?" The lawyer's quizzical gaze burned Spencer.

It had been too long. Guilt swept through Spencer and shook his resolve. He inclined his head, accepting the lawyer's question with regret. "Four years."

"I see." The lawyer cleared his throat. "Well, your father was in the pink of health when he had his accident. The horse had to be put down, and it was the infection that took your father. I was there that last day, and his faculties were fully functional. The will was made a year ago, though, and has not been altered since."

A year ago… Right about when Spencer had begun doubting his place in life. He'd had a particularly rough patch with gaming debts and irrational, clinging women. A brewing scandal had convinced him to take a little trip to the Americas…probably the best decision he'd ever made.

He frowned, tapping his fingers against his trousers.

"It looks as though I'm well and completely snookered," he said. "Thank you for seeing me on such short notice. If I do not marry, what shall happen?"

"You will have the entailed property from your mother, and you shall keep your title as Earl of Hartsacre. There is no money with that property except for what it makes. Your standing would be diminished."

Standing. Spencer grunted and pushed to his feet. He did not care a fig for social status, but he did love his home, and the thought of losing Ashwhite… He gripped the edges of his coat. It could not happen. He schooled his features and held out a hand. The lawyer stood and they shook.

"You may send a copy of the banns when you've found a bride, but keep in mind you must be married in three months' time, not engaged."

"I understand." Spencer gave the lawyer a curt nod and let himself out.

If he was to save his property, then he must marry. And to marry, he must find a suitable bride. For all his travels and his transformation that had taken place in the Americas, he felt himself at a crossroads.

What would the God he'd chosen to follow in the Americas think of this choice to marry? Was marrying to keep his lands and fortune safe rather than for love acceptable? Falling in love was unlikely, but surely there must be something in the Bible about parameters for marrying. *Talk to God. Confess to Him your needs.*

The American preacher's voice, filled with conviction, filtered through his memory. Perhaps prayer was the answer. Outside the office and right on the street, he closed his eyes. Took a deep breath. Let it sink deep in his chest before exhaling.

Lord, the preacher said You know my desires and needs. Right now, more than anything, I'm in need of wisdom. And some help. Please show me the way, if You would?

Spencer opened his eyes. He waited and didn't feel any kind of answer, but he did have a strange contentment that he must assume came from praying. Perhaps it was an answer in and of itself.

Smiling, Spencer relaxed. His friends might never believe him about this, but surely there was a God, and surely He heard prayers.

He walked to where he'd parked the phaeton. The morning mist felt cool upon his face, perfect weather for a quick ride around Hyde Park. He made sure his tiger, Jacob, was safely situated at the back of the phaeton before he snapped the reins. The bays launched into a steady prance, and his shoulders eased back. Confinement in his town house proved to be more stifling now. After a year in the Americas, that land of stubborn colonials, he'd come to appreciate the scent of fresh air and the wildness of being free.

For so many years, he'd wasted his mornings with sleep. Spent his evenings gaming and carousing with women of ill repute. Missed the golden drench of sunrise, the newness God brought each day. Even now it was hard to remember why he hadn't thought of God, how he'd strolled through life living only in the moment, thankful for nothing, expecting everything.

He inhaled a deep breath of morning air, tasting its richness imbued with the flavor of summer flowers. Around him the streets remained quiet. It was the height of the Season, after all, and the *ton* and their servants would still be sleeping off their late nights.

One of his horses snuffled softly. This exercise would keep them strong and healthy. He turned them to circle the park and reminisced upon last night.

He'd gotten nowhere in talking to Eversham. His friend was being surprisingly tight-lipped about his sister and her situation. Maybe Waverly knew something, though he doubted it. While he'd been in the Americas discovering a new way of life, his friend Waverly had continued to stay busy following his normal, debauched path.

A path Spencer had stepped away from forever.

Thoughtful, he turned the bays in the direction of Mayfair. The one piece of information he'd received from Eversham last night was Lady Amelia's address, though it had been reluctantly given and accompanied by a suspicious frown.

Spencer couldn't stop his smirk.

Poor Eversham. On one side a needy spouse and on the other a far too independent sister. Spencer had always wanted siblings, but now he thought perhaps it was better he had none. They were far too emotionally costly. By the time he found Lady Amelia's townhome, sunlight had melted away the mist and coaxed a fine layer of perspiration to his brow. He brought the phaeton to the curb. His tiger leaped down, and he handed the reins to him.

"Jacob, is it?" he asked as he climbed down.

"Yes, my lord."

"Mrs. Cubb's son? You've grown."

"Thank you, my lord." The young man flushed and bowed.

"Have you driven a phaeton before?"

"Yes, my lord."

"And can you handle these horses?"

Jacob's eyes brightened. "That I can."

"Be a good lad, then, and take my phaeton home for me. I shall walk back or catch a hackney."

A mile-wide grin bunched the boy's cheeks. Smiling, Spencer turned toward the house and listened as the phaeton pulled away. The joys of childhood left too quickly, as young Jacob would discover.

He rapped at the door, and an aging yet capable butler received him. After presenting his card, he followed the butler to a small library.

"Her ladyship may not be receiving callers today," the butler told Spencer. "I shall return with an answer."

"Thank you." Spencer took a seat and looked around. Evidently Lady Amelia appreciated literature. Her library was…excessive. Books not only lined the walls but also topped every table in the room. Some of the shelves held double rows of books.

Intriguing.

He wasn't sure if he'd ever met a woman before who read so very much. Then again, most of his intimates had not been keen on intellectual discussions. He frowned, remembering his former ways.

Many had called him a rake. Maybe that was why his father had added the marriage clause to his will. Spencer hoped his reputation wouldn't impede any progress in the marriage quest.

The door to the library opened once again. The butler gave him a steady look. "Lady Amelia is indisposed and wishes for you to return at a later time."

Spencer bit back a sudden grin. So that was how she intended to play things? Well, Lady Amelia was sadly mistaken if she thought she could ignore him. He had too much to lose to fall over and play dead to her whims.

He arched a brow, leaned back and propped one ankle across the other. "I shall wait."

The butler tilted his head. "Her ladyship does not wish to be disturbed."

Knowing it was the height of rudeness and not caring one whit, Spencer gave him a slow, lazy smile. "I've come to discuss important business. If she will not see me this morning, then I shall wait until this afternoon. And if not this afternoon, then I shall arrive again the next morning. I shall come every day until Lady Amelia recovers from her indisposition and is ready to receive my call."

To his surprise, the old butler chuckled. "I will give her the message, my lord."

"Very good." And he settled back, certain he would not have to wait long.

* * *

"My lady."

The whispered words filtered through the haze of sleep anchoring Amelia to her bed. Her blankets bunched up around her, creating a comfortable haven of warmth. She scrunched her eyes closed, praying she had only dreamed the sound of Dukes's voice. Now, where had she been… Oh, yes, dancing. She burrowed into her pillow, remembering that delicious low rumble of her partner's voice…

"My lady, I apologize, but Lord Ashwhite is in the library."

She groaned. "Again?"

'Twas the third day the persistent man had shown up at her doorstep. Yesterday he'd stayed until evening. Abominable creature. She groaned again and pressed her face against the pillow.

"My lady, shall I tell him you're indisposed?"

"Please," she whispered. Two could play at this game. Perhaps if she didn't know what he wanted, she might be compelled by curiosity to see him, but the problem remained that she *did* know, and she could not help him.

Aiding Cousin Lydia was risky enough, especially since she wasn't receiving a payment for her services. As much as she needed the money, she certainly could not allow Eversham's best friend to hire her. When her brother found out, then her fate would be sealed. Her independence decimated by Harriet's voracious need for control.

The sound of something plopping against her coverlets raised her head.

"My lady," Dukes said. "I've brought your morning mail in case you do not plan to leave your room again."

"Thank you." She pulled the covers over her head,

scowling into the darkness. How uncouth of Lord Ash-white, how utterly irritating, that he persisted in this non-sense. She refused to be bound to her bedroom simply because he could not take no for an answer.

On the other hand, she had no wish to face him. It was bad enough that she dreamed of his voice, but to look into that startling, laughing green gaze of his and refuse to help might be her undoing.

If he wasn't her brother's good friend, she'd call the constable...oh, no.

She was to meet with her Bow Street runner today regarding Lord Dudley!

She whipped into a sitting position, startling the stack of mail into slipping off the bed. It crashed to the floor. Her hair knotted about her head in a wild mass that divided her line of vision. She swiped it away and jumped out of bed, almost colliding with the boudoir as she rang for Sally.

While waiting, she scooped up the mail. Nothing important except a letter from her brother. She sighed, went to her vanity and plucked up her letter opener. She slit the envelope and read his scrawling script, each of his words tightening her chest until she felt as though she wore a corset three sizes too small.

She closed her eyes. *Deep breaths.* It would not do to have a fit of the vapors. Her fingers clenched the letter opener. The cool metal dug into her skin. She would not be hysterical. She would not.

Her brother's threats to end her life as she knew it, forcing her into that cage he called a home, were not idle after all. His demand that she pack within the week was ludicrous.

He cared not that she wasn't earning money helping Lydia. He only worried for their family's reputation...a reputation that was perfectly unharmed by her actions. He and Harriet were behaving in such an unreasonable way.

"My lady, are you all right?" Sally stood in the doorway, brow puckered.

"Perfectly fine," she answered crisply. She would not allow Eversham to bully her. Surely she could make him see reason. "I need my hair done quickly, though, not a moment to lose, for I must find my brother and talk some sense into him. And could you ask Dukes to keep Lord Ashwhite in the library? It appears I'll need to speak with him after all."

Not only that, but her Bow Street runner was scheduled to arrive at ten o'clock. It wasn't like her to be so disorganized. She frowned as she looked for a dress to wear. Perhaps a modest muslin of a robust shade. Something to lift her mood and give her confidence for the battle to come.

Thirty minutes later, armed with her spectacles and a magnificent fan she'd bought with Cousin Lydia in Bath, Amelia descended the stairs and marched into the library.

As expected, Lord Ashwhite lounged in a chair. Unexpectedly, he held one of her novels in his hands. Open.

Her eyes narrowed. "You wished to see me?"

"Two days ago." In a smoothly relaxed move, he laid the book, facedown, on the side table. He regarded her with laughing eyes. "Do you read much of that rubbish?"

Cheeks burning, Amelia set her jaw. "My reading materials are none of your concern."

"Should I hire you—and after reading that, it's a questionable venture—I would need to know that your ability to pick a spouse is not based on some impractical frippery that only exists within a woman's imagination." He tented his fingers. "Or perhaps these stories inspire you?"

His languid tone, the way his lips curved as if he were trying to hold his laugh in, set her teeth on edge. His aristocratic snobbery filled her with a sizzling need to throw a book at his head, which she didn't understand. Why, she barely knew this man. She'd shared one dance with him, had one conversation, and yet she was beginning to comprehend why the jewel-laden woman at the ball the other night had slapped him.

Wetting her lips, she moved farther into the room. "As you are a good friend to my brother, I will pretend you have not insulted me within my own home. I will overlook the fact that you've been rude and hostile, and I will answer your questions. But first, have you need of refreshment? Surely the time you've spent encamping in my home has famished you?" She ended with a soft little smile even though she was seething on the inside. And those butterflies were waltzing in her stomach again, aggravating her even more. Her fingers clenched within the folds of her dress.

He studied her, the posture of his hands suggesting a more serious mood. Good. She could handle a man with a real goal, but a tease? No, she was ill equipped for that. Her mind flashed back to Lord Markham, and she grimaced.

"I am in no need of refreshment, my lady." Lord Ashwhite stood and pointed to the other chair. "Would you care to have a seat so that we might discuss business?"

"We have nothing to discuss. You have asked and I have declined."

"These books look costly." Lord Ashwhite ran a supine finger down the length of her bookcase. "Does the money you receive from your brother cover your purchases?"

"That is hardly your concern." But she found herself captivated by the movements of his hand. He touched her books lovingly, as a man who understood the value of such things.

"There is no Lord Byron here," he murmured.

"No, I find his poems tedious and fanciful. Despite what you may think, Lord Ashwhite, I am a practical woman." She injected sternness into her voice and forced herself to stop staring at Eversham's friend. "And therein lies your problem. You want a wife, but I do not find wives. I find husbands for women who would like to marry well and marry happily. Furthermore, there has been a…change of plans for me. I am not presently taking on new clients."

He swiveled that direct gaze of his toward her. She picked up her chin and gave him what she hoped was a glare that bespoke finality.

"But there is some sort of stress in your life, am I correct?" He advanced toward her in a slow manner, a glide almost. She resisted the urge to back away. "I have been given the impression that you may be forced to change residences soon. Which would be rather sad, seeing as you've made a home for yourself here. And would you be able to paint at your brother's estate?"

She blinked. "What do you know of my painting?"

"I know your fingernails are stained. The books you read are not practical but romantic. You are not what you present to the world, my lady."

Her breath came quick and uneven. "What are you suggesting?"

A languorous smile touched his face. His fingers spread in a supplicating manner. "I propose we work together in finding me a wife. The amount I pay you will be adequate in covering whatever is forcing you from your home. We shall both walk away happy from this partnership."

Before she could form an answer—and in truth, she did not know what to say—Dukes appeared in the doorway.

"My lady, your runner is here," he said.

Chapter Five

Her runner? As in Bow Street? Spencer forced his face to blankness despite the questions ricocheting through his mind. Lady Amelia might have much more happening in her life than strained familial relationships.

She nodded to Dukes, back straight and that no-nonsense tilt to her chin lending her an air of authority. "Very well. Would you show him to the parlor while I finish with Lord Ashwhite?"

"Certainly." Dukes bowed and disappeared from the doorway.

"Before we were interrupted, you made a proposition." Lady Amelia turned to him. Whatever vulnerabilities he'd sensed only moments ago were gone, replaced by the sheen of pragmatism. "I must decline…again. As I said, I am not taking on new clients. It very well could be that this business of mine is ended. While I admire your persistence, you must stop now, for I do not foresee a change of mind or plans." With that, she gave a quick jerk with her head as if to underscore the firmness of her words.

"I am not one to give up lightly," he warned her.

"And neither am I."

Perplexed, feeling at a crossroads, he studied her. He

had the strongest intuition that this lady could help him, and yet she refused. *Lord, what now?*

He had a responsibility to the people of Ashwhite. Furthermore, he did not trust Dudley to look over the property the way he could. His fingers tapped against his legs as he worked through the situation. Lady Amelia looked flustered, though knowing her, she'd deny such a feeling.

Her hands gave her away. She sported the most interesting look of sternness upon her face, but her fingers knotted within the folds of her dress, a rather pretty shade of pink that put roses in her cheeks. Or mayhap it was his words doing that.

He met her eyes and saw the determination there. There was only one way he could think of to sway her. He moved closer so that she might see the sincerity upon his face.

"My lady, might you consider my plight more seriously? It would probably be well to explain my need of a wife."

Her lids flickered and there was the barest hesitation of breath, so he proceeded. "It is not only for my well-being but also for the people who depend upon my property for their livelihoods. Ashwhite is a prosperous estate near Kent. Through different ventures and progressive farming methods, I've increased its profits and created a home for many."

Lady Amelia looked away, but her fingers had stilled their fidgeting.

"It is my fear that should the estate leave my hands, the one to whom it is going may not manage it as well. I love my childhood home, and I love the people there." His voice unexpectedly caught, for at that moment images from boyhood rose to his mind. Cook, with her flushed cheeks and wide smile. His old nanny, who now lived a

happy life in a small cottage on the grounds. His childhood friends who'd grown to become the barons and rec-
tors living nearby.

"Truthfully, my lord, you make a compelling argument." Lady Amelia raised her gaze to his, worrying
her bottom lip. He saw the compassion radiating in her
direct look and felt the first stirrings of hope. "I still
must decline, however, for should I take on your case, it
could ruin me."

"I don't understand," he said slowly.

"The wherefores are too complicated to speak of now,
but I would like you to know I respect your desire to
protect your people. If I could help, if I thought it were
profitable for both of us, I would. Please believe me, my
lord." She placed her hand upon his arm.

He looked down, felt the heat of her imprint against
his sleeve. Her hand was small and delicate, with taper-
ing fingers that hinted at her artistic temperament.

"Perhaps someday I shall see your paintings," he said,
looking deeply into her eyes. A heady sensation was taking over him, one he well recognized but did not care to
resist. "Perhaps when I find a wife, I shall commission
you for a portrait?"

A fine blush spread across her face, and he decided
that she felt the same strange pull he did. Not only that,
but he'd rendered her speechless. His stare dropped to
her lips, which parted ever so slightly.

She stepped back quickly and would have lost her
balance had her hand not still rested upon his arm. Her
grip tightened. "My guest is waiting for me. I must go,
but thank you…" She trailed off, sounding uncertain and
perhaps afraid.

He had much more experience than she in the ways
of attraction. Whether she knew that about him or not,

he wasn't sure, but he bore the responsibility to put her at ease. He gave her a short bow and gently removed her touch from his arm. The absence of her hold left a curiously cool place upon his sleeve.

Swallowing past the tightness of his throat, he smiled. "Thank you, my lady, for your time. I hope you might change your mind."

Her head shake was curt. "I fear not." She backed to the door. "Perhaps I shall see you next week at Almack's. Fare thee well, my lord."

He nodded as she left the room in a graceful sway of skirts. What an enigma, and yet…he had no idea why Eversham found her exasperating. Then again, he'd just discovered that his feelings toward her were not quite brotherly.

He'd had these feelings before with other women. The emotions were short-lived and passed quickly. No doubt they would for Lady Amelia, as well. He let out a heavy sigh. It appeared this avenue led to a dead end. He might have to go about finding a wife the old-fashioned way.

Soirees, balls and, worst of all, the throat-clutching, loathsome house party.

Stifling a groan, he stalked out of the library. As he entered the small hallway, he noticed the parlor door remained open. Lady Amelia's skirt was visible just past the entrance. A man's voice carried into the hall.

Had he said "Dudley"?

Spencer glanced around. Not seeing the aging butler or any other servant, he ventured closer to the door.

"Are you quite sure, Mr. Ladd?"

"Yes, my lady. My information has been verified several times."

Lady Amelia responded, her voice low and refined.

Spencer couldn't catch her words. A puckish intention overrode good sense, and he strode into the parlor.

They turned toward him, shocked. Lady Amelia with her sharp eyes and pretty mouth both rounding, and the runner who was surprisingly young and fit looking with a wild mane of hair that rode about a curiously blank face.

Spencer made a neat bow and then straightened. "Please pardon my rudeness. I could not help but overhear your dialogue concerning Lord Dudley."

Lady Amelia, to her credit, remained composed. She curtsied and then beckoned him in. "Lord Ashwhite, this is Mr. Ladd. He is in my service on a special project."

They exchanged civilities, and then he looked to Lady Amelia and waited.

She arched a brow at him. Sunlight streaming in through large windows glinted off the edge of her spectacles. Very well. He'd make the conversational overture. It did not matter to him in the least if Mr. Ladd found him rude.

"I have an interest in Lord Dudley and will pay to hear what you have discovered about him, Ladd," he said.

The runner leaned on his heels and rocked a bit, his face a quiet study of consideration. At last he held out a palm. "A farthing will do."

"Done." Spencer retrieved his money purse from his pocket and gave the man what he had asked for. He slipped a glance at Lady Amelia. Her face looked a tad pinched. He had the feeling she wanted to reprimand him, but not in front of the runner. An absurd sense of satisfaction settled over him.

Mr. Ladd gave the piece a nip and then slid it into his pocket. His eyes, a remote brown, took in Spencer. He allowed the perusal and did his own. Shabby coat but expensive shoes. Clean nails and unkempt hair that looked, nevertheless, washed. This man might be a trusted source for Lady Amelia.

"Mr. Ladd, if it is all the same to you, I will fill Lord Ashwhite in. I'm sure you have other matters to attend to this morning."

"An excellent notion, my lady." The runner retrieved the coin but Spencer shook his head.

"Keep it," he said.

After a brief hesitation, Ladd nodded. He gave Spencer what felt like a warning look and then smiled at Lady Amelia. "Are you sure you'll be safe in his company?"

Spencer bristled. Did this man disapprove of him?

Lady Amelia let out a delicate chuckle. "But of course, Mr. Ladd. He is a family friend. I do thank you for your most excellent work once again. You're an asset to the agency."

To Spencer's surprise, and possibly chagrin, he watched as Mr. Ladd's impassive features took on a flush. The man bowed to Lady Amelia, murmured, "At your service" and left the room.

Once again, Spencer was alone with Lady Amelia. Exactly what he wanted. A grin overtook his features. "My lady, you have information to share?"

"Tell me again why I am riding with you?" Lord Ashwhite sat in the corner of the open hackney Amelia had hailed. He looked quite perturbed, most likely because she hadn't shared with him yet about Lord Dudley's financial straits.

Instead, she'd hustled out of the house, the need to see her brother more important than indulging a marquis's curiosity.

She did not own her own phaeton or curricle, which did not usually pose a problem because she was in walking distance of most everywhere she wished to go. When she traveled to Bath, she borrowed her brother's landau.

Arcs of sunlight from the window splayed against her dress but left the marquis across from her in shadows. She scowled at the man, whose arresting gaze irritated her to no end. Or did it stimulate? She shrugged off the unwelcome thought. Stuff and nonsense, that was all. Her life did not resemble a fluffy novel with its exciting tales and dashing heroes. No, real life required choices and practicality.

"Well?" Lord Ashwhite prompted her.

"I—uh—" Amelia's mind scuttled for an answer whilst hardly remembering the question. Oh, yes. His annoying presence in the hackney.

Summoning a bit of steel to her spine, she gave him an arch look. "You've disrupted my business for three days. If you must know, it is paramount that I see my brother this morn. I don't have time to dillydally with you and your games."

"I told you, this is not a game," he said languidly.

"My mistake." Her tone softened, for how could she not empathize with wanting to save a childhood home? "I have been blessed in that my brother inherited my father's estate when my father died. He loves the people there as much as I do."

His bright eyes centered upon her face. "Then, you can imagine how I feel?"

"Indeed." She nodded slowly, gripping the seat as the hackney jolted over some unevenness in the road. "My trouble lies in wondering why you do not go about the traditional way of obtaining a wife. There are plenty of young women who would be delighted to marry you. A title, wealth and a good disposition cause many mammas to salivate."

His nose wrinkled, which caught Amelia by surprise. She felt an unwilling urge to smile.

"As I have only three months in which to marry, there isn't time to get to know the lady. I am not looking for a young miss. Ideally, my wife will be refined and mature. She must have a good sense of humor and live in a godly way."

Amelia cocked her head. "Do you mean to say her church attendance is important to you?"

"No." He leaned forward, propping his arms on his knees and clasping his hands together. "She must have a personal interest in God. A relationship with Jesus, if you will, that influences her daily living."

How absolutely intriguing. Amelia eyed him carefully. A marquis who felt Christian values were important. That Christianity should be a part of living rather than a Sunday ritual. Her own parents had been pious. She remembered the large ornate Bible on a table in the library... Where had that disappeared to?

"Have I embarrassed you, Lady Amelia?" Lord Ashwhite's winning smile bunched his cheeks. "Your brother finds my religious fervor baffling, and my friend Waverly finds it annoying."

"Not at all. I find it most impressive." And attractive, though she certainly couldn't say so.

"Meeting such a lady is bound to be difficult, as most seem to bend their beliefs to reflect their company."

"Perhaps try a church?" Overhead the sunlight shifted with the hackney's movements, and she adjusted her hat. Lord Ashwhite's face moved out of shadow. "There are many societies that aid the less fortunate, and within those I've found a number of young women living out their lives in godly service."

"Might I attend such a meeting with you?" The question, while casually delivered, came with such a mischievous smirk that she felt tempted to rap his arm with her fan. Rather, she gave him a sidelong glance that felt a tad flirtatious.

"Perhaps one day, my lord."

The hackney rumbled to a stop. Lord Ashwhite exited, and then held out his hand to her. The barest hesitation rippled through her. His mannerly approach could not stifle the fluttering that had resumed in her belly or the reluctance she felt in making contact with him.

Nonsense.

She summoned resolve and put her hand in his. Through her gloves she felt the gentle strength of his grip, his thumb resting lightly on her hand, his fingers curled around her palm, insurance against a fall. She could not meet his eyes for the emotion coursing through her. It would do no good to let this marquis see feeling plastered across her face.

He spoke intelligently, listened to her ideas, danced like a dream and cared for his people. What of it? Many men did the same. There was no logic to the emotions stilting her thoughts. As soon as her slippers touched the cobblestones, he released her hand. She paid the hackney driver, and then they commenced to her brother's front door.

"I will pay back your fare," Lord Ashwhite said as they mounted the steps to the door.

"Certainly not."

"Indeed, or shall I call for my landau and offer you a ride home?"

He was too charming, with that sun-induced twinkle in his eyes and that handsome curve about his lips. She adjusted her hat and gave him a prim look. "You'll do no such thing, my lord."

Twisting forward, she rapped smartly on her brother's door and steeled herself for a conflict.

"You didn't tell me about Lord Dudley," he said abruptly.

"Oh, dear… Well, now is not a good time. I do not wish to bandy about information where the servants might hear."

"I'm quite sure they know more than you do." He paused. "That runner, Mr. Ladd, seems protective of you."

"Surely your imagination." She rapped on the door again, harder this time, more desperately.

"Have you been doing business with him for a long time?"

"You ask too many questions." She raised her hand to knock again, but the door swung open, much to her relief. Confounded man. Why had he taken such an interest? It would not bode well for her should he decide to impart what he knew to her brother.

Eversham's butler showed her into the library, her favorite room, as he well knew. He left the door open while he went to rouse her brother.

"I see old Ev's sleeping habits haven't changed."

"They attended Lady Blight's rout last evening." Amelia perused the shelves for something new to borrow. Unfortunately her sister-in-law was more of a talker than a reader. More was the pity.

"And you?" Lord Ashwhite questioned.

"My, but speculation does seem to be your favorite game."

"Whilst you excel at charades."

Despite herself, she smiled. "Really, my lord, must we engage in verbal battle?" She turned and unexpectedly found him behind her. Breath caught, heart pumping, she paused.

"Yes, my lady, we really must, for I intend to win at this game."

"I do not lose easily," she said, refusing to back up. In fact, she'd give him a taste of his own antics. An exciting quiver of anticipation arched through her as she stepped forward. Only inches away.

His cravat was tied exceptionally well. The breadth of his shoulders surpassed her own, and she pointed her face upward, fixing him with a determined look that she hoped did not belie the curious thrum stretching her nerves wire taut. To her surprise, an indefinable look crossed his face.

What was that in his eyes? For a moment, it seemed as though he swayed toward her. But then his features smoothed, and politeness blanketed his expression.

He backed up and made a terse little bow. "Forgive me for intruding upon your space."

Suddenly uncertain, she nodded a pardon.

"Am I interrupting?" Her brother stood in the doorway, looking displeased. His forehead creased as it was wont to do when he became upset. Deep circles ringed his eyes.

"Not at all." Smoothly Amelia skirted Lord Ashwhite and went to her brother. She clasped his hands and drew him into the room. "And I do apologize for waking you, but this cannot wait. Is Lady Eversham asleep still?"

"Yes, and not to be disturbed."

They sat on the couch while Lord Ashwhite continued his elegant stance against the wall shelves. Amelia acutely felt the heat of his gaze upon her but chose to ignore it. She hoped Ev would dismiss his friend, but when her brother called for morning tea, that hope withered.

She took a deep, fortifying breath. Very well. Lord Ashwhite would find out her circumstances soon enough should things not go the way she wished.

"Did Ash come with you, Amelia?" Ev steepled his fingers. She noted the clumsy knot of his cravat and felt a pang of guilt for showing up so early.

"Yes."

His brows rose, waiting, but she wouldn't say more. He'd already interfered in her life enough. And she'd let him know that, regardless of Lord Ashwhite's presence.

"We had business to discuss." The low rumble of his voice interrupted the tension between her and Eversham.

Amelia gave Lord Ashwhite a warning look before turning to her brother. "I received your note, brother, and am most disturbed. Could we discuss your plans in private?" Perhaps not the politest way of ridding the room of Lord Ashwhite, but she had to at least try. He was distracting in too many ways.

"Ash can hear whatever you have to say. It's good for him to learn what happens when forced to choose between relatives and a wife."

Amelia frowned. "But this is family business."

"Yes, and business is what got you here in the first place. I meant what I said in my letter, Amelia." He gave her an annoyingly stern glower. She hated that look.

"You're being insufferable," she said quietly. Anger was stirring in her belly, hot and viscous. "My life is not yours to dictate."

A flicker of empathy crossed Ev's face before being tamped down by an even worse emotion: resolve. "I know you don't like it, but I have responsibilities now. Four years ago I wouldn't have cared, but I've the properties to look out for as well as my wife. Your ridiculous rants against the prison system, not to mention this…*business* of finding husbands… It has to stop."

"But one week—"

"Is more than enough to pack up your house," he finished for her. "I'm going back to bed unless, Ash, you have something to add?"

"I've heard quite enough," said Lord Ashwhite.

Amelia hardly dared look at him—at anything, really, lest the men see the burning anger that swept through her at the unfairness of it all. A week to move in with her brother and his wife. No choice at all. Even if she stopped all her activities, he would not give her a stipend large enough to rent her own home. What was she going to do?

Chapter Six

Two nights later, as Amelia and an excited Lydia swept into Almack's, the question of Amelia's future dampened her enjoyment of the evening. They mingled, and Amelia introduced Lydia to several notable ladies, who in turn introduced Lydia to eligible family members. It wasn't long before her dance card was filled.

Amelia had deliberately left her card near the punch bowl. She didn't intend to dance with anyone. Look at what one quadrille with a marquis had done—sent her into a romantic fit of emotions that could do no good for her, especially with the threat of losing her home a pall that continued to darken her mood.

No, indeed. Her dancing days were over, just like her courting days. Spinsterhood beckoned with all its freedoms…though not so many now her brother had become involved. She frowned.

"Are you feeling all right?" Lydia touched her shoulder. "Perhaps we should get a bit of air?"

Amelia gave her cousin a rueful smile. "I am simply pondering the recent turn of events."

"I am so sorry."

She had filled Lydia in on her brother's machinations.

Sometimes two heads worked better than one, but in this case, neither woman had been able to think of a suitable plan to change the situation.

Now Lydia's face brightened. She looked beautiful, her blond hair coiffed perfectly, her complexion healthy and smooth. "There is always teaching at a girls' school. You would do exceptionally well."

Amelia blanched. "But there are so many rules to follow. Etiquette and languages…not to mention the noise. When would I read or paint?"

"Life cannot always be pleasure," Lydia said gently. "You must work for some things."

"Of course I know that, but if I can find work I enjoy, so much the better." That was true, right? She hoped she wasn't being lazy or unthankful, but to live miserably seemed such a waste if she could live happily. "Perhaps I am being a spoiled earl's daughter. In truth, I think I'd find a noisy school of adolescent girls preferable to living with my brother. He is overbearing at times."

"It won't be all bad." Lydia squeezed her arm. "You'll have your own wing to live in, plenty of space to breathe. You'll be able to go riding and visiting. We shall plan a vacation to Bath and wade in an ocean somewhere."

Amelia tried to smile but wasn't quite able. "You make valid points, though I cannot but help feel suffocated. The past few years' taste of freedom has ruined me, I fear." When her first Season had ended with no engagement, she'd been disappointed. The second Season, she'd fared the same. But the third Season… That was when she'd met Lord Markham. The year she'd decided she would never marry anyone.

And now, at the ripe age of five-and-twenty, after she'd lived four years independently, the thought of submitting to her sister-in-law's reign gave her the shudders. But a lady had no choice. She should count herself blessed that she did not live on the streets as so many in London did, or that her family had not squandered their fortunes and left her in ruin.

"'Tis not so bad, being a woman," said Lydia. "Even as a country baron's daughter, I have been spoiled and cosseted. My family is loving and kind, and I would do anything for them."

This time Amelia managed a chuckle. "Even throw yourself into the marriage mart."

Lydia cringed, her smile wry. "Even that, though I wish I did not have to do so. But that is why I have you." Her palm swept the air. "You shall introduce me to a man whom I will love forever. We will be happy, and this won't seem like such a great sacrifice."

"I truly hope so." For if she ever found that she'd brought two together who could not find happiness, then she'd gladly quit this business.

The music started, and an eager-looking young lord claimed Lydia for her dance. Amelia watched them for a moment, feeling a stirring of sorrow in her chest, for when had she ever experienced such an enthusiastic response from a man?

She could think of only two, and she did not wish to think of either. Biting her lip, she meandered to a quiet alcove to sit on a brocaded chair. The corner partially obscured her from view, and she could lend her attention to the dilemma she faced.

When she'd left her brother's the other day, Lord Ashwhite had tried to hire a hackney for her, but she had decided to walk home. She'd hoped sunshine might soothe the storm inside, but even though she'd walked briskly, she hadn't been able to shake the tension upon her shoulders.

Sighing now, she watched Lydia swirl around the ballroom floor. The girl didn't want to marry, yet she would lay her life down for her family. Amelia frowned, thinking of her own selfishness. She wanted to paint and make her own decisions.

Poor Ev had married a shrew to bolster their family's flagging finances and to fix up their estates. He'd performed his sacrifice. But what of her? Yes, she was involved with several societies that helped those less fortunate, but she must be missing something. What, she wasn't sure.

She must have a personal interest in God.

Lord Ashwhite's words about his future wife rounded through her. He'd looked so very earnest as he said that. Remembering his expression caused her discomfort, and she could not pinpoint why.

"Ah, at last I've found you." The rumble of a deep voice interrupted her self-analysis. The subject of her thoughts settled beside her, his cologne fragrant and light. She sniffed appreciatively, telling her heart to stop its ridiculous pattering over nothing more than a pleasant aroma.

Lord Ashwhite tipped a lazy smile toward her. While dressed handsomely, he did not cross the line into the dandy style that she found so abhorrent. His clothes fit him perfectly, and someone had tied his cravat neatly.

She gave him an arch look. "What are you doing here?"

"Where are those manners you teach your clients?" he countered. His relaxed posture suggested good humor.

"Did you find a wife, then?" she couldn't resist asking. "You're looking awfully happy with yourself." Which made her feel rather disgruntled. To cover her emotions, she searched for Cousin Lydia. Satisfied her charge was safe and behaving above reproach, she returned her attention to the marquis and his smug expression.

"No wife, but I do believe I shall be able to help you with your dilemma." His eyes, full of amusement, met hers.

"I am not in a dilemma," she said, feeling stubborn. "And if I was, I wouldn't need your help."

His hand went to his chest. "You wound me, my lady."

"I heartily doubt that," she muttered beneath her breath. Oh, how she wished her heart would stop its dreadful knocking against her sternum! One dance, one conversation, and now she could not escape this peculiar excitement she felt whenever she saw him. Like a silly miss out for her first Season, head turned by her very first suitor.

"On to a serious note." Lord Ashwhite straightened in his chair and propped his elbows on his knees. "I have a proposition for you."

"You are fairly bursting with propositions."

"This is one that will suit your needs very well." A slow smile spread across his face. "I have thought about buying your house—"

"My house?" She covered her lips, alarmed by the screech she'd uttered.

"Very attractive, my lady."

She scowled at him. "Go on."

"But after consideration, I thought it might be better to engage your sympathies once more. You see, you never told me the details of what your runner discovered about Lord Dudley. And I never told you why I wanted to know."

Curiosity piqued, she studied him. "This is true. And I do apologize, but I had much on my mind."

Surprisingly, his look was gentle. "I know that, which is why I determined to give you a few days' rest before—"

"Hunting me down?" she offered.

"Fair enough." He inclined his head, though she didn't see a trace of repentance in his face. "Here is my conundrum. Lord Dudley is a distant cousin, but he is the direct heir to Ashwhite should I fail to fulfill the obligations of my father's will."

"To marry within three months."

"Yes. Less than that now."

She fanned herself, spotted Lydia dancing with a different young man, who wore the same look of eagerness as the last and chewed her lip. The right thing to do would be to help Lord Ashwhite. Especially in light of what she'd learned of Lord Dudley. "This information does change how I view your problem, but I must have a night to think on it. Could you meet me tomorrow, say around four in the afternoon, in my parlor? I will be prepared to give you an answer as well as share Mr. Ladd's findings on Lord Dudley."

Her gaze drifted past Lord Ashwhite and locked on Lord Dudley, who had spotted her hiding spot and now marched toward her with determination.

How had Lord Dudley gained entrance to Almack's? Granted, he was an earl whose proclivities remained unknown to most of the *ton*. She was beginning to tire of seeing him at every event she went to, especially now that he was out of the running for Cousin Lydia.

Lord Ashwhite followed her look. "Trouble, Lady Amelia?"

"Not at all." She stood quickly and gave Lord Ashwhite what she hoped was a confident smile. "Handling suitors is my specialty." Head high, she swept out of the alcove to meet the earl who couldn't seem to understand her very firm *no*. And as she left, she felt Lord Ashwhite's stare upon her.

Tomorrow.

Tomorrow she'd have to decide whether to work with Lord Ashwhite or not. She might have to accept his offer in order to avoid the dregs of a caged life.

Spencer watched as Lady Amelia glided away. The way she moved spoke of gracefulness and poise. One might never guess from the way she walked that she indulged in intellectual and political pursuits. From the outside, she appeared to be a fashionable lady of the *ton*. He saw the exchanges she made, how the dowagers greeted her with warmth and comfort. They trusted her status and knowledge. There were no suspicious or haughty glances directed toward her. Not like the ones his mother used to endure. How would that change if they discovered her less than ladylike activities?

The memory of her direct gaze and delightfully straightforward talk brought a smile to his lips but heaviness to his heart. It might be that engaging her services could cast a gloom about her reputation. After all, those same ladies who offered her their approval tended to frown at him.

It was far too close to how they'd looked at his mother. But she'd flouted society's conventions in numerous ways, bringing shame to his father and pain to Spencer. Their disapproval of her was of a far different nature than their disapproval of him. After all, he did manage to coax a grudging twinkle in their eyes when he put his mind to it.

He stood, keeping his gaze on the maddening Lady Amelia. He was beginning to understand Eversham's frustration with his sister. He stepped into the ballroom and headed toward the entrance. He'd done what he'd hoped for, proffered an exchange of information, at the least.

As he rounded the room, he noticed the gentleman standing near Lady Amelia. Something about the way he stood... It was familiar, and it was too close. Spencer frowned and immediately reversed direction. As he neared, he realized that the man next to Lady Amelia was none other than Lord Dudley. His distant cousin bothered Lady Amelia, though Spencer noticed she took great pains not to show her unease.

Perhaps it was the stiffness of her shoulders that gave her away. Or the tight press of her lips. Either way, his gut told him to move quickly. Jaw tight, he pushed past a group of giggling misses. He dodged a dowager who was giving him the evil eye, no doubt wondering how he'd snagged an invitation to Almack's.

A marquis title came in handy every so often.

Finally he reached Lady Amelia in time to hear her curtly say, "No, Lord Dudley, I am overheated at the moment. Really, a dance would be too much."

"But my lady, I saw you dance last week, and you are adept at it." His facetious cousin bestowed a sickeningly sweet smile on Lady Amelia. "I long to share such an experience with you."

Her fan came out, nearly smacking Spencer's face. "Really, my lord, you flatter me. But I must insist you find another partner." She hadn't noticed Spencer yet; she was too busy fanning her face, which looked remarkably red beneath the elaborate glass lights.

"Shall we retreat to a cooler spot in which to rest?" The hopeful look on Lord Dudley's face, and Lady Amelia's barely controlled grimace, spurred Spencer to action.

"May I borrow Lady Amelia for a moment?"

Dudley had not recognized him. Spencer gave a terse nod. He ignored Dudley's surprise and reached for Lady Amelia's arm, lightly turning her toward him. "There is a family matter I wished to discuss with her."

Though Lord Dudley's cheeks drooped, he gave a grudging nod. "Farewell, my bonny lady. Perhaps later this evening we might share a waltz?"

Spencer didn't give her time to respond. He propelled her toward the balcony, where a light breeze fluttered the simple curtains. They passed the orchestra and moved into the cool evening air. Her arm felt small and fragile beneath his grip. She moved away as soon as they passed through the doors.

"That was unnecessary," she said, looking up at him.

He wanted to take the spectacles from her face and get a good look at her eyes. They were very dark, fathomless, and he could not tell her mood.

Unsettled by his forward thoughts, he looked down. "You seemed as though you needed an escape from my cousin."

A short, humorless laugh rushed out of her. "Perhaps I did, and perhaps I should thank fortune you provided it."

"They say God works in mysterious ways."

"Yes… God." Her eyes met his, and he saw no anger on her features, only blatant curiosity. "You speak of Him in a way I'm unused to. Sometimes at the prison, I overhear the women discussing the Bible. They share verses they've studied or different theologies they're pondering. Their experiences while praying. It all seems much more personal than what I've witnessed in my life."

The breeze blew a dark strand of hair across her shoulder. He almost reached to brush it back but stopped himself in time. This was no actress or lowborn woman. Every movement or word said could have devastating consequences for her. He peeked into Almack's and, as expected, caught a patroness studying them.

Clearing his throat, he crossed his arms and thought about her words. "Neither had I, but my trip to the Americas changed my outlook."

"That must have been quite the change for you."

"It was." He thought back to the past year, which already seemed a long time ago. "I learned much about myself. I found out I wasn't who God made me to be. My priorities changed when God changed my heart."

Her head cocked to the side. "Your heart?"

Spencer fumbled for words, feeling awkward and far from the smooth rake he'd been rumored to be. Something about this woman caught him off guard. There was more than attraction between them, but he couldn't tell just yet if it was curiosity or something rarer.

"I don't know how to explain what happened, only that when I needed God, when I realized my own sinfulness and cried out to Jesus, He was there."

Lady Amelia's eyes widened, and then her features took on a blank look. "You had an emotional experience."

"It was real," he told her quietly, all awkwardness gone as he realized just how true that was.

She pushed her spectacles upward. The look she gave him was very serious. "From what I have seen, emotions are not to be trusted or to be used as proof of anything."

The breeze caught the barest hint of her perfume, and it lingered beneath his nose, tantalizing and sweet.

"I hesitate to argue with you, my lady, but your supposition is based on experience, and experiences are interpreted by feelings."

"A valid point. I shall concede to that." She worried her lower lip with her teeth, which Spencer found unexpectedly adorable. "Thank you for your rescue earlier."

"Why do you dislike Lord Dudley?"

"Trust you to ask the impertinent questions." She sighed, but he could tell she was not irritated. "In truth, I am not sure. There is something in his expression that warns me away. And perhaps I should not have investigated his financial background, but I did, and what I found makes me wary."

Spencer's brows rose. "Do you investigate all your suitors?"

Her nose wrinkled. "He was intended for Miss Lydia, and I investigate all marital prospects." She quirked a smile his way. "But yes, I have a curious nature, and if someone intrigues me, I will look into their lives a little more closely than the casual acquaintance."

"And what about me? Have you investigated my background?" His throat felt oddly tight as he awaited her answer.

Her smile wavered the slightest bit before turning cheeky. "Only men who intrigue me, my lord. I believe you to be an open book."

Before he could refute that erroneous assumption, her cousin came rushing out of the ballroom.

"Oh, Amelia," she gushed, seeming not to notice him. "It has finally happened." Her breaths were quick and light. Apparently Lady Amelia felt the same alarm he did, for she hurried forward and took Miss Stanley's arm.

"You must take deep breaths or you shall faint." Lady Amelia delivered the instruction in that strident tone he'd come to admire. "Now, what has happened? Are you well?"

"Better than I have ever been." Miss Stanley beamed a radiant smile that transformed her into a gorgeous creature. "I have met him."

"Who?" Lady Amelia cast Spencer a quick, searching look before returning her attention to Miss Stanley.

"The love of my life. The man I'm going to marry." At that, Miss Stanley's eyes fluttered closed and she collapsed, dragging the smaller Lady Amelia down with her.

Chapter Seven

Corsets were a nuisance.

Amelia relaxed in the drawing room, thankful she rarely wore one. Styles had certainly changed for the better, and many day dresses did not require one. If Cousin Lydia's hadn't been pulled so tight last evening, she wouldn't have fainted. And all over a man. A man with whose name Amelia had never heard. She touched the sore spot where Lydia's elbow had connected with her brow on their downward trip to the floor.

"My lady." Dukes appeared in the doorway. "Lord Ashwhite has arrived."

She straightened. "Send him in, and then please instruct Sally to bring us refreshment." For a bit more in earnings, Sally served as both housemaid and personal maid. Her Yorkshire accent and practicality added much to Amelia's household. She did not look forward to losing Sally when she moved to Ev's home.

If, she reminded herself. No use counting chickens before they hatched. She adjusted her spectacles as she waited for Lord Ashwhite. And then she shifted on the chair. Perhaps she should stand. But then she'd have to look up at him. Better to sit, forcing him to sit as well, and they could face each other eye to eye.

Her fingers played with the paperwork carefully balanced on her lap. Only a few pages that told quite a story.

"My lady." Lord Ashwhite entered the room, bowing and then striding toward the other chair. He wore a crooked smile that bespoke mischief. It was both utterly attractive and supremely irritating. "I pray this afternoon finds you and Miss Stanley well?"

Huffing in a quick breath, she nodded to him as he sat. If only her pulse would slow. A spinster such as herself should not have these reactions...should she? She became aware of the afternoon sunlight highlighting the marquis's face and making his eyes shimmer.

Such color...such texture. Stubble darkened his chin. Sunbeams skimmed over his cheekbones, carving hollowed shadows. An attractive man with a charming personality. Any woman would be susceptible, she assured herself.

"Is that a bruise?" Lord Ashwhite lifted forward as if to come inspect her face, of all things. She held up a hand.

"My lord, pray stay seated. It is merely a swelling." Which Sally had been told to powder, but evidently she had not been liberal enough with the concealment.

"From last night?"

"An unfortunate collision with Lydia's elbow."

"Ah, yes, Miss Stanley." He relaxed back in his chair, crossing his legs at the ankle. "Does she fancy herself in love?"

"You are full of questions. They never cease from you." Though she sounded disapproving, Amelia was surprised by the feeling of kinship sweeping through her. For didn't she also have many questions? She could understand such curiosity. "I think it would be best for Miss Lydia to discuss her emotions with you herself."

Lord Ashwhite's brow moved upward. "And yet you are without opinion?"

"I did not say that." She shifted in her seat. "You are well acquainted with my thoughts on the validity of emotions."

"Somewhat, though I would learn more." He studied her, head cocked to the side as though examining an unusual specimen. "Your stance creates great curiosity. What must have happened to turn a young woman into an unfeeling—"

"I am not unfeeling," she retorted. Her face felt extremely hot again. His doing, no doubt. The man enraged her. "Do not look at me as though I am a curiosity to you, some insect to be studied. I have feelings, but I do not allow them to rule my decisions."

"Because you don't trust them."

She blinked. "Well...yes." Wasn't that obvious?

His grimace lowered her ire. "My lady, I apologize. You are not unfeeling, and that was an insensitive word choice. I greatly admire your work at Newgate."

"It is not only my work," she felt obliged to point out. "Mrs. Elizabeth Fry has led the movement, though she is very often busy with her children. But I believe she has great plans for helping the prisoners, and it seems a practical way to show love."

"Yes, it does. I'd like to be involved." He paused. "You cannot tell me your emotions are not related to your decision to help."

She frowned, feeling at a loss suddenly. "Our conversation has veered off track."

"Your tea, my lady." Sally came in with a tray and placed it on the small table. "Shall I pour?"

"Please." Amelia nodded. Normally she would do the task, but at the moment she felt quite shaky. It was not every day someone questioned her motives or challenged beliefs she'd clung to for years.

Discombobulated. That was how she felt presently.

In an effort to look calm, she took the tea Sally offered and sipped slowly. Once Sally had served Lord Ashwhite and left the room, Amelia carefully set her cup on the table. She picked up the papers and held them out to Lord Ashwhite.

"You may peruse these if you wish." Her voice sounded steady, which was a blessing.

He took the papers and flipped through them, giving her several moments to scrutinize him. The thick hair, the finely pressed clothes. The strong line of his jaw and tanned fingers. Lean and long... Suddenly she knew she must paint him.

It would have to be from memory. He could never know she'd memorized him in oils. Feeling flushed, she averted her eyes. The drawing room was her favorite room in the house. Whoever had owned the home before her brother had decorated in the Adam style. The rich splashes of turquoise-robed peacocks enriched the dark wood furniture. When the thick green curtains were drawn, sunshine spilled into the room through overly large windows.

The thing she adored most about this room was the closet. Not many drawing rooms had one, but this one did, and she stashed her easel and paints within its confines. Though she kept the turpentine outside, its odor stubbornly remained and reminded her of her greatest love.

Lord Ashwhite slapped the papers on the table and planted his hands on his knees. "This is precisely why

I need a wife. I had no idea of his financial troubles, or that he had brought them upon himself. And it appears that he may be collecting money for a sham investment."

Bringing her mind to the present, Amelia nodded sadly. "Yes, I'm looking further into who is involved in the scheme. It was distressing to learn of this. Lord Dudley has such a bright and open face. One never knows what lies beneath such a facade."

"For all have sinned," Lord Ashwhite murmured, almost to himself.

"Is that from the Bible?"

He nodded. "No one is perfect. He might not purposefully wear a facade, but it is hard to escape our own natures."

"But some people are better than others," she pointed out, thinking of Mrs. Elizabeth Fry.

"True, but our goodness can never be good enough to be holy. Never enough to bring us to God."

"Such heavy matters on a bright day," she said lightly, hoping to change the subject. This conversation struck something deep within. It discomforted her, though she could not pinpoint why. "Let us return to the topic at hand. We should discuss our possible partnership and what it will entail."

"Very well." His lips curved as he regarded her with eyes a touch too merry. "I propose you find me a wife so that my lands will be safe and my people properly cared for. In return, I will pay you handsomely."

"I thought you were going to buy my house?"

"My lady, a gentleman is allowed to change his mind."

Cad. But she could not blame him as it had seemed an extravagant offer. She understood practicality.

"How much will you pay me?" she asked cautiously.

Her breath hung suspended within her chest, and she did not move as she awaited his answer.

He named a figure that drew the air from her lungs in a sudden gasp. Why, such an amount would go far in securing her own home, even if it was but a tiny cottage in the country. Ev would have no say in her life then. And though everything within her protested working with Lord Ashwhite, could she honestly refuse a plea that helped both her and so many others?

He must have seen her discomfort, for he cleared his throat.

"If you are uncertain, perhaps you'd like visit Ashwhite tomorrow afternoon for a tour. Your brother will be there on business matters, and I am sure you could accompany him."

Amelia pressed her lips together, battling her rising elation. She'd been on the cusp of saying yes to his proposition, but the thought of seeing his estate, of being more in his company, was proving irresistible.

"That sounds like a splendid idea," she finally said. "I will give you my decision tomorrow, on one condition."

He tilted his head in question.

"You must not tell Eversham about our discussion. He is a tad upset about my side business, and I've no notion to upset him further." Soon enough she'd have enough money saved to move out, and then she'd deal with Eversham's wounded pride. When Lord Ashwhite looked hesitant, she rushed on. "I do not ask you to lie to him, for I don't condone dishonesty, but should the subject arise, I would appreciate discretion."

There was a pause. Then he dipped his head in concession. "Very well. I shall exercise discernment and try to keep your trust without betraying my conscience."

She allowed herself a relieved smile. "I shall be there in the morning, then."

"Wonderful." He flashed her a grin so bright her heart fluttered. "What kind of mount shall I have ready for you?"

"I prefer a horse with spirit." She gave him a no-nonsense look so he would take her seriously. "And a sensitive mouth."

"Somehow I am not surprised." His grin widened.

They stood, and she reached out her hand. "My papers, please."

He set them in her palm. "Come hungry. My cook prepares the most delicious meals. He came from the Continent, escaping the revolution."

"How intriguing. And you did not turn him away?"

"No, he brought his family, and they have been a blessing to the estate."

She nodded, digesting this information. Such compassion moved her greatly. They said their goodbyes, and she tried hard to memorize the planes of his face before he left. As soon as his curricle pulled away, she rushed to her desk in the library, penned a note to her brother about tomorrow's trip and gave it to Dukes to have delivered.

Then she went to her drawing room. Though it was five in the evening, darkness had not quite arrived. She went to the closet and studied her canvases. Perhaps a portrait would do for now. She pulled out the right size and set to work priming it so that it would be ready within a few days for painting.

By the time she'd finished, darkness had fallen. The excitement she'd felt at the thought of her new painting faded with the sun and, tired, she ate the dinner Sally brought her and then crawled into bed.

Sleep did not come easily, though.

Too many plans; too many things that could go wrong. Lydia, for one. She must find time to investigate this suitor who had caught her cousin's eye. From what she understood, he was the second son of an earl. More than likely he was enlisted in the military. Surely Lydia could not want to be married to someone with so few monies to his name, no title and a job that might send him all over the world? Had she forgotten her entire reason for marrying? To save her family. And how could she accomplish that with a second son?

Amelia frowned into her pillow. The sound of carriages in the street filtered through the walls. The Season was in full swing, but she had no parties to attend this evening. Her thoughts turned to Lord Ashwhite and his peculiar words about sin.

Of course, she knew no one was perfect, but Lord Dudley's gambling problems seemed a little more than just imperfection. Why, he could ruin his new estate that way. Leave his people with no employment opportunities and starving.

She might be imperfect, but she would never do that to anyone.

Gambling.

She made a little noise with her mouth and rolled over. Bunching her pillow with her fists, she closed her eyes. Lord Ashwhite's face swam before her, his expression laughing and kind. What compassion he had to offer refuge to his cook and family.

He spoke of God and sin as real things. She believed there was a God, but had she ever felt as though she could speak of Him as she would a friend? Not hardly. She squeezed her eyes tighter, nuzzling the softness of her pillow, willing sleep to take these thoughts from her.

Everyone sinned, but some sinned more than others.

She wanted the notion to make her feel better, but all it did was tangle her stomach and push the comfort of sleep further from her. Her nerves were awash with worry. What would Ev say if he discovered her plans to help Lord Ashwhite? And how would she feel when she saw the marquis in the morn? What else might he say to her?

Questions that must wait for answers.

Spencer thought he might like Lady Amelia very much indeed. Not enough to want to marry someone like her, though. A woman with such strong opinions often left the family to suffer while she tried to convince everyone else how right she was.

That had been his experience with his mother. Ideology left little room for basic responsibilities, like caring for her husband and child. Even now, he felt the painful sense of abandonment he'd grown up with. Always hoping for his mother's return from whatever adventure she'd left on. The way he'd covered his ears at night when she was home so as not to hear the terrible arguments between her and Father.

Childish feelings he stuffed away. He didn't care for their reemergence now.

He grimaced. He would need to vet carefully the women Lady Amelia chose. Certainly good works were admirable, but he did not want someone who would put those things above her family as his mother had.

He watched her control her mount with finesse and gentleness. While he and Ev discussed politics and the upcoming issues in the House of Lords, Lady Amelia wandered ahead, expression alive with excitement. She rode with perfect posture, as well.

He smiled, thinking of how much he'd enjoyed showing her the estate thus far.

"Did you hear me?" Eversham's disgruntled words cut through his musings.

"What was that?"

"Just as I thought." Ev frowned. "You're ogling my sister."

"Certainly not." But Spencer couldn't stop his smile. "She's very amusing." At the moment, said person had dismounted by herself and was picking gooseberries.

"Her manners apparently deserted her when we left London this morning." But even Ev's mouth twitched. "I still don't understand why you invited her. This was to be a ride for us. And Harriet was none too happy to see her arrive, especially since she could not come herself."

Spencer urged his horse to go a bit faster, hoping Eversham wouldn't press for more details. Ev followed him, though.

Spencer cleared his throat as they neared Lady Amelia. "Why didn't Lady Eversham join us?"

Ev shrugged, looking pensive. "She has a touch of sickness and hasn't been able to leave her room."

"Gooseberries, anyone?" Lady Amelia held up a handful. Her lips were stained with their juice, and the sparkle in her eyes grabbed Spencer's attention. She looked quite pretty. The rosy flush on her cheeks and wide smile disarmed him a bit.

"No, thanks," said Ev in a glum tone.

Spencer shot him a look. He must really be upset over his wife's ill health.

"Come now." Lady Amelia gave him a teasing grin. "These are your favorites. I might be persuaded to make you a pie if we gather enough."

"I said no." The sharpness in her brother's tone wiped the smile from Lady Amelia's face. Spencer felt an unusual urge to knock some sense into Ev for ruining his sister's enjoyment.

"Why are you even here?" Eversham gave her a pointed look, then swiveled to Spencer. "Since when did you two become friends? I'd like to know what's going on, right now."

He glanced at Lady Amelia, expecting her to remount and leave him to answer somehow. But no, her eyes were blazing, and the gooseberries lay forgotten in her clenched hands. Spencer calmed his horse with a soft stroke to his neck, who had picked up on the tension and begun prancing uneasily.

"You go too far, John." She addressed Eversham by his given name—not a good sign. "First you attempt to take my home, and now you'd like to pick my acquaintances? I think not."

Ev's eyes flickered to Spencer, clearly uncomfortable.

"Quite frankly, it is none of your business whom I spend time with."

"It is when you choose your company unwisely," Ev countered.

Her eyes narrowed. "And have I thus far? I am a pillar in the *ton*, a bastion of good sense and propriety." She said it without any pride, in a humble, no-nonsense manner.

It was the truth, which led him to wonder what exactly Ev meant by his comment. Spencer watched him closely, his nerves thrumming. As far as he understood, Lady Amelia knew nothing of his past. How that was possible, he wasn't sure, but he didn't want to tell her now, not with her so close to agreeing to help find him a wife. His past wasn't relevant, anyhow. It had nothing to do with fulfilling the terms of the will.

"Oh, forget it," Ev said. "You'll do what you want no matter what I say. I'm just warning you."

"About what?" A thread of vulnerability entered her voice.

Ev shrugged and looked away, meeting neither her gaze nor Spencer's. "Let's get on with things."

Lady Amelia hurled her brother an unladylike scowl. "This is a wonderful outing, and I appreciate the chance to see Lord Ashwhite's home." She tossed the gooseberries toward the bush and, pulling a handkerchief from some hidden pocket in her dress, proceeded to wipe her hands violently. "Let us continue the tour without your negative attitude."

Giving Eversham an imperious glance that almost made Spencer chuckle, she swiftly remounted and clucked her horse forward. They followed, though Spencer felt the stiff silence beside him. Ev was clearly attempting to hold his temper.

He frowned. That had been close, and he hadn't expected to be thrown into the mix. Of course he realized that he wasn't Ev's first choice of a friend for his sister, but then again, they weren't friends. They were forming a mutually beneficial alliance.

But he couldn't tell Ev that without betraying Lady Amelia's trust. Groaning, he nudged his horse into a canter.

They spent the afternoon touring the grounds and meeting his tenants. Lady Amelia charmed them all, surprising Spencer. She praised the look of the land, the fruitfulness of gardens and the cleanliness of their homes. She even held Hilda Smith's newborn while chatting about the differences between goat's milk and cow's milk.

Spencer grew more and more impressed, and by the

time they were heading back to his home, he knew with great certainty that she was the one to pick out a wife for him.

They left their horses with the groomsmen, and as they entered the house, Lady Amelia's smile broadened. "Oh, this is a lovely home!"

He looked at the house through her eyes. He hadn't been here for a while, being busy in London with his political responsibilities. Now he took in the warmly hued walls, decorated by his mother. The pastels contrasted nicely with the light oak furniture. There was an openness to the rooms. He'd forgotten how large the windows were.

"So much light," Lady Amelia said.

He felt the customary pride. "Ashwhite has been in our family for five generations."

"Such a lineage." She smiled, and his chest felt unaccountably tight.

Madness, he told himself, backing away. Madness to feel drawn to a woman such as Lady Amelia. A bluestocking and an artist. Like his mother, who, while holding many good attributes, also clung to her independent ways, which led to the demise of her marriage.

"We have rooms like this," Eversham said from where he stood inside the library. "You'll be able to paint at our home."

All at once Lady Amelia's expression fell. "If *she'll* let me."

"Why wouldn't she?" asked Eversham.

"Do you remember last Christmas? What about when I visited during the spring? She kept me busy planning menus and calling on neighbors."

Eversham laughed. "I'd forgotten about that."

"Don't even mention the budget," Lady Amelia warned, her face dark.

Spencer couldn't resist. "What about the budget?"

Both faces turned toward him, one amused, the other disgruntled.

"Family business," Lady Amelia declared and abruptly turned to leave the room.

"My sister and numbers do not mix well. Harriet keeps a close eye on the ledgers and is now determined that Amelia shall never touch the accounts again." Ev smiled and watched Lady Amelia depart. "She'll look in your parlor next."

Sure enough, she wandered across the hall and disappeared from view.

"You know her well."

Ev nodded, and his gaze turned serious. "She's my twin, and I know her like the property lines of my estate. I wasn't born yesterday."

Spencer stiffened. "Meaning?"

"I can put two and two together. You want Amelia to find you a wife. She needs money to maintain her lifestyle. You're working together."

Spencer forced his features to remain placid. Trust Ev to figure things out so quickly. "When is she moving in with you?"

"She has four more days. I've told her to quit this business of husband hunting, and I didn't expect you to go behind my back and encourage her."

"I have a little over two months to find someone whom I can say vows before God with in good conscience," Spencer said quietly. He met Ev's gaze. "If your sister chooses to, she can help me."

"And your reputation? That won't help her. If she discovers—"

"She won't," Spencer said curtly. A deep regret over his past rolled across him, dousing any hope he felt for a new life.

"How are you going to stop that from happening?"

"She doesn't know yet. There's no reason for it to be brought up, especially since it has no bearing on the present."

"You'd better not hurt her." Eversham glanced past him to where they could see Lady Amelia looking out the window, lost in a daydream. "I've seen her with many people, but with you, her guard is down. She's...different somehow."

Spencer frowned. "You're one to talk of hurt. How do you think she's taking your dictate that she leave her home? She's unhappy, and it has nothing to do with me."

"It can't be helped." Eversham grimaced. "There are things I can't tell you just now, but you'll have to trust that I need her at home for a time."

Spencer nodded. Though he didn't understand, he wouldn't press Ev. He'd give him the privacy he wanted, and he'd expect the same treatment. He watched Lady Amelia, how the sunshine swathed her in light. Even outside he'd noticed her hair was not the plain brown he'd assumed. Golden strands threaded through her chignon and glimmered in the spring sun.

He stood at the edge of a precipice. One false move and things could go badly indeed. But with the correct step, everything could be righted. He'd save the futures of his tenants and friends. His title came with responsibility, and he couldn't shirk that.

He tore his gaze from Lady Amelia's pretty hair. His attraction to her was a complication he couldn't afford. Not now. Not ever.

Chapter Eight

Amelia tasted the lemon ice Lord Ashwhite had bought her from Gunter's. Delicious tartness coated her tongue, and its chill made the afternoon heat more bearable. Though seated beneath a shady oak, she felt the pure blueness of the day multiplied the strength of the afternoon sun.

Yesterday's tour of his home had been lovely. Before leaving, she'd informed Lord Ashwhite that she would help him. This morning he'd sent a note inviting her to enjoy afternoon ices.

She was not one to turn down a free dessert.

"Gunter's is my favorite place to stop," Lord Ashwhite said beside her.

They'd found a nice place in the park across from the tea shop to conduct business. While anyone could see them, Amelia felt certain a tête-à-tête here would not arouse suspicion or gossip. This was a safe arena for all, and quite popular.

"And mine, as well." She took another lick before the melting ice could dribble upon her fingers. "Thank you for this treat."

"You're quite welcome. I am indebted to you." A peculiar intensity entered his gaze.

She looked away, focusing on finishing her treat while watching other picnickers enjoy their day. Someone's dog had been let loose and ran yapping across the verdant lawn. A child laughed and chased it.

Amelia smiled at the scene. "I had a pup as a child. Rooster."

"Rooster. Dare I ask how such a name came to be?"

"His bark." At the memory, Amelia couldn't stop a snicker from tumbling past her lips.

Lord Ashwhite chuckled. "That would be something to hear. My dogs were utterly normal, and I gave them names like Buster, Mutton... It's hard when they die, though."

"It is."

The somber turn stopped their talk, and they finished their ices in silence. Amelia saw many new faces here. She'd been so focused on finding Cousin Lydia a husband that she hadn't paid attention to the newest additions to the *ton*. Even while presenting Cousin Lydia to the queen, she hadn't noticed the misses fresh from their schoolrooms.

Not an efficient way to establish a business. And now she had only two days left before Eversham came and carted her away. She peered at her ice, frowning.

"Do you think Eversham shall physically carry me from the house in two days' time?" she asked. "Or will he arrive with a bevy of servants and start unloading my home?"

"You know your brother better than I do," Lord Ashwhite said carefully.

Irritated that he was right, Amelia glowered. "He shall arrive and begin taking things. That is how he will do it.

He will give my servants their letters of reference and no doubt secure them employment somewhere. He will force my hand—"

"To do what?"

"To go with him. What do you think?" She hated the feeling of powerlessness burning through her, a mad fire within her chest, cutting off her air. "Even with the money you'll pay me, I don't know if the owner will re-negotiate the contract. I will have to move in with Ev."

"Do you want an advance?" There was no cautious-ness on Lord Ashwhite's face, only curiosity. His trust in her dampened the flames of resentment.

"Thank you, and I do appreciate that, but no. I accept payment only upon success. If I do not find you a suit-able wife, then I shall not charge you."

"Those are high expectations, my lady. And very little reward for the work you put into this."

"Nevertheless, it is my policy. That is something you should know up front." She glanced down at the paper on her lap before lifting her pen. "How about we start with attributes you're looking for? Hair color?"

"Looks are of no importance."

Amelia's head jerked up. "Surely you jest?"

"I don't." He grinned at her. "What, my lady? You have never heard of marriage based on more than a lik-ing of looks?"

"It's unnatural," she said, frowning. "You will be mar-ried to this woman for the rest of your life. Certainly you'd want to enjoy looking at her?"

"I believe our respect for each other will lead to a har-monious relationship in all areas." His eyes crinkled, and the dappled sunlight filtering through the leaves of the tree behind them caused his eyes to sparkle. "But if you insist on a physical preference, I would say I quite like brown hair with strands of gold throughout."

"That is very particular, my lord," she grumbled, but she grudgingly wrote "strands of gold" on her paper. "For the eye color, let's stick to one shade. A man too particular has a slimmer chance of catching a wife."

"Yes, my lady," he said in a voice so docile and false that an unwilling smile edged her lips.

"Blue, green or brown?"

"Irrelevant," he said firmly. "I'd like a normal-looking woman with more sense than most in the *ton*. A heart bigger than her fortune. Hands quick to help those in need. Not a gossiper."

"That last one will be nigh impossible."

"Then, I shall need a woman who does not speak."

They laughed, and though Amelia doubted she'd ever forget his list, she wrote the attributes down anyway. What a strange man he was. This task might be more difficult than she'd anticipated.

"I forgot one thing," he said quietly beside her.

Looking at him, at the smiling seriousness of those eyes, Amelia knew what he planned to say. "Her relationship with God."

"Yes."

"How shall I know if she has one?"

He tipped his head, holding her gaze. "It may be evident in her conversation, but most likely in her actions. Her spirituality will be something I will be responsible for noticing."

Amelia wet her lips, feeling strangely relieved. What did she know of religion or God? Perhaps in childhood, at the bedside, through songs her mother sang. A faint memory that she pushed away. Her times at church were spent daydreaming or planning lists to write later. "Religion is very important to you."

Lord Ashwhite broke visual contact and stared out over the grass. "Not religion, no. But discovering God's love…that changed me."

Now she was curious. She hadn't bothered to investigate Lord Ashwhite. Her funds were dwindling, and she planned to stop by Mr. Ladd's flat to discuss Lydia's newest suitor. The one she was in love with. He'd already taken her cousin for a ride in Hyde Park, or so she'd written Amelia in a quick letter that had come in the morning's post.

Amelia had read the note with foreboding. The courtship was moving entirely too fast.

Forcing her mind to the subject at hand, she studied Lord Ashwhite. "You speak of God's love. How can such a thing change a man? And from what were you changed?" She certainly couldn't see this kind and respectful person beside her as someone in need of a metamorphosis.

"Oh, in different ways." Lord Ashwhite paused as though weighing his words. "In the past I was very selfish. Uncaring. I used others for my own ends."

She thought of his cook, the immigrant from France. "That does not sound like the man I know."

It seemed a struggle for him to smile. "I hope not." He cleared his throat. "What about you? If you were to marry, what qualities would you look for in your groom?"

A sharp laugh slipped out before she could stop it. She gave him an incredulous look. "Marriage is out of the question. I will never be tied down in such a way."

"You are saying you've never considered it?" His brows rose.

"I did consider the ordeal and had no problem dismissing the thought." Not quite the whole truth, but she did not wish to spread her shame out like a picnic for him to feast upon. She pushed herself to a standing position, clutching paper and pen.

He stood also, holding out his hand to take her finished ice. "What made you dismiss marriage? You would make a good wife."

"You say such unsuitable things." She fanned herself with the paper, glad the heat covered what she was sure was a blush spreading across her cheeks.

"Is the truth unsuitable?"

They picked their way across the park's lawn while Amelia tried to think of a response. How could she tell him that she'd longed for a husband and that she'd thought she found the perfect man, only to discover him in the gardens with another woman…?

"Have I offended you with my candidness, Lady Amelia?"

"Not at all," she said briskly. "Honesty is something I've come to cherish. I am merely sorting through my schedule." Not entirely a lie. She did have much to accomplish.

"A schedule that is no doubt robust with activities." They were nearing his curricle. He dropped their waste with a waiter whose sole duty was to serve those who chose to eat in the park rather than at Gunter's. "I'd be happy to assist you."

"I'm sure you have more to do than follow me around." And she didn't want his unsettling presence anyhow. "But we will need to finish our list."

"What else is there?"

"Rank, dowry, expectations of children." She ticked off the list on her fingers. "And that is only the beginning."

"You're very thorough."

If she wasn't mistaken, she heard laughter in his voice.

"I do try," she said with her chin in the air.

Grinning, he helped her into his curricle. His hand was warm and firm, his grip ever so much larger than hers. She removed her fingers as quickly as possible and found her seat. When he climbed in beside her, she shifted to the side a bit to make sure her dress did not touch his impressively expensive breeches.

Not that she cared one whit how much his clothes cost. Perhaps vanity was his flaw, for surely he must have one. Every man did.

"Where to, my lady?"

"Home."

"Nonsense. Let me ride a bit more with you."

"People may talk."

"Unlikely. We've been out for little more than an hour." He winked at her, and she felt her resolve melting.

Perhaps his accompaniment might be helpful, for she did need to travel to a more dangerous area. "Very well. But you are not to interfere while I speak with Mr. Ladd."

"Your runner?"

She nodded and gave the driver the address, and they set out. The movement and flow of air kept the heat from stifling her, but never once was she unaware of Lord Ashwhite beside her. His lips were compressed quite firmly.

"Do you disapprove of my activities?" she finally asked.

"They're dangerous." He turned to her, the blade of his nose as sharp as the look in his eyes. "What would you do if I were not with you? Please do not say you traverse these streets without protection."

She countered his glare with one of her own. "Perhaps you don't understand how many women and children live here? They cross those streets daily just to survive. If you must know, I don threadbare clothing to walk in the area. There's no cause for worry."

"Worry?" He scrubbed his face with his palms. "You've not the clue of it. And is Eversham aware of these jaunts?"

"Why should he be?" A prickle of guilt scuttled through her, but she squashed it determinedly. "He is not my father and is no longer my guardian. In fact, I am not sure I shall even move in with him. If he forces me out, I have friends to stay with. Perhaps even Cousin Lydia. And after I find you a wife, I shall have enough funds for a new home."

"Not in Mayfair." He squinted at her as they rounded a corner and sunlight hampered his vision. "What if Eversham cuts you off completely?"

"I still have a small stipend of my own apart from him, which I inherited from my mother."

"You seem as though you've thought of this deeply."

"I have," she assured him, though a small niggling voice prodded her to rethink her strategy. But how could she give in to Ev based on nothing more than his fears of social status? No, indeed. She was made of sterner stuff.

The curricle jostled and bumped as the roads deteriorated. This part of London was not her favorite, but hopefully her familiarity would keep her safe. Her fancy clothes certainly wouldn't. She glanced at Lord Ashwhite and saw his face had hardened somehow, become more astute.

Considering the way he looked at this moment, she doubted anyone but a fool would accost them.

"Well, here we are," she said brightly, aiming to lighten the mood.

The driver pulled the curricle to a halt, and she didn't wait for Lord Ashwhite to help her down. No need for such nonsense, she told herself, refusing to acknowledge the small pleasure his gentlemanly assistance usually brought her.

She stepped down, careful in her flats, and straightened her skirts. Lord Ashwhite appeared beside her, his face a study in disapproval.

She felt a bit bad for him. "Really, my lord, there are worse places than this. Why, this isn't even considered the slums."

"But it's close," he muttered.

"We shall only be a few moments," she told the driver. Then she looked at Lord Ashwhite. "Will he be able to protect himself in this place?"

"All my men are trained with pistols, if that's what you mean. But should anyone take my curricle, they will not last long." He beckoned toward his seal on the side of the curricle, the visual mark of his rank.

"Quite correct. Follow me, then, and try to wipe the frown from your face."

"I hope you do not come here often." His voice sounded as surly as his expression.

"Not that often," she said, rapping on a rotting door in the broken building facing her.

"Who's it?" a gruff voice called from the other side.

"Miss Amelia."

A series of thumps and bangs followed, and then the door swung open and three wonderful, smelly children launched themselves at her.

"Not often, huh?" Lord Ashwhite stepped back to avoid their feet as they hopped about, squealing and begging for a bit of candy.

She handed out the pieces she'd stowed in her pocket, and then beckoned her disgruntled companion. "Come along, now. Business won't wait."

Chapter Nine

Spencer leaned against a flowery wall while Amelia scanned Lady Cuthbert's drawing room, making notations upon the small pad of paper she'd brought with her. Her stance in the corner sufficiently hid her from view and yet allowed her to detail the available females of the room.

Or so she'd told him.

He thought she rather liked being incognito and had missed her calling as a spy. This seemed to suit her well enough. Yesterday had been enlightening as to this lady's nature. The children adored her and the runner, Mr. Ladd, had been as protective as the last time Spencer saw him. Though he didn't detect anything of a romantic nature in Mr. Ladd's manner, there was certainly a high level of respect.

Spencer glanced at Lady Amelia again. She appeared lost in thought, her gaze unfocused and dreamy. He considered nudging her but found that he liked looking at her more. When she wore that rapt expression, her features softened and she looked exceptionally pretty.

Such a shame some gentleman hadn't nabbed her when she was younger. He recalled the guarded look upon her face at the park yesterday. Certainly there was a story there. A kind of heartbreak. He felt a frown curl his lips at the thought of some cad hurting this kind woman.

"What about Lady Whitney?" Lady Amelia interrupted his thoughts. Her pen pointed directly ahead to a stunning young woman with light brown curls cascading down her back. She danced artlessly, and the smile upon her face looked genuine.

"Why do you think she might suit?" Her hair was not even the right color, though why that should irritate him, he wasn't sure.

Lady Amelia sported a perky smile. "Her mother helps at the prison, and sometimes she comes with. Her breeding is impeccable, and her voice soft. I hear she's an excellent singer and does well with the pianoforte."

"Those items were not on my list."

"But how nice would it be to have a bit of music in the home? Many comfortable evenings could be spent listening to her splendorous voice." She arched a brow. "And admiring her generous curls."

Spencer shifted on his feet, wanting to sit and possibly disappear from this gruesome event. "I like that she helps at the prison. How can we get an introduction?"

"I shall arrange it. A house party at my brother's, and then we shall also plan one at your estate."

"Oh, no." He held up his hands. "Absolutely no parties at Ashwhite."

"Come now. How do you expect to meet a potential bride? Remember, the banns must be posted in two months' time. This gives you little preparation. It shall have to be a whirlwind romance." Her gaze shifted and unfocused as some daydream caught up to her and pulled her in its wake.

Unexpectedly enthralled, he noticed the soft glow of

her skin and the way her lips, rosy in the lamplight, tilted in a tender smile.

"My lady," he said quietly, watching as her attention returned to him, "you appeared to lose yourself for a moment."

A hint of color passed across her face. She blinked and then stood quickly. "I only remembered a story I recently read about a similar situation."

"One of your novels?"

"Do not laugh at my reading choices, or I shall laugh at your choice of clothes." Her gaze traveled the length of him and then returned, smug, to his face.

"What about them?" Should he be offended? It was hard to be so when she flashed that adorable smirk.

"I shall not say unless you persist in your mockery of my literature. I'll have you know that I've come up with many a great idea while in the throes of one of those novels."

"No doubt," he said drily, thinking of Mr. Ladd and this lady's unusual activities. "And you believe a house party shall do me well?"

"Yes. We will schedule one at Eversham's first. Yours will be at the end of the month. This gives you time to enter into a month-long courtship with a young lady before announcing an engagement."

A horrific thought occurred to him. "And what if the young lady says no? What if she rejects my invitation?"

Lady Amelia's head tilted. Behind her spectacles, her gaze looked quizzical. "I hardly see that happening. Why, you're an eligible marquis… Say you enjoy the company of Lady Whitney. She is the eldest daughter of an earl, but her family has been impoverished. It is only through good relations that she is able to have a Season this year. Do you not think she'd be most grateful for your offer of marriage? With such an honor, she and her family will be provided for, and her life will be secure once again."

"I hadn't considered that." He rubbed his chin. Did he want to be in the position of rescuer? He didn't know much about marriage, but it seemed an unwise start to their relationship. "I don't favor a woman fawning over me." He'd had enough of that to last a lifetime.

"Of course not. But could a touch of thankfulness hurt?" Lady Amelia smiled up at him.

The effect of that smile hit him hard. Like a punch to the gut, or something worse—a pull on his heartstrings. With effort, he forced a smile. "I suppose not. Do you have any other potential wives?"

"Yes, indeed." She named off other women, some in their first Season and others whom he'd heard of but never met. Finally she read the last name and offered him the paper. "Would you care to look over this?"

He gave an impatient head shake. "Keep it. Those women are strangers."

"Not for long, my lord. I am a highly capable husband hunter, and I am determined to do no less in finding you a wife. Remember, I need that money."

"Is your brother due tomorrow?"

"Yes."

"Because you refuse to quit this side business?"

Her eyes widened, and she jerked her chin toward the dance floor, where dancers swirled past them in flurries of dresses and glittering hairpieces. "Keep your voice down."

"You think they don't know?"

"Most of them don't, and I plan to keep it that way. My services are irregular and potentially damaging to my reputation. Word of mouth is the only way to hire me, and I depend upon my clients to use discretion." She squinted at him. "What is that look you're giving me? Are you laughing at me again?"

"No." He cleared his throat, swallowing his chuckle. "I find you interesting. That is all."

"Oh, well, in that case…" She shot him a crooked grin. "I shall forgive your lack of manners."

"Keep your forgiveness handy, for my manners are deplorable and liable to lapse at any time."

She giggled, a bona fide giggle, and he couldn't stop the chuckle this time. If anyone could find him a wife, it was Lady Amelia. The more he discovered about her, the more he liked her.

The music changed to a quadrille, drawing his thoughts to the first and only dance he'd shared with her. She looked at him, and he could see she remembered, as well.

"Would you care to dance?" he asked.

She shook her head. "I think I shall go check on Cousin Lydia. I left her by the refreshments. Thankfully her suitor is not here this evening. I haven't heard from Mr. Ladd yet, but I don't believe he's a good candidate for her."

"And you are basing this on…?"

"It's merely a feeling, and I'll need to find some evidence to back it up."

"You don't trust feelings, remember?"

"Which is why I shall uncover proof that he is unsuitable. In the meantime, keep your options open. There are many eligible young ladies here tonight. A compatible match awaits you."

Spencer yawned. "There is no point in my staying here. We've already covered your list."

"Fiddlesticks. If you stand near Lady Whitney, there is the possibility someone will introduce you."

"Society rules," he grumbled. It could take all night to get an introduction.

"We must work within our confines," Lady Amelia said a little too sweetly.

"I have been thinking—"

"Oh, no."

He grinned. "Oh, yes. And I believe a visit to your prison is in order. Allow me to accompany you on your next visit."

"The ladies there are a bit older than this set, but perhaps that is not an issue for you?" She tapped her chin thoughtfully with her fan. "Yes, a splendid notion. Keep up your thinking." She turned and left him standing in the corner, feeling immensely satisfied with himself.

The more he considered going to Newgate, the better he felt. A prison might prove a better place than a ballroom to find a good wife and to save Ashwhite from ruin.

"Stop! Don't touch that!" Amelia careened around the corner, arms outstretched to catch her painting before it crashed to the floor. A manservant whose name she did not know dodged out of her way. The young man holding her painting froze.

Her heart pounding, she grasped the wooden frame and bestowed a disapproving look upon the servant. "I specifically said no one is to touch these paintings."

Face red, he mumbled an apology before whirling and heading toward the kitchen. She let out a shaky sigh and rested her forehead against the wall, propping the frame carefully beside her.

Eversham had arrived this morning, just as she'd predicted, his servants in tow and several carriages ready to cart away her worldly goods. The furniture would stay, though. It had come with the home and would go to the next tenants.

Her throat felt raw from the tears she refused to shed. Her overbearing brother did not seem to care about her feelings at all but stood at the entrance calmly issuing orders. He had never, ever treated her with such insensitivity before.

She vowed this would not happen again. To be forced from her home, punished merely because she lived her life as she saw fit? It made no logical sense, but all her efforts to speak to him about his inane behavior resulted in a controlled and haughty attitude. He acted as though he owned her.

She cast a scowl in his direction, hardly daring to admit that in a sense he did own her. An unmarried woman such as herself had few opportunities for independence. To be a governess or teacher of some sort could prove a practical choice, but then again, she'd still live beneath the rule of another.

A heavy sigh slipped past her lips as she slumped against the wall. Defeat had never tasted so bitter.

"Why the dreary sigh?" Lord Ashwhite's voice came from behind her. She straightened, adjusting her spectacles and pushing the frown from her face. No need to let him see the depths of her despair.

"That man almost ruined my painting. What are you doing here?"

"Thought I'd come and help, as it were." He granted the painting a thoughtful look. "It appears untouched. Would you like me to move it for you?"

"I'll manage." She lifted it, the thick wooden frame digging into her palms, and he grasped the other end. Stubborn man. Nevertheless, she allowed him to help, and really, his added strength did make the job so much easier.

"You're appearing to take this move in stride," he remarked as they shuffled carefully down the hall.

She shrugged. His concern brought a suspicious burn to her eyes that she quickly blinked away. "I have little choice in the matter."

"I am sorry for that."

His sympathetic tone almost unraveled her self-control. Biting her lower lip, she struggled to get her feelings in check. After all, he certainly shouldn't care about her personal dilemmas. Their partnership was of a business nature, and after she found him a wife, she doubted she'd see much more of him.

It would be as before, when Eversham and his life ran a parallel course with hers. She did not attend his dinner parties and outings, and neither did he bother with her reading group nor prison-reform fund-raisers.

After this, she might never see Lord Ashwhite again.

The thought did not cheer her.

"Where would you like this?" Lord Ashwhite scrutinized the front entrance for a good spot to set the frame.

"Perhaps here." She used her chin to show him where she meant. "Then I shall supervise the servants who carry it to the carriage." They propped it up and then stepped back. Out of the corner of her eye, she noticed Lord Ashwhite's attention focused on the painting.

It wasn't one of her best. A simple oil of a cloudy afternoon. She'd been inspired one day by heavy winds and sharp-edged sunbeams cut by clouds.

"This is magnificent," he said.

She blinked. "Are you quite mad, my lord?"

"Not at all." He moved forward, his finger reaching toward the canvas, tracing the curves of her paint. "There is texture and color here. Deep emotions caught in the strokes of your brush. How did you make the sky glow in such a way?" He turned to her, his eyes alight with interest, and she wet her lips.

"I'm not sure. It is how I paint." She studied the painting again, trying to see what he found so "magnificent" about it.

"You don't use watercolors?"

"Of course she doesn't." Eversham joined them, a rueful smile upon his face. "If she did, she might have more pin money."

"Watercolors don't capture the essence of my ideas," she said stiffly. Who cared if her perturbation with Ev showed? She lifted her chin and refused to meet his look, opting instead to glance at Lord Ashwhite.

A sympathetic smile edged his full lips. Unsettled by the feelings his look wrought within her, she returned her attention to the painting. "Ev, I'd like it very carefully loaded. Cover the entire thing with cloth beforehand."

"It shall be done. I've arranged a carriage to take you to Eversham—"

"Your country estate? Now?"

"Interrupting is rude."

Amelia wanted to smack the priggish look right off her brother's face. She folded her hands together instead. "I'd like to finish the Season in London. I've several parties to attend. Can I not stay at your London house?"

"Send your condolences, because you're done with this Season." His eyes narrowed, causing a familiar sense of hopelessness to swamp Amelia's will to fight. "There are bets on the books at White's about your behavior. It will reach some old biddy's ears soon enough, and then your invitations will slow. The best plan is to put you up at the country estate and try to control the fire here.

If you're not around, then it's hard to prove you've been conducting a business or visiting the slums of London."

Amelia gasped and swiveled to Lord Ashwhite. "How dare you?"

His brow knit. "How dare I what?"

Teeth grinding, she provided her brother the darkest look she could muster before whirling and making for the curricle awaiting outside.

Everything within her ached. For Lord Ashwhite to tattle on her to her brother was reprehensible. Certainly beyond the pale. Why, she should wash her hands of him at this very moment. And she would if she didn't need his money.

But she did, and desperately so. Deliberately she forced her jaw to relax and her fingers to unclench her skirt. At the moment, she entertained several fanciful ideas for revenge upon those two meddling men. Immediately she regretted the thoughts.

No, the best course of action involved restraining her feelings and behaving in a logical manner. She must pursue her goal of independence and leave the men to play their own games. With a servant's help, she climbed into her brother's curricle. As she settled upon the brocaded seat, though, she did not feel comforted by future plans. Pain invaded her heart, and as she was driven to her brother's estate, she realized that she felt betrayed by Lord Ashwhite.

Without intending to, she had trusted him to keep her confidences. A most foolish move she must never make again.

Chapter Ten

Falling in love destroyed the best-laid plans.

Amelia filed paperwork in her desk, half an ear closed as Cousin Lydia droned on about the man she'd met. Mr. Brighton, the epitome of honor and goodness. So handsome that just his visage made Lydia's knees weak.

And so forth.

Pressing her lips firmly together, Amelia closed the drawer to her desk a little too hard. The smack of wood colliding with wood sent a satisfied sensation through her, though. One duty completed, a million more to go.

"Are you listening?" Cousin Lydia had draped herself across the small couch on the farthest wall. Now she pushed herself into a sitting position and eyed Amelia.

"I certainly am listening, and I have to say that his qualities are simply overwhelming me." She pushed her spectacles up to more firmly look at her cousin. "You *do* realize his attributes do not negate his faults, correct?"

"Oh, stop being so prissy." Lydia's blue eyes twinkled, and a saucy smile played about her lips. "The goal was to find me a husband, not a fortune. If it were not for your contacts and careful planning, I would never have been allowed entrance into Almack's. Then I would not have met my future husband. And I am certain Mr. Brighton shall be proposing, for he has orders to ship out at the end of the year. I plan to go with him." A lovelorn sigh erupted as she slumped back onto the couch, her gaze drifting off to a different place.

The future, if Amelia had to guess, full of frothy dresses and giggling children.

Amelia frowned and looked away. Once upon a time she had dreamed of the same, but no more. To find a trustworthy male proved almost impossible, she'd come to realize. Banishing the thought of Lord Ashwhite's wayward tongue, she surveyed her new desk.

Rather big, it fit nicely with her needs and had been a kind concession on Eversham's part. Though she'd been at his estate for only three days, she found herself longing for her London home with its huge windows and promise of private independence. The thought of picking up her paintbrush filled her with a desperate hunger for space and light, for aloneness.

At least Cousin Lydia had met her at the estate and helped her settle in, but she'd be leaving this morning to return to London.

Swiping the invitations she'd recently finished writing, Amelia stood. "Try not to give this suitor of yours any promises until I hear from Mr. Ladd. For all you know, this Brighton is out to cause a scandal."

She grimaced at Lydia's unladylike snort.

"I very much doubt that," Lydia said. "He is the second son of an earl and adores his career. He absolutely would not seek a scandal. In fact, you should not waste your money on Mr. Ladd, for there is nothing that will stop me from marrying Mr. Brighton."

Amelia had to bite back her frustration. Cousin Lydia

was much more stubborn than she'd originally realized. "He is simply not what I envisioned for you."

"Well, you can't control everything. Surely you realize that?"

Amelia made for the door and beckoned Lydia to follow. "Control is not my intent. I simply want to see you happy." Even as she said it, though, she wondered. Why *should* she care if Lydia found happiness with a common man? Was she so shallow to look for only titles and fortunes?

Shrugging the unpleasant thought aside, she turned to her cousin. "Remember, it is my job to help you find the proper husband, one you can love forever, not one for whom you've developed an affection."

For such emotions were useless in practical living. They complicated life and caused heartache. She squared her shoulders and marched into the giant hall of her brother's mansion. She'd grown up here, and it rankled to find herself once again at home, feeling like an unwanted child.

Eversham stood at the foot of the stairs, examining his watch.

"Brother," she called out. "To whom shall I give these invitations?" They'd taken longer than she expected. A marquis's presence would bring a large turnout, which was what she wanted. After this house party, she imagined she'd have a good idea of whom to invite to Lord Ashwhite's party. Perhaps even make it a weeklong affair with games and music.

Eversham looked up. His hair was tousled this morning, and his cravat was crooked. Amelia frowned at the absentminded look upon her twin's face.

"Is everything all right?"

"Quite fine. I'm a bit late, that's all."

"I am planning a party for next week. The invitations are ready and need to be rushed out."

Ev's forehead wrinkled. "A party here?"

"Yes," she said, exasperated. "Where have you been? I've toiled with these since I arrived, and if your wife would ever emerge from her room, I could consult her. But she hasn't, and so I made plans on my own."

He groaned and raised a palm to his forehead. "The budget?"

"Do not fear. I am working with your housekeeper on that."

"Very well." Eversham let out a deep sigh, as though her very presence caused him grief. "Keep the affair small and light. I don't want Harriet disturbed."

Amelia gave him a curt nod and watched as he strode past, his hand briefly lifting in farewell. She glanced at the stack in her hand.

"How will you do that?" Lydia asked from the doorway.

Amelia shrugged, feeling both annoyed and pained by Eversham's treatment of her. What had gotten into him? Granted, they had never been close friends, but there had always been a bond forged by trust and understanding. "I cannot rewrite all the invitations or change the plans for a soiree. He simply must understand that this is my home now, and if he insists I live here, then things may change."

Lydia only lifted a brow.

"I tried repeatedly to speak with Harriet. She has refused to give me an audience," Amelia felt compelled to explain. In fact, she'd been made to feel unwelcome here and couldn't understand why Ev didn't let her stay at his London house. It was those ridiculous wagers at White's. What did those gentlemen know, who did nothing more than sit around arguing politics and gambling away their money?

"Do you have your visit to Newgate today?" Lydia's gentle voice brought Amelia back to the present.

She nodded. "Do you wish to join me?"

"No, Mother has planned an outing for us this afternoon." Amelia handed her stack of invitations to the butler, who walked around the stairs at that moment. "Please see that these are delivered immediately," she told him. She returned her attention to Lydia. "Now, do you have a meeting with Mr. Brighton today?"

"Tomorrow."

"Can you put it off until I see Mr. Ladd?"

"Absolutely not. I told you, nothing he says will change my mind."

"But something is not right," Amelia persisted despite the mulish expression upon her cousin's face. "At least let me prove that he's suitable for you."

"I feel in my heart that he is. Really, cousin, you must know that not all people are hiding some horrible secret in their past. He is who he says. Why can you not accept that?"

"It makes no sense to merely take him at his word." Amelia felt irritation building and tried to suppress her temper. Logic and order. That was what was needed here, not a willy-nilly emotional outburst.

"I trust him," Lydia said with remarkable calm. And it was in her eyes as well, a peaceful look Amelia found herself envying. "You will have someone to trust someday, too. Don't shake your head at me. You will." Lydia hugged Amelia. "I enjoyed our morning together. I'm going to scrounge for some more of those delicious cookies while I wait for Mother to show up. Enjoy your time at Newgate."

"I'll try…" It was often painful to see how the women and children at Newgate were treated. Though she wrote letters on their behalf, Amelia often thought she should be doing something more. Mrs. Fry spoke of organizing a kind of aid society, and Amelia felt that would be beneficial. She'd considered starting it herself, but since Mrs. Fry evinced formidable organizational skills, she'd leave the details to her.

She glanced once more up the stairs, wondering at Harriet's absence of late. Was she ill? If so, wouldn't Ev say so? She grimaced. With the way things stood between them, perhaps not.

She retrieved her things from the parlor. The curricle was to be ready at noon, which must be nearing. Arms full of clothing and the fresh bread she'd snagged from Cook this morning, she walked outside and waited for Ev's curricle to be brought around.

The day was filled with the sounds of twittering birds and the whisper of a soft breeze sweeping through the branches of stately oaks. Sunshine glowed against the grassy lawn.

How many times had she played here in her youth? Chasing Ev, laughing and dreaming? No worries of grass in her skirts, of maintaining proper posture or impressing stuffy old ladies. Years when Ev had been her playmate and not her keeper. Then their parents had died, and everything had changed.

A hackney came bouncing down the drive, sending clouds of dirt to trail behind its rushed progress. Amelia squinted but saw no crest upon its side. The driver stopped in front of the terrace and the side door opened.

Spencer dismounted from the hackney, great rushes of relief spiraling through him when he saw Lady Amelia standing on the porch. His worry had escalated over the past three days, and he'd finally decided a visit was in order. The last time he'd seen her, she'd rushed off in a huff, and a bad feeling had plagued him thereafter. Especially when Eversham had been quick to turn on him for knowing about Lady Amelia's jaunts and not saying anything.

That had not been fun to explain.

He paid the driver and waved him off before turning his attention to the woman before him. Her foot tapped, and she wore a scowl. Spectacles glinting beneath the sun's hot rays, mouth tight, she quite obviously held a grudge against him. He bowed to her and grinned when her scowl deepened.

"My lady, you look resplendent," he said. And she truly did. Though she'd chosen a simple dress in a pale lavender shade, it complemented the fairness of her complexion. Her hair was done up, pulled away from her face—

"Don't patronize me, Ashwhite." In her miff, she left the title off his name. He found he rather liked it. He also liked the determined glare upon her face. "I know exactly how I look, and it is an appearance suitable for a jail, not a ballroom. What reason are you here, pray tell? For I am to be on my way in minutes."

He advanced up the steps and noted how she stepped back. "I apologize for my tardiness, but I've come to speak of the other day. Unfortunately politics stole my time, but now we've a break, and I wanted to speak with you."

"About business, I'm sure." She looked at him over the rim of her glasses.

An alarming urge to knock the spectacles off her face

and kiss her silly slammed into him. He frowned. "Not quite."

"Well, stop staring at me that way." Her chin lifted, and she looked past him. "We are business partners. That is it. Do not think you can go traipsing with me on any more adventures. If I'd thought you'd go tattling to my brother at your first opportunity—"

"Now, hold on." Spencer held up a hand. Irritation spiked through him. "What are you talking about?"

"Are you pretending you don't know?" Her brows furrowed, and those pretty lips of hers pursed again. "Very well. I shall spell it out for you. My visit to see Mr. Ladd is none of Ev's business, and I certainly did not expect you to share that with him."

Well, this explained her strange behavior. He didn't like it. Growling low in his throat, he stepped closer. "I don't tell tales, my lady. Perhaps you should work on your assumptions."

"You deny it?" She set her chin and threw him a belligerent look.

"Vehemently."

She glanced away from him, a soft flush suffusing her cheeks. "I find myself wanting to believe you, but it doesn't change the lesson learned."

Spencer took a deep breath to calm his temper. At the moment he battled two instincts: pull her close and kiss the downturn of her lips away or throw his hands in the air and stomp off. Obtuse woman. He moved back, plunging his fists into the pockets of his light waistcoat.

"Dare I ask what this lesson was?" he asked drily.

"Never trust a stranger."

"I'm a stranger?" Incredulity lit his temper once again. "Madam, you are illogical and entirely ruled by your emotions."

"I certainly am not." She glared at him, hugging her arms to herself. "My practical nature is one of my assets, I assure you."

"That's a humble way to see yourself."

"You insulting man. I trusted you to keep our trip to Mr. Ladd's a secret."

"And I did," he enunciated very slowly.

Her eyes flashed. "How else would Eversham know my whereabouts? There is only one other way…" She trailed off.

"He's following you," Spencer supplied, giving her an arch look.

"Could he be?" Surprise, maybe hurt, scattered across her face and pulled those lovely lips into a frown. "But why? Can he care so much about reputation?" The confused sadness of her face gripped Spencer in a way he didn't care to examine.

Throat tight, he gestured to a bench situated against the stone wall of the terrace. "Have a seat."

She seemed not to hear him, and so he carefully took her arm, which felt small and light beneath his touch, and guided her to the bench. Sitting beside her, he waited.

"He's been so distant lately," she finally said. "And he looks at me as though I'm an unwanted responsibility, a burden. Never before has he treated me so."

"What do you think has changed?"

"When he married four years ago, I believe he saw that I am not an ideal lady." She looked at him with sadness in her dark eyes, which contrasted so beautifully with her skin.

He mentally shook himself. Where was he going with all these thoughts? He had a wife to find, and Lady Amelia had been quite clear about her stance on marriage. Still…he took in how he felt sitting beside her, the gentle curve of her cheek as she stared out over the lawn and that tapping foot of hers, which signaled an active and ready mind.

He probably liked her more than he'd ever liked another woman. And there had been plenty of women to like.

Yet he empathized with Eversham. His own childhood had been rife with tension as his parents had battled over his mother's bids for independence. He himself wanted a lady of a certain quality, one who did not make too much of a social fuss but who had a good head on her shoulders.

Leaning back against the bench, he stretched out his legs and mused on the situation. Was Ev's relationship with his sister so untenable? Yes, Lady Amelia drove him a bit mad, but she was also interesting, with an honorable core that intrigued him.

Deeply intrigued him.

"What do you think, Lord Ashwhite?" Lady Amelia prodded him with her elbow. "Has Eversham fallen beneath the evil influence of his wife, or does he just detest me that much?" Though she smiled, he heard the vulnerable timbre of her tone.

"It remains to be seen, my lady, but I do not think you should overly concern yourself with him just now. Look." He pointed at the curricle barreling up the lane. "There is your ride to Newgate. Let us visit those in need, and perhaps it is there I will find a woman who steals my heart."

Lady Amelia scoffed. "I shall be the judge of that. Stealing hearts is not a good basis for marriage."

They stood and walked to the steps, where the curricle parked. She scooped up a pile of items he hadn't noticed resting against the stone wall. Deftly he plucked the stack from her arms.

"The gentleman should carry the load," he said. "What constitutes a good marriage, in your mind?"

It seemed her shoulders stiffened as though she did not wish to answer. "Friendship, mutual interests."

"Attraction?" he put in, biting back his grin at the firm shake of her head.

"That will follow with those other things, my lord. Now hand me my items, please."

"I will accompany you," he persisted, and gestured to the curricle, where the footman waited to help her in. "I see your lady's maid is already inside. Let us join her."

"Very well." Lady Amelia offered him a somber look. "But prepare yourself for the dankness that is Newgate."

"I will." He bit back his humor at the melodramatic words. She had a point, though. He must ready himself to trust a woman who resisted matters of the heart to find him a wife. A woman who denied her own emotions, though it was plain to see she wore them on her sleeve. At this juncture, he had only God and Lady Amelia to trust to sort out this situation.

He couldn't live with himself if he lost the family home. Once again he bemoaned the ultimatum to gaining his inheritance. Though there was his mother's family estate, a cousin presently cared for it, and he did not wish to usurp another family. The entire situation was ridiculously complicated, and he could blame only himself.

His carefree ways had disappointed both his parents. Now his father was gone, but his mother, despite the unsettled feelings he held toward her, deserved a son she could be proud of.

He would be that son, even if it meant being tied down to someone he disliked the rest of his life. With Lady Amelia on the case, though, he hoped for at least a convenient marriage.

Chapter Eleven

Amelia did not care one whit for convenience.

She surveyed the young lady handing out clean clothes next to Lord Ashwhite. Her glossy dark hair shone with health, cascading down her back in an enviable shimmer of beauty. Rose-hued ribbons accented her chocolate eyes and flawless skin.

A convenient wife did not measure against a smart, compassionate one. And Lady Hope was all that and more. She'd been helping at Newgate for as long as Amelia, though they'd never taken the time to strike up a friendship. They held a mutual respect for one another, though.

Amelia eyed Lord Ashwhite and Lady Hope as they conversed quietly with the young children waiting in line for their portion of goods. They worked well together and appeared to take a mutual liking to each other.

A twinge tightened Amelia's chest. She rubbed at her collarbone before returning to her own sorting. The other ladies had brought a variety of clothes for the poor children who lived here with their convict mothers. There was also lye to distribute and a few loaves of bread. Not enough, though. Never enough for the sweet children who behaved, at times, more like starving mongrels in the streets.

Their mothers were no better. Rarely did Amelia come in contact with a woman prisoner, for they could be dangerous. Though Mrs. Elizabeth Fry did seek to change the situation. Amelia had heard plans to start a school at the prison, which seemed a wonderful idea. She slanted another look toward Lord Ashwhite, just in time to catch his laugh at something Lady Hope said.

Frowning, she handed the last item to a child and then surveyed the tiny room for anything she'd missed.

"Are we finished here?" Lord Ashwhite's deep voice startled her, and she jumped.

"I believe so," she answered despite the race of her heartbeat. "Did you enjoy your conversation with Lady Hope? Shall I add her to our list?"

"Absolutely. She's a lovely woman." Crescents dipped into his cheeks.

Ignoring the flutters beneath her ribs, Amelia managed a brisk nod. "Very well. I shall make sure she receives an invitation to your country party."

"About that…"

Amelia quirked an eyebrow. "Surely you are not backing out of such a necessary endeavor?"

"It seems over the top." He grimaced.

"Fiddlesticks. You'll be able to mingle with many prospects, get a taste for their personalities and characters." She thought of Lady Hope and searched their small group of volunteers with her eyes until she found the young woman. She was staring at Lord Ashwhite with a smitten expression.

"I think our mission may be easier than we expect," she muttered under her breath, averting her gaze and swinging toward the exit. "Do not forget to make eye contact with her as you leave. Perhaps that little smirk you dish out so often?"

"A smirk, is it?" He took her elbow and guided her through the door.

She tried not to notice the firm pressure of his fingers against her sleeve, or how the nearness of his person brought the flavor of his cologne to her nose. Nevertheless, there was a hitch to her breath the entire ride home.

Even with her lady's maid in the carriage, she had trouble breathing. This attraction was becoming quite the nuisance. She wanted to stop it somehow. Needed to keep from repeating the mistakes of her past.

She was not meant to be romantically involved with anyone. Or to marry. Better to keep her nose in her novels, where adventurous heroes with hearts of gold rescued perfect heroines. Her paintings satisfied her in ways no relationship could, and she knew once she began selling them, she'd feel a wholeness inside that always seemed to elude her.

But as they neared her home, she found herself doubting the mental assertions. Because when she sat next to Lord Ashwhite, when she answered his questions and engaged in conversation with him, nothing seemed as wonderful as being near him.

Most certainly this needed to stop.

He smiled at her in the carriage, the flash of his teeth inciting a memory of Lord Markham. Hadn't he smiled in such a way? Confident, with ease, and he had looked at her as though only she existed in his world.

What a fool she had been to believe that.

The carriage stopped at the house. With relief she took the driver's hand and dismounted, the lady's maid ahead of her and Lord Ashwhite behind her. She could feel his smile at her back, and an absurd desire to pop him on the shoulder with her fan tickled her.

He came to her side, and together they entered the house.

"Where is the butler?" Lord Ashwhite asked.

"The staff has been given today off. Once a month they receive a half-Saturday reprieve. It is rather late in the day, and I presume everyone has left for the village. I am sure that is where my lady's maid has gone." Amelia looked around, feeling the emptiness of the house. Its loneliness.

"Does your maid have a name?"

She shrugged, avoiding his curious gaze. "I have been careful not to become attached. As soon as I've acquired the funds, I shall be rehiring Dukes and Sally."

"To work here?" Surprise laced his tone. "And will your brother approve such an endeavor?"

"No, but that is irrelevant, because I have found a small cottage in Yorkshire in which to live. The stipend I receive is comfortable enough to allow me a house with Sally and Dukes."

"And food, I hope?" Sarcasm had entered his voice, and she dared a look at him.

He thumbed the pockets of his waistcoat, and a lone lock fell over his forehead. Those piercing green eyes of his studied her with great solemnity. How she wanted to capture that expression. Her fingers fairly itched to reproduce his features upon canvas. To find the exact shade of green, that lovely deepness that was neither emerald nor moss but somehow a mixture.

"My lady?" His eyes crinkled. "Is there a smudge upon my cheek?"

For a moment she was stymied. And then the most ridiculous urge to press her thumb against his brow and rub an imaginary stain away overtook her. The desire was so strong that her hand raised, halfway to its destination, before she came to her senses.

She shook her head and pivoted on her heel. "Lost in thought, my lord. That is all."

"Indeed." His voice was soft.

"My cottage is lovely. I visited yesterday. There will be plenty of room for roses, and the windows are quite large. I shall have the privacy I need—"

He touched her elbow, his hand closing around her forearm. Then he turned her to him, drawing her closer than any gentleman had the right to do. She should protest this manhandling, she should yank herself from his grasp, but her mouth had dried, and her heartbeat had taken on an unnatural pace beneath her sternum.

"And what of your husband finding?" He stared deeply at her.

She could not look away.

"I—I…" Before she could formulate a thought, before she could even catch her breath, a loud thump followed by a muffled cry echoed from above stairs.

Her gaze ripped away from Lord Ashwhite's. Together they mounted the stairs. He took two at a time, and she stayed at his heels. They hurried down the hall, past her bedroom and rounded the corner. Then Lord Ashwhite skidded to a stop.

Amelia crashed into the sturdiness of his broad back. His hands found her. Steadied her. She looked past him and gasped. Pushing away, she hurried forward.

Harriet lay sprawled on her belly across the floor, her face utterly bereft of color. Even her lips held a sickly pallor.

"Are you ill?" She dropped to her knees, panic making her movements jerky.

"Roll her onto her back," said Lord Ashwhite, who had appeared at her sister-in-law's side.

Amelia did as he said, pushing against Harriet's limp body. The lady seemed less than formidable now. Frail and vulnerable.

She looked up at Lord Ashwhite, her insides twisting. "What's wrong with her?"

Face grim, he shook his head. "I don't know."

"Shall we lift her to the bed?"

"No. If something is broken, we don't want to make it worse. We should fetch a doctor."

Amelia nodded, though coherent thought seemed to have deserted her. She glanced down the length of her sister-in-law's body, searching for any broken or twisted limbs. Her frothy dress disguised any malformations. Impatiently Amelia pushed it aside.

"Oh." Her hands flew to her mouth.

"I'm getting a physician immediately. Watch her closely."

Vaguely Amelia heard his departure, the quick thud of his shoes down the stairs, but she could not take her eyes from the crimson stain spreading across Harriet's nightdress. A numbness overtook her.

Breath shallow, she took her sister-in-law's cold hand and waited.

A sense of helplessness engulfed Spencer. He didn't much like the feeling, wished he could shrug it off, but the irritating emotion persisted in perching on his shoulders. Chest tight, hands fisted, he waited in the upstairs hall while Doctor Brimes examined Lady Eversham.

Lady Amelia's voice filtered through the heavy doors, followed by the doctor's deeper tones. The door opened, and they stepped out.

The doctor gave him a brisk nod and then left, tromping down the stairs to outside, where the curricle waited to escort him back to the village.

He turned to Lady Amelia. "How bad is it?"

Her heavy sigh nudged the pain in his gut, twisting it tighter until all he wanted was a sweaty pugilistic bout with someone. Anything to rid himself of this sorrow for Ev and his wife.

"Let us go downstairs." She cast a worried glance at the door. Tendrils of hair had escaped her serviceable chignon, curling against the nape of her neck. If only he could wipe the worry from her features.

Once settled in the parlor, she leaned her head back and let out a long and gusty groan. A smile tipped at Spencer's lips. The unladylike sound was refreshing and halved his tension. He lounged in his chair, glad his heart rate had finally slowed. He waited for Lady Amelia to collect her thoughts.

"I find myself in a selfish quandary," she finally said, straightening her body into the posture of a lady. "Harriet is not sick, but she has been pregnant and now is no longer. She has not woken, but the doctor informed me that this is her third loss…" Her lids closed and her face tightened as though the next words pained her. She opened her eyes, and the loss in her gaze sent goose bumps scuttling across his forearms. "I believe when she wakes she will be devastated. Furthermore, Eversham still needs to be informed, and I feel incapable of imparting this news."

Spencer leaned forward, elbows on knees. "I wish I could fix this."

"It is not fixable." She hesitated. "I had accepted an invitation to a soiree this evening but must cancel. My brother may need me. However, I have it on good authority that Lady Whitney shall be attending."

"Which one is she? From Newgate?"

What passed as a smile flirted with Lady Amelia's cheeks. "No, my lord. You met her a few days ago at the ball we attended. Did you ever procure an invitation?"

Ah, the one with the light brown curls. Not his favorite color, but he'd been told not to be picky. "Yes, introduced and even finagled a dance."

"Very good." Lady Amelia's face took on that distracted look he was coming to know so well. "I will arrange for Ev's steward to take you home now. Lydia shall be there as well once I find a companion for her. I have high hopes of distracting her from this suitor of hers."

"Still in love, is she?"

Lady Amelia grimaced. "Unfortunately."

And so it was that five hours later, Spencer found himself in a crowded, perfumed room. Irritated, he wedged himself against the wall and gulped his punch. This crush would be so much more amusing if Lady Amelia had attended.

Strangely enough, at that very moment he saw her pass through the room. Perhaps it wasn't her, but he was bored enough to follow. He pushed away from the wall and slipped into the crowd. She had disappeared into a mass of large hats and odious matrons. When he approached the refreshment table, one lady recognized him. He knew this because she quickly ushered her daughter away.

Good. More punch for him. He filled his cup and surveyed the room while sipping the sugary brew.

"There you are!" Lady Amelia appeared at his side.

He turned to her. "I thought I saw you."

"Yes, Ev believed it better for me to attend and keep an eye on Cousin Lydia. He said there was nothing I could do by staying home." She frowned as though she disagreed.

He cleared he throat. "How are Ev and his wife?"

"She was sleeping when I left. My brother is heartbroken." Amelia fiddled with her fan. "We shan't speak of it now. Tell me, have you danced tonight with anyone?"

"Sadly, no." He did not hide his sarcasm.

She touched his shoulder with her fan. "Come, now, my lord. You cannot avoid women forever. There are two very good prospects for you to choose from right over there." He trailed the direction of her finger to a cluster of girls overly adorned with hats and feathers and giggles. "And forgive me, but I did forget to ask how you feel about widows?"

At the moment, his feelings weren't the best to go by. All he wanted was to escape this ordeal. To forget the shattered faces of hungry children and Lady Eversham's loss. "Let us focus on finding a suitable wife. Her status and looks are not important."

"Time is slipping away."

"Thank you for pointing that out," he said drily.

"Well, go on, my lord. Don't be shy." Her teeth flashed up at him, and again he was struck by the darkness of her eyes behind their spectacles.

Gathering his wits, he gave her what he knew she deemed a smirk. "My lady, I have never been accused of suffering from shyness. However, the thought of conversing with those giggling females puts me in mind of Newgate and prison doors."

Her lips pressed together, yet merriment danced across her face. "Very well. I wasn't going to do this, but I see you need added incentive."

"Besides saving my property from the likes of Lord Dudley?"

"Yes, and I have just the adventure for you. But first you must trust my taste. Go over there and strike up a conversation with Lady Whitney and Lady Hope. They are both kind and gentle young women who I do believe possess some modicum of intelligence."

Charmed by the sparkle in her eyes, Spencer nodded. "I shall speak with them, but then I expect this adventure you promised."

"Hopefully it will not scare you too much." Her smile widened before she twirled away and disappeared into the throng of ruffles and lace.

Perhaps he should have been disturbed by that smile, but instead he found himself looking forward to the evening ahead. Surprisingly, getting to know Lady Hope and Lady Whitney proved unpainful. One was shy and the other garrulous, but both conversed in interesting ways. They were not afraid to broach the topic of politics, though Lady Hope seemed to back away from arguing while Lady Whitney pushed past the edges of decorum to defend her views.

He bid them adieu after a time and went in search of Lady Amelia. He found her in a small alcove, talking to an odd-looking gentleman with her cousin by her side. Wild gesticulations accompanied her speech. Animation brought her face alive, and for a moment Spencer found himself transfixed.

She caught him staring, and her words trailed into nothingness. He saw the look in her eyes—something very similar to what he'd seen in Lady Hope's. Was it possible?

Something stirred in his chest, something elemental and quick. He tipped his chin toward her. She excused herself and, with Miss Stanley, joined him.

"Well?"

He raised his brows. "Is there a question in that word?"

"I believe she wants to know if she's been successful in her matchmaking." Miss Stanley flashed him a grin.

"More than you might guess," Spencer told her. "Now, for that adventure you promised?"

Lady Amelia cleared her throat and then looked over the top of her spectacles at Miss Stanley. "Are you ready to leave?"

"Yes, I am unfortunately still smitten with an undeserving second son."

Spencer bit back a laugh at the sarcasm in Miss Stanley's voice. He rather liked this cousin of Lady Amelia's. If she hadn't fallen in love, she might have made an excellent prospect for marriage.

"There is no need to be saucy with me." Lady Amelia turned to him. "We shall discuss our plans in the curricle after we drop off Lydia."

"And why can't I join in this adventure?" Miss Stanley asked.

"We must keep your reputation spotless."

"What of yours?"

"Mine is staining rather quickly, I fear."

And yet Spencer heard no remorse in Lady Amelia's voice. Rather, an undercurrent of excitement tinged her tone, and he found himself wondering what on earth she might be planning. Was this how his father had felt with his mother's antics? Apprehension surged through him. He hadn't asked for an adventure that could stain a reputation.

"Shall I brace myself?" he asked.

Lady Amelia's hands waved in a confident arc. "My lord, when accompanying me, you must always prepare yourself for surprises."

He rather did not like the sound of that.

Chapter Twelve

Lord Ashwhite obviously did not care for spontaneity. Amelia observed his grimace when they dropped Lydia at her home. She'd chosen to rent a hackney for tonight's enterprise. No need to set tongues wagging more than they already were.

There was also the fact that she'd decided not to bring her lady's maid tonight. The girl was no Sally. Hired by her brother, no doubt she'd go straight to him and inform him of what Amelia had done.

And Amelia was in more than enough trouble. She didn't want to remember Ev's accusations when he'd arrived home to find his wife abed, but they bounced through her memory anyway. *Her fault, all her fault...*

Sharp daggers of pain lanced through her, so physical she had to contain her gasp. Instead, she focused on taking deep breaths, willing the pain, the guilt, to ease, if only enough for tonight's mission.

"So where are we off to?" Lord Ashwhite leaned against the squab, arms crossed in a relaxed manner. He didn't seem ill at ease to be alone in a carriage with a lady. Whereas her nerves felt at the point of shattering. Whether with remorse or anxiety, she could not tell.

Amelia shifted, measuring her words. Weighing the amount of trust she could put in this man.

"I am bringing you with me tonight for a purpose." She paused. "You must understand that normally—"

"Normally?" Within the shadows of the hackney, his jaw hardened.

She was struck by the play of monochromatic tones across his face, those varying shades of black, and how they charcoaled his bone structure. She would remember this evening. She would sketch the mood of this moment, the deep contrasts, forever on vellum.

"My lady, you seem to have lost your train of thought."

The throaty depth of his voice sent a pleasant feeling to curl in her belly. "I did no such thing."

"Why do you do that?"

"What?" The warm feeling in her belly dissipated.

"Deny the truth." He straightened, and even in the darkness she could feel his gaze pinning her to her spot. "Pretend to be someone other than you are."

"Are you suggesting I live in pretense?" She tried to keep the hurt from her voice, but it managed to slip out. Perhaps he would not notice.

"I am not maligning you. I am simply curious. You're a caring person with great emotional ranges. It's in your paintings and in the way you treat children. Yet you wear a facade of practical indifference. You pretend that daydreams are not for you."

Somehow Amelia swallowed past the boulder that crowded her windpipe. She peered out the small window. Weren't they close to their destination now? She did not want to answer his accusations, did not know how.

Her silence tainted the air.

Lord Ashwhite cleared his throat. "Forgive me, my lady. I've spoken out of turn."

"You certainly have," she said pertly. And could not think of another thing to say. Did not know which words to formulate and could not bring herself to acquit him of his intrusion. A gentleman would not be so common, so… personal. Hadn't he acted this way from the start, though?

She'd found his blunt and unpracticed ways refreshing.

Not when they came so close to the truth, though. Not when his words pierced the armor that kept her safe from pain.

The carriage drew to a halt. *Finally.*

"You may want to move to the side, as we'll be having company."

"Your brother?" Lord Ashwhite peered out his window, and the lamplight caught his frown. "No, we are on the other side of town. What is going on here?"

"Exactly what I want. Mr. Ladd shall be accompanying us."

"Please tell me this is lawful."

"And what did you think I'd be doing in the middle of the night, pray tell? Combing my hair? Dancing at some crush? No, indeed." Excitement stirred within her. She leaned forward, commanding his attention. "I have much bigger goals to pursue. In fact, my worries about Lord Dudley may be well founded. There is something strange going on, and I shall tell you about it as soon as Mr. Ladd arrives."

"If it is a problem for the constable, then you should allow him care of the matter."

"Perhaps, if the situation comes to that, but at this point I am simply searching…"

"Searching?"

"For something." She pushed her spectacles firmly against her nose. "I know not what. But I will."

The carriage door opened, and Mr. Ladd stepped inside. "We are heading to White's?"

"Yes, our usual," she said while briskly waving him in.

She noted the glance he gave Lord Ashwhite before settling beside him. She rapped the top of the carriage, and off they went. As before, her pulse began to quicken and her palms sweat. Nerves, or perhaps the pants she wore beneath her skirt.

She could feel Lord Ashwhite's disapproval, and it did not settle well. "Do not stare at me so. This is a common practice of ours, and if all goes to plan, I will be averting a great disaster."

The priggish quality to her tone caused her to flinch. Did she normally sound so stuffy? So much like Eversham? A snuffled snort told her that someone was laughing at her. She scowled into the darkened hackney.

"Forgive me, my lady. I just did not take you for melodrama." The amusement dripping from Lord Ashwhite's tone carved the frown deeper into her face. She could feel her lips pressing tight. No doubt an unattractive quality, but then again, she'd never been known for beauty.

"What you have taken me for is of no consequence to me. The reason I invited you is because you are good friends with Ev, and I'd like a witness, as this will personally affect all of us."

"I am confused."

She sighed. "You need not know the details, only that you shall silently witness a confession from a man who I am quite sure is not only disreputable but also a criminal. I shall not allow him to take advantage of my brother."

"What are you talking about? I ask again, my lady, why isn't the law involved?"

"I am the law." Mr. Ladd's answer didn't dent the palpable tension in the carriage.

"You're a runner. Nothing more."

"That is only one of my many occupations," he said, voice cold.

Amelia watched the two men as best she could in the darkened carriage and hoped things went to plan. She couldn't stop now. Somehow she must repair the damage she'd caused to her relationship with Eversham.

"Very well." Lord Ashwhite let out a heartfelt sigh. "Do you care to disclose what exactly we will be doing and where we are going?"

Amelia swallowed away her regrets and forced the no-nonsense tone that more often than not got her the results she desired. "First we shall go into White's and make conversation. During the course of mingling, we will spread out and find Lord Dudley. Whoever finds him first must mention that he has heard of his new venture and would like to invest in it."

"Wait." Lord Ashwhite held up his palm. "And how do you plan to get into White's?"

"A disguise, of course."

"You realize this is disreputable and dangerous."

The corner of her lips tickled. "Never fear, my lord. Ladd and I have everything under control."

Lady Amelia and Mr. Ladd had thrown Spencer's world into chaos. Disbelievingly he watched the two round the room, stopping to talk to various gentleman. Not a one seemed to realize that Lady Amelia was a woman. How could they fail to notice?

Granted, the room was not well lit, and most of the gentlemen had been in their cups a tad too long. But who could miss the fine structure of her jaw or the fullness of her lips? And the way she walked… If she was going to wear trousers and pass herself off as a man, she must do better than this.

Before his very eyes, he watched a man greet her with a broad grin. It looked as though he called her by a false name… Spencer frowned. How long had she been doing this? Ladd needed a thorough talking-to. Surely he knew such a game was not safe.

Jaw tight, Spencer gripped his drink and harnessed every ounce of self-control he had to keep from dashing over, scooping her up and getting out of there.

"Cards not going your way this eve?" Lord Dudley came up beside him, a supercilious smile on his face.

"Not quite," Spencer answered. He was supposed to say something but for the life of him could not remember what. Lady Amelia and her plans! He ground his teeth and tore his gaze from where she stood with a foolish group of young men too stupid to realize they told ribald jokes to a lady.

"Lord Ashwhite, correct?" The man beside him shifted on his feet. "Though we are distant cousins, we've not been introduced. You are newly a marquis."

Spencer nodded. Dudley recognized him after all. A sudden ache crept into his chest at the remembrance of how he'd become a marquis. He rubbed at the spot. "And you are Lord Dudley."

"Yes, I saw you briefly at Almack's. You're a family friend of Lady Amelia?"

"That's right." Spencer studied the man beside him, feeling a dark foreboding sweep over him. "I have a matter of a sensitive nature to discuss with you. It is fortuitous that we've met tonight." He gestured to a quieter corner. "Perhaps we can discuss it somewhere…private?"

"Quite fine, my lord."

Spencer saw the greed lighting the earl's squinty eyes.

Feeling grim, he led the man toward Mr. Ladd, who had spotted them and waited by a potted palm tree well removed from the bustle of the gaming tables. There was something amiss here, something he had no doubt the indomitable Lady Amelia should not be dabbling in. So why did she?

What was driving her to take these risks with her reputation? Not to mention her safety. A gentleman's club was no place for a lady. He gave Mr. Ladd a brisk nod, then turned to Lord Dudley.

"This is my business partner."

"Ladd." They shook hands.

"Now, about that sensitive subject…"

It was an hour later when the three of them finally made it back to the hackney. Spencer was so angry he could hardly form a coherent word. Whether at Lord Dudley or Lady Amelia, he could not fathom. They clambered into the carriage, each silent and withdrawn into their own thoughts.

Once on their way, Spencer turned to Mr. Ladd. The man was uncomfortably close. He'd rather sit next to Lady Amelia, who was a sight smaller than Mr. Ladd and more pleasant overall.

"What do you make of it?" he asked the runner, studying him carefully for any signs of dissembling.

"Definitely a scam. Though to stop it will take some work."

"I agree. Any chance you can get the constable involved?"

"I'll send him a note, give him a tip, but the plot is fairly thick, and the ones involved aren't going to be happy about this. They might fight the information in the hopes of retaining their dignity and money."

Both men glanced at Lady Amelia, whose face remained in the shadows. He'd pay a purse of farthings to know what she was thinking. Surely her practicality could see a way out of this for her brother.

Spencer's gut twisted at the thought. His friend Ev stood to lose a great deal with this investment. Besides that, there was Lady Eversham and her miscarriages. Spencer's mouth tightened. Ev was a fine man. Good-hearted. He didn't deserve to be completely wrecked.

"Any ideas on how to force Lord Dudley to return everyone's money before it sinks with that false ship?" Several peers believed they were investing in a cargo of tea to be shipped to the Americas.

"I have a few," said Lady Amelia. Her perky voice set his teeth on edge.

"This is not a game, my lady."

"I'm well aware of that." Her chin lifted. "I have a dear friend who is married to a captain. He is the one who informed me that Lord Dudley's ship does not exist. I shall check with him again, but in the meantime, I believe we should force Lord Dudley's hand somehow."

"Blackmail?" Incredulity laced Mr. Ladd's voice.

"No, sir. I believe we can find a legal way to convince Lord Dudley that it is in his best interests to pay everyone back their investments."

"It is naive to believe he still has that money," said Spencer.

"I'm with you." The hackney shuddered to a stop, and Mr. Ladd rose. "Lord Ashwhite has friends in high places. It could be they'll accomplish more than the constable and his men."

"I'll see what I can find out," said Spencer. This was a delicate situation.

Mr. Ladd jumped out. "Take care of her."

The hackney leaped forward, leaving Mr. Ladd at his door.

"Take care of me? Whatever is he thinking?"

Spencer's anger revived. "My lady, I believe he is worried about your safety." He gestured to the trousers that did nothing to conceal her womanly form, and to the hat she wore, in which she'd tucked up her hair earlier when she'd changed. He wished he and Ladd had never stepped out of the hackney to allow her the "moment of privacy" she'd requested. Now her dress lay in a frothy heap beside her. "How often have you visited White's? And do you think it will go unnoticed? You will create a scandal for yourself, and I'm at a loss as to why you're taking such risks. It's not practical. You pride yourself on pragmatism and doing the logical thing, but your actions are born of emotion."

"I do not need to explain myself to you," she said quietly.

"On the contrary. You have dragged me into this. An explanation is most certainly owed." He hated the stern tone of his voice and the long, thick silence that ensued.

He would rather have Lady Amelia's eyes flashing at him with mirth or her mouth forming witty and saucy words that she flung at him like well-aimed bullets.

Not this deep quiet pebbled with the sound of hoof and wheel against cobblestone.

"You are right," she said at last. Her voice sounded strained. "I have importuned you in the worst way. It seemed the right decision at the time, but I see now the mistake I've made. Forgive me, my lord."

"An answer, Lady Amelia, is what I'd like."

"Shall I drop you at home first?"

Changing the subject. A rudimentary diversionary tactic. "No, I've instructed the driver to drop you off first."

"He's not your driver to instruct."

"I feel responsible for you, especially since you seem to have no care for your own safety. This was to be a simple arrangement. You find me a wife. I pay you. Not strange adventures in the middle of the night." Irritation and concern mingled together, making his voice gruff and unyielding. Lady Amelia was no sensitive miss, though, and he did not get the impression he was hurting her sensibilities.

In fact, he had the distinct impression her chin was lifting, and as they passed beneath lamps, their flickering glow played across her face. He thought he saw her eyes flash.

"Do not take that tone with me. You had the opportunity to back out and you did not take it. In fact, your curiosity compelled you to join Mr. Ladd and me on our excursion. Is this not true?"

He bit back a groan. "What is the reason for this? Why not just tell Ev the whole thing is a hoax? Why seek out Lord Dudley and gain…what? What exactly did we gain? No proof it's a scam, certainly. Besides what you already have, which is the word of a captain who may not have all the information at hand. I fail to see the reason behind this trip. Or the logic behind your clothing and sneaking into White's."

He fixed her with a hard stare. She was not a young woman ignorant of repercussions. No, she was smart and independent, and that was why he could not explain this odd behavior.

"I…"

"You…" he prompted her, ignoring a twinge of conscience at how he pressed her for information. But they were almost to Ev's, and he owed his friend at least the responsibility of watching over his sister.

A broken sigh. The sound of her feet shifting on the floor. And then, "Very well. I shall tell you something I haven't told anyone else."

He leaned forward, his gut twisting at the tone of her voice.

"Eversham is… He is very angry with me. Perhaps he even hates me." The fleeting shadows showed her hands twisting in her lap. "I must fix this somehow."

"By sneaking into White's dressed as a man?"

"No, by getting proof. By saving him. I have already damaged so much…" Her voice trailed off, and the strange, forlorn quality to her tone sent ice down Spencer's spine. This was not his normal Lady Amelia.

He reached for her, then withdrew. "Damaged?"

"Don't you see?" Her pitch rose. "My antics have caused Lady Eversham to miscarry. Not once, but three times."

They rolled to a stop, and Spencer had no time to speak past his shock when the hackney doors opened. Ev stood before them, peering into the carriage, face haughty with anger.

"Amelia, get into the house. Ash, I shall speak with you in my library. At once."

Chapter Thirteen

Amelia watched her brother settle at his massive desk. A cold and desperate dread scuttled through her, weighting her limbs as she plastered herself against the farthest wall. Lord Ashwhite seemed completely disaffected. He sprawled on Ev's armchair, a relaxed look upon his features.

She wished she could be so blasé about the situation, but she was quaking. Such an unknown feeling. She had felt this massive fear of the future when she and Eversham were twelve and their parents died. Where would they go? How would they survive? But Eversham had been capable and strong. He'd overtaken their estate duties and given her a Season at eighteen.

And she'd failed him.

Hadn't caught a husband, had done nothing to add to their waning coffers. Wasted money on clothing and fripperies and parties. Then, when she'd had The Great Disappointment, she'd languished. Poor Ev had had to lift her from melancholy. He'd rented the London house for her, and she'd thrown herself into painting and reading, gradually earning money by helping a friend with her Season.

Things had progressed until she'd felt independent and no longer a drain on her busy brother. He'd married, and while she dodged Harriet's various attempts at control, she had overall felt successful at being someone of whom her brother could be proud.

Until now.

Everything within her protested meeting her brother's eyes, but she made herself lift her gaze, only to find Ev staring hard at Lord Ashwhite.

"What exactly is going on, Spencer?"

Her brother's use of Lord Ashwhite's given name took Amelia aback. This was serious indeed. And his name was Spencer? She rolled the name in her head, tasted it silently on her tongue. The temptation to call him by name was already growing inside. She must not be so ostentatious as to use his given name.

Lord Ashwhite—Spencer—gave Ev an indolent grin. "A mad adventure that's over now. There's no need for you to worry or get angry. Let your sister go to bed and me return home. I don't have patience for histrionics."

A muscle in Ev's jaw quivered. "You were out *alone* with my sister. Care to explain?"

"Actually, I don't."

"Why, you—"

Amelia jumped forward, grabbing her brother's arm and positioning herself between the two men. "Please, Ev..." She swallowed hard, glancing back at Lord Ashwhite before turning her attention away. "It's not Lord Ashwhite's fault. He is merely trying to protect me, which he doesn't need to do. The truth is, I did this for you."

"For me?" Eversham snorted. "Do you pretend this is the first time you've snuck into places dressed as someone other than yourself?"

Amelia blanched. "How do you know these things?"

"Never mind that. My biggest concern now is that my supposed friend has been escorting you around alone. Doing who knows what, setting tongues wagging." Eversham brought a hand to his forehead. Then he pivoted and went to a chair, his shoulders more bent than any young man's should be.

Amelia bit her lip and willed the tears far from her eyes. Her willful ways had done this to her brother. With a sinking heart, she realized what she must do. She turned to Ashwhite.

"You can go. I shall explain the situation to Eversham."

Lord Ashwhite's beautiful green eyes held hers. No twinkle now, only a steady soberness that made her breath catch. He looked concerned. For her?

He straightened, rising above her, looking down at her. His hand came up and then dropped as though he'd thought better of touching her. Which would have been absolutely unacceptable.

"Do not feel overly burdened, my lady," he said.

"It's too late," she whispered.

And she realized it was. She couldn't bear to do this to her brother, not even for her own happiness. Distressing him, distressing his wife to the point of losing their child.

Casting Lord Ashwhite one last glance, noting the concern in his eyes, she gave him what she hoped passed for a reassuring smile and went to her brother.

He would not allow it.

Spencer spurred his horse across his land, wind rushing past his face, his heart thudding with the pounding of hooves. No, Lady Amelia was not backing out of their agreement, no matter what she'd told her brother.

The very next morning he'd received a letter in which the lady had politely explained how she no longer was at liberty to help him.

She'd penned no other news, and for days he'd stewed on how best to approach her.

Tonight he planned to attend a soiree at which several young women on Lady Amelia's list were to be present. He had it on good knowledge that Lady Amelia might also attend. Eversham was nursing a grudge and refused to see him or let him explain.

He could only hope Lady Amelia had shared her discoveries about Ev's investment with him. For himself, Spencer had done what he could by sharing his concerns with the constable and planting a few seeds in the ears of some fellow peers. It was the most he could do at this stage, though.

He reined in his mount, turning and surveying the land. Acres and acres of emerald green hills unfolded before him. Bright and healthy. His crops and gardens shimmered in the distance. Well cared for and orderly, bringing in food and revenue for the people who were his responsibility.

He didn't know if Lord Dudley was aware of this potential inheritance and, if God willed it, he never would. Jaw firm, Spencer motioned his mount toward the estate. If only his mother was home. She had a way of reading people that might be useful in his choosing a wife, but alas, she was still journeying the Continent with a friend of hers.

Never mind. With Lady Amelia's help, and he would most certainly insist on her help, he wouldn't worry about events outside his control. Tonight he'd go to that soiree. He'd speak with those young ladies and figure out who might suit as a marriage partner.

* * *

And so it was that five hours later, Spencer found himself drinking watered-down lemonade and eating stale cake while some bright-eyed girl played a tedious song on the pianoforte.

He eyed the doorway, waiting for Lady Amelia to show her face. For such a paragon of virtue, she was uncommonly late. He sipped his drink again, tapping his foot and cringing when the girl hit a false note. If only Amelia would get here… He caught himself, realizing he'd used only her first name in his thoughts.

It wasn't exactly appropriate, but then again, they'd become friends of a sort. Business partners, at least.

A familiar blonde swept into the room. Miss Stanley. Spencer craned his head, searching for Lady Amelia. No sign of her, though. He strode forward, intent on answers.

One of the women on Amelia's list stepped in front of him, a hopeful smile on her pretty lips. What was her name? He couldn't remember, and it took all his restraint not to brush past her. He forced himself to stop and reciprocate the smile. It wouldn't do for a marquis to give the girl what some might call a *cut direct* just because he was in a hurry.

"Lord Ashwhite, how good to see you here." Blushing, she fluttered her lashes at him.

Even in his wilder days, he'd never flirted with girls in their first Season. Certainly didn't chat with them or show them the slightest attention. Young girls fell in love easily, and he'd learned a long time ago to stay away from the snare of fancy. By instinct, he gave her a remote smile and then caught himself.

What if this girl was the one he'd spend forever with? His mind bucked at the idea. No, her hair was too light. All the same shade.

"And good to see you." He gave her a friendly nod and continued through the press of oversize dresses and heavy colognes. The girl probably had wanted him to stay and talk, but first he must find Amelia.

Spencer empathized with Ev's anger. It was regrettable that Lady Eversham and his friend must go through so much pain. If it wasn't for the sake of the people on his estate, Spencer might not press for Lady Amelia's help. He hated to cause his friend more grief. If only there was a way to gain Lady Amelia's help without causing a rift...

There! He spotted her familiar locks and busy fan. He stopped midwalk, irritation galvanizing him.

Not shock, though. These feelings did not surprise him. He was aware of a certain attraction to the artistic and stubborn Lady Amelia, and the emotion was getting in the way of his goals. Finding a wife proved hard enough and was made worse when his mind kept wandering to unlikely places.

Though he didn't think the lady was immune to him... Of course, he hadn't turned on too much charm. Maybe it was time to start.

No. What was he thinking?

She was too similar to his mother, and he well remembered the strain on his parents' marriage. To the point that his mother had traveled abroad and his father spent most of his time at the House of Lords, leaving Spencer to play with the village children and sneak Cook's raspberry tarts.

Annoyed beyond reason, he brushed past several tittering ladies and didn't make eye contact. After what seemed an absurd amount of time, he finally reached Lady Amelia.

"My lady, might we have a word?" he asked during a lull in her conversation with a gray-haired matriarch who found no trouble in giving him the *cut direct*. Her brows rose, and her lips quivered before she turned her back on him.

Lady Amelia's fan looped precariously through the air.

He didn't have time for this nonsense. He gently took her arm and prompted her to follow him. They needed somewhere private to talk. But not too private. It was obvious his reputation still preceded him, and even though Lady Amelia acted as though her reputation didn't matter, he wouldn't be the cause of any mean-spirited gossip about her.

"Whatever was that for?" she sputtered.

Spencer was acutely aware of the warmth of her arm beneath his hand. She moved gracefully, too, which put him in mind of the quadrille they'd shared.

Gritting his teeth, he steered her through guests toward a small settee in a corner alcove. She sat delicately, her flouncy dress settling beside her in gauzy purple lines.

"We need to talk." He sat beside her, an appropriate distance between them.

"I am not stopping you, my lord." Though her tone was kind, a flash of mischief lifted the corners of her lips.

If he wasn't so annoyed he might have smiled. "You've left me in the lurch."

"I?" Her hand fluttered to her collarbone, traces of paint discoloring her thumbnail.

"Yes, you. We had an arrangement. A deal. And for you to back out now… I only have a month and a half left or I'll lose Ashwhite. I am here to insist you fulfill your part of the bargain."

The mischief fled her face, replaced by resistance. "It is not fair to ask me to continue something that so disturbs my family. You're quite fine on your own. You have all the qualities necessary to land a wife. Both the ladies here are good candidates."

"I can't remember their names," he said under his breath.

"What was that?"

He repeated himself and glared when a little snort escaped her. "Not ladylike, that."

"Oh, pshaw. You'll do fine." She patted his hand as if she was a dowager comforting a child. He didn't like that feeling, didn't like her playing to his emotions or even acting as though touching him was like taking care of an infant.

Before she could react, he flipped his palm neatly and caught her hand. His thumb stroked the tender spot between her thumb and forefinger. Her eyes widened. She jerked her hand, but he held more tightly.

"My lord," she whispered with a false smile, "kindly let go."

"Not until you find me a wife."

"No." She yanked her hand again.

It was a shame, really. He kept her hand within his, gently but firmly, admiring how neatly she fit. How the warmth of her fingers melted into his. Maybe he'd been approaching things from the wrong angle.

"Why exactly don't you wish to marry?" he asked.

Her brows ratcheted upward, and her mouth rounded. Then, as though catching herself, she smoothed her features, and he had the sense she was hiding behind spectacles and primness.

"I beg your pardon?"

Oh, yes. Definitely hiding. That tone amused him, and his mouth quirked. "I am certain you heard what I said. My lady," he added just to irritate her.

It worked. Her lips puckered, and she jerked her hand again. This time he let go.

"I have my reasons, and they mostly have to do with control." She scoured the room. "You shouldn't have done this. Someone might take note and talk."

"Since you don't intend to marry, I fail to see the issue," he answered in a lazy voice, knowing it would infuriate her.

He was right. She turned toward him, mouth firm. "My reputation matters."

"Your behavior suggests otherwise."

"I don't want to be banned from polite society merely based on a…a joke of yours," she answered sharply.

"But what if it wasn't a joke?" he said softly. He leaned forward, finding himself unable to resist the sweet scent of the rosewater she used or the tender flush to her skin. "What if I enjoy holding your hand and wish to do so again?"

The pink tint to her cheeks deepened to rouge. "That is a bold thing to say."

"Do you object?"

She wet her lips, stymied by his flirtation. He swallowed, feeling suddenly unsure if he was doing the right thing. He didn't wish to trifle with her affections, only to see where this feeling might lead.

"My lord," she finally said, "I believe you should focus on the goal at hand. Namely, finding yourself a wife. For myself, I am working on making my brother happy, thereby making his wife happy."

"But you've reneged," he pointed out.

"I am deeply sorry, but I don't see how I can fulfill my part of the bargain."

"Amelia…" At her startled look, Spencer cringed. "That is, Lady Amelia, it is hard for me to believe you have single-handedly caused her ladyship to miscarry." She started to protest his words, and he held up a finger. "No, hear me out. There are causes for that, and an independent sister is not one of those."

"But stress is. And I've stressed her deeply."

He shook his head. "Nonsense."

"It's not nonsense." She took a deep breath. "Eversham was quite clear with me about my part in the matter. Some of my letters to Parliament were aggressive in nature. In particular, toward a certain person." Her eyes flickered. With pain? "I publicly castigated Lady Eversham's father, and shortly after, she suffered her first... malady. A few months ago she discovered somehow that I had found a friend of hers a husband. When she realized I'd been paid to do so, she lost the next child. And now... Well, I moved in and sent invitations for a party designed to find you a wife, and you see what happened." Her fingers were clasped, her knuckles white.

"This isn't logical." He wanted to get up and hit something. "You are not the only hardship in her life, and it's silly to say you're causing this to happen."

Her dark eyes met his, serious behind the lenses of her glasses. "You're right. It is illogical and silly and for anyone else, I would laugh it away. But this is my family. I cannot ignore my part in their pain."

Mindful of curious eyes, Spencer refrained from throwing his hands in the air. "Surely you can't believe in your heart that this is your fault."

"I don't know what to believe," she whispered. "Only that I have caused Ev pain, and that is something I deeply regret. You don't understand..."

"Explain it to me, then." His voice came out clipped. He prayed for patience.

"Ev is my only family. My mother and father died

when I was twelve. A carriage accident." Her gaze left his, staring into the distance, unfocused and far away. "With the help of a guardian, Eversham took over the estate and all the duties of an earl. He should have been in the schoolroom. As he grew older, he should have been traveling, learning. Finding his place in the world. Instead, he spent his growing years recouping our family's dwindling fortunes. He launched me into a spectacular Season, during which I failed to secure a husband. I cannot fail him again or cause him more distress. He had to marry Lady Eversham." She bit her lip as though stopping herself from speaking ill of the lady.

Spencer was at a loss for what to say. He'd known Ev had come to the earldom at a young age, much as he had, though thankfully his mother still lived. He hadn't known Lady Amelia carried such guilt over things outside her control.

Silence suspended between them, though not complete. The soiree was in full swing. Another young woman played the pianoforte, this time with more skill. Chattering and the rustling movements of stiff dresses filled the hole in their conversation.

Spencer studied the young ladies. Their youthful faces and innocent eyes. Where had he been during Lady Amelia's come-out? Graduation from university, perhaps? He vaguely remembered Ev leaving for a semester to supervise his sister's Season.

He took in her glossy hair and the strong, aquiline nose she wore like royalty. The direct gaze and slender fingers.

"I wish I had met you then." The impetuous words surprised him.

Her brows arched, and for the first time that evening, a real smile broke her sober mood. "You wouldn't have liked me."

"I've always liked a challenge, and that's probably what you were."

"Most men wouldn't say such a thing."

"Most men are easily fooled by pretty looks."

She blanched.

"Not that you don't have pretty looks," he rushed on, wondering how he'd made such a blunder so quickly.

Her hand waved dismissively. "Never fear. I am quite aware my brains exceed my beauty."

He coughed out a laugh, surprised by her words and disagreeing completely, though not in a way she'd probably understand.

"My lady," a voice whispered from behind them. Spencer swiveled, as did Lady Amelia. A maid peered at them from behind a potted plant.

"Sally?" Lady Amelia's pitch rose. "Is that you?"

"It is indeed, and I have dreadful news. Just dreadful." The branches rustled. "Can ye meet me in the coatroom?"

"Certainly." Lady Amelia rose. "Please excuse me, Lord Ashwhite."

He stood also, a head taller than the stubborn lady and just as determined. "I'm coming with."

Their conversation wasn't over by half.

Chapter Fourteen

Amelia was acutely aware of Spencer at her side as she rushed to the coatroom. Mortified by the conversation they'd had and yet strangely calmed, she refused to look at him. How could she, anyhow, with all the people at the soiree to skirt? Somehow this had become a crush of the worst sort.

She reached the coatroom and spotted Sally near the back, her face splotchy.

"Oh, dear." Chest clenching, Amelia dodged an errant coat poking in the way. "Whatever is wrong?"

"It's Dukes." The girl sniffled.

Something tight and hard balled in Amelia's stomach at the mention of her faithful butler. He had been with their family since she was a little girl. After hearing of her parents' deaths, Dukes had held her while she wept. She would never forget his hand patting her back or the scent of his cologne. Eversham was to have given him a spectacular letter of reference.

"Tell me at once," she said.

But her former servant had seemingly lost control of her faculties, for she collapsed to the floor in a mess of tears and skirts.

Had Dukes…died? Amelia swayed and blindly reached for a coat, something, anything to hold her up. What she found was Lord Ashwhite's sleeve, to which she clung, for her knees trembled violently. Mouth dry, she blinked hard and willed some starch into her backbone.

Mustering every ounce of willpower she possessed, she released Lord Ashwhite's shirt and marched over to the maid. "Sally, stand up at once and tell me whatever is the matter. Now, girl."

Sally blinked up at her and rose to her feet, fingers balling in the front of her dress. "He's been taken, my lady."

"Taken?"

"Yes, my lady, to Newgate."

Amelia's jaw dropped. "But whatever for? He was to have been employed somewhere… My brother was to see to it."

Sally shook her head, eyes wide in her splotchy face. "Dukes found a job briefly, but his arthritis was too much. He dropped an heirloom and the family fired him. When he came to me, he was hungry and dirty, but I have no room at my flat. I live with my mother, sisters and grandfather. I'm not sure what happened next, but this evening the cook was talking. Seems she knew of Dukes many years past and is right saddened to hear of his arrest."

"There must be some mistake." Dukes would never steal…but perhaps hunger had forced him to it? Though she was gladdened he hadn't passed away, her hands remained clammy. Newgate would not keep a feeble old man alive for long. What could she do?

Summoning her resolve, she took a deep breath and patted Sally's shoulder. "Thank you, Sally. You've done the right thing in coming to me. I shall remedy this at once." With what money remained to be seen.

"Oh, thank ye!" Sally bobbed her head and curtsied. "I better return to my duties."

"It was good to see you."

"And ye, my lady."

The maid scurried out, and with her retreat, Amelia's strength waned. Trembling, she leaned against the wall and dragged in a heavy breath.

"How can I help?" Lord Ashwhite took her hand, his thumb rubbing circles against the tops of her fingers.

"I have relied too much on you." She closed her eyes. Just for a moment. Just to gather her wits. Which, unfortunately, were being scattered by Lord Ashwhite's quite comforting touch. She yanked her hand away. "Why did you follow me? Our discussion is done. I am not finding you a wife. I realize it is dishonorable of me to go back on my contract." She swallowed hard, for her spontaneous declaration the other night certainly rankled now. "However, my brother's wife's health is more important than my…hobbies."

Lord Ashwhite's eyes narrowed. "We had a deal."

She wet her lips. "You're right, but please understand my position."

"I do." His face softened, and the gentle look in his eyes curled warmth through her belly. "You're doing what you feel is the right thing. But I have to do what I think is right, as well. And saving my land, the people who rely on me—that's my priority. I won't stop until it's done."

She shook her head, despising the discombobulated feeling lurking inside. Normally decisions appeared cut-and-dried for her. But now there was so much to weigh. Her brother. Lord Ashwhite's tenants. And Dukes. She had to take care of Dukes somehow.

The stipend she had from her mother… Would that be enough? She squared her shoulders.

"First I must make a list." Yes, that was what she would do. A list. She pushed past Lord Ashwhite and strode into the main room. The scent of perfume and flickering candlelight battered her senses, and suddenly the walls were tilting toward her…

"My lady, you are not well. Perhaps a bit of fresh air will do." Ashwhite took her elbow and prodded her toward a door that led to a patio. His fingers were firm and strong. She knew from experience gardens waited outside, with curved walking paths and ornate benches. The dizzy feeling persisted, a heavy pressure against her skull.

It was the silly old corset she wore. The new maid had drawn the strings far too tight. She tried to take a deeper breath and only managed to see stars. Her steps faltered.

"Take care, my lady." Ashwhite's breath ruffled past her ear, intimate, and his grip tightened. "We're almost to a bench."

They moved through the door, and humid air engulfed them. The moon cast a bright radiance that clarified the path before them whilst darkening the shrubbery into muted shadows.

"Spectacular, isn't it?" Lord Ashwhite tilted his head up, staring.

Amelia studied the moon, too, feeling the quietness of the moment, the gentle hum of insects and muffled sounds of music. Lord Ashwhite's arm was still linked with hers. The lunar glow illuminated his features. And then he turned to look at her. There was a sparkle in his eyes, a quirk to his lips, that caused a different type of dizziness to pass over her.

Was she floating? Because she felt the solid ground

beneath her feet, but her head was…starry, or was it her heart beating unnaturally fast? Yes, that was it. Too much blood flow to the brain.

"Are you feeling better now?" he asked.

"I think I should sit," she murmured. Perhaps that would calm her racing heart. This beastly attraction. It was certainly causing problems with her equilibrium. "Stop smiling like that," she said, crossness snipping her words.

"Like what?" His eyes creased at the corners.

Oafish man.

She shot him a scowl but allowed him to lead her to a bench swathed in moon glow. Gratefully she sank onto its cool surface, resting her fingers on the edge. Lord Ashwhite sat beside her, and his scent surrounded her. Sandalwood soap, mostly. Perhaps the slightest hint of cologne.

Discreetly she inhaled.

"What happened in there?"

"Too much perfume," she said simply. Her vision was clearing nicely and her pulse slowing. Very good. All she'd needed was to sit and catch her breath.

"You're not having corset troubles again, are you?" He chuckled at his reference to the first time they'd met and his comment that dancing could relieve an overly starched corset. She resisted the urge to swat him. That would be quite unladylike, though, *oh*, so tempting.

"This is not a laughing matter," she said sternly. "Dukes is in real trouble. I must deliver him from New-gate. Somehow." She felt a frown tugging at her lips, but she would not give in to such an insidious expression of defeat.

"What do you propose to do? Break him out?" Lord Ashwhite let out a short laugh. "If Dukes committed a crime, getting him released might be nigh unto impossible."

"But if he only owes money, if he stole because he was hungry, it may be that I can pay his fines. Then I must bring him home. I don't know why Eversham didn't hire him in the first place."

"Your brother is strapped for cash."

"How do you know that?"

"Hazarding a guess. He has invested in Lord Dudley's scheme, which tells me he's looking for quick money. How did the estate's crops do this year?"

"Why, I don't know…but Ev has an income from serving in the House of Lords, does he not?"

"It wouldn't cover the costs of maintaining an estate. Food, clothes, servants."

"Doctor's fees." Poor Harriet.

"Do you really believe you've caused her miscarriages?" Ashwhite peered at her, his face kind and handsome.

She swallowed hard. "Logically, I know I cannot have caused such a thing. But it is said extreme stress can provoke illnesses, and I worry that my being a burden on Ev has transferred to her. And now there is Dukes and whatever costs he might incur." Her chest constricted. "I cannot leave him there. I just cannot."

"You're very devoted to him."

"He's been with my family since I was a little girl."

"And when your parents died?"

"Yes." She blinked, surprised by how the memory snuck up on her and stole her breath. She hadn't expected still to feel pain over such a long-ago tragedy.

His hand covered hers. "I'm sorry for your loss, my lady."

"Thank you, Ashwhite."

"About this list you mentioned."

"Rescue Dukes is the first thing I must do."

"And then?"

"The cottage I looked into has unfortunately been let to someone else. With Lady Eversham's malady, I didn't feel right in leaving. Once she is recovered, I think I should permanently remove myself from their lives."

"Now you're being ridiculous."

"I beg your pardon?"

"You're speaking from emotion and not practicality."

"It's not practical to leave so that she and my brother can live a restful life, free from worrying over me and my wayward decisions? Then, what, pray tell, do you suggest I do?"

"As much as you love your independence, it is my observation that your wish for a 'permanent' leave is due to hurt feelings. It's as simple as that."

She felt her spine stiffening. "That's an insufferable thing to say."

"But it is the truth, isn't it, my lady?" He leaned forward, his eyes piercing, the pupils huge and dark. "This outer mask of pragmatism you wear hides a tender and hurting heart. You should tell your brother how you feel. Stop trying to control everything."

He was very close to her.

An odd sensation stole over her, traveling through her limbs and filling her with a heady anticipation. Her heart tapped a sluggish beat against her sternum. Her stomach clenched as she waited…

Her throat was tight, and her senses reeled from the onslaught of moonlight and sandalwood. The moment stretched between them, suspended by a connection she could not bring herself to break.

Then he blinked. Backed away. Took the initiative she

could not find. Her pulse roared in her ears. From relief or disappointment, she wasn't sure.

"I'll help you with Dukes," he said.

In his eyes she saw resolution. Steadiness. She wet her lips and nodded. "Thank you."

Now she owed him. Perhaps she could still assist him in finding a wife. If she didn't accept payment, then technically she wouldn't be violating her word to her brother. It was only fair to follow through on her promise to Lord Ashwhite.

His tenants didn't deserve Lord Dudley's management. Not when Lord Ashwhite loved his home and wanted to care for it. And she could make it happen. She did not doubt her abilities to find him a wife one whit.

So why did she suddenly feel so hesitant?

The next morning found Amelia creeping up to Harriet's door. She carried a breakfast tray. A truce of sorts. She also needed to ask her sister-in-law about the upcoming house party. There was still time to cancel. Though invitations had been sent, a menu must be created and an orchestra appointed.

Why had she planned this soiree? She reminded herself that she'd been forced into this house. Manipulated, even. Once she spoke with Harriet, she intended to pay Lord Ashwhite a visit. After last night's promise of help, she knew she'd need to move fast to rescue Dukes. He couldn't withstand Newgate for long.

She nudged the bedroom door open, hoping her sister-in-law would not order her out. They'd engaged in many verbal battles in the past, neither backing down from an argument. Sometimes Amelia felt it hadn't been her fault. Harriet had waltzed into her life with ready-made ideas on how the sister of an earl should behave. Though Amelia was her senior, that hadn't stopped the lady from expressing dissatisfaction. Which had only spurred Amelia to continue on her own way, in her own time.

But to think of all Harriet had suffered recently…well, Amelia could only do what she could to make amends. As she entered the room, the stale odor rushed to greet her. This would not do at all. She set the tray of food beside the bed and then went to draw the blinds. They opened to reveal sunlight at its zenith. Such a beautiful summer day should be enjoyed. Sunshine spilled into the room, exposing the aimless dust motes that traveled through the undisturbed air.

"I prefer those closed." A sullen voice emerged from the four-poster bed.

"Darkness will do you no good." Amelia swept toward that voice, ignoring the tiny twinge of fear inside. Fear of what? Of being chastised yet again?

"You are not in control here. Close my curtains."

"Take a hint of light, my lady." Amelia settled on a chair next to the bed. "You are in need of it."

"Go away." Harriet pouted, turning her delicate face away from Amelia. "And remove that food. I'm not hungry."

What could Amelia say? How she longed to fix things, if only a little? But Harriet's querulous nature grated deeply. A strong craving to grasp the lacy coverlets and yank them off her sister-in-law's uncombed head washed over Amelia. With gritted teeth, she tamped back the urge. "Would you care for a bit of story? I have an exciting tale of a damsel—"

"No," Harriet interrupted. She peeked out of the coverlets, her eyebrows narrowed into accusing lines that gouged her forehead. "This entire disaster is your fault, and if Ev didn't tell you so, then he is a bigger coward than I thought."

The angry words slapped her across the face. She couldn't breathe. The chair in which she sat dug into her spine, its ridges hard and unyielding.

"Not only have you dragged this family's reputation into danger, but my babies—" at this, Harriet's voice caught in a half sob "—are dead. Dead! I have been overcome with worry trying to understand your activities and nonsense, but we've had enough. If you ever want another farthing to spend on those ridiculous, ugly paintings, you must understand that your silly letters and uncouth notions better stop." Her head lolled back and she uttered a deep sigh, as though speaking to Amelia had cost her a great deal of energy.

Horrible waves of regret rolled through Amelia, drowning any good intentions she might have had for her brother's wife.

If it was true… Amelia swallowed hard, tearing her gaze from the now-silent lady. Those words of hers had severed any possible attempts to bridge their relationship. Despite what Lord Ashwhite had said, Amelia knew that she had played a part in her family's loss.

Again.

Tears didn't often visit Amelia. She was far too pragmatic, but at the moment her throat felt curiously tight. Thick with emotion. Blinking hard, she swallowed back the tears, willing them to a hidden place never to be visited.

Her sister-in-law suddenly sat up, throwing her blankets aside. She glared at Amelia. "Oh, whatever are you staring at? Leave at once, and do not bother me again."

"I only came to remind you that we will be hosting a party in two weeks' time," she managed through numbed lips.

"And who, pray tell, gave permission for this party to be held here?" asked Harriet in a cold voice.

Amelia wet her lips, summoning a strength she did not feel. "I shall cancel it immediately if you wish. I'm so sorry—"

"If I had a wish, it would be never to hear of you again. In fact, if I was a man, I'd put you on a ship to another country and tell everyone that you'd gone overseas to visit relatives." Light caught Harriet's icy blue eyes, turning them into shards of glittering anger. "Believe me when I tell you that I shall be speaking to your brother about this…thing…you have planned."

"Whatever you feel is best." Amelia stood, spun on her heel and marched out the door before Harriet could see the stricken state of her soul. Certainly she had experienced pain, but to treat Amelia thus? It was unwarranted…and yet there was that tiny part of her insisting she deserved it.

Deserved it for bucking tradition and societal norms. For engaging in less than ladylike behavior. Had her parents been alive, they might not have allowed her to behave so. As much as she disliked remembering them for the hurt it wrought, a memory stymied her path down the stairway.

Mother sitting in the garden, the family Bible in her lap. Father singing a hymn as he pruned overzealous bushes. She didn't know where Ev had been, but she'd been playing near the pond when she had seen the most exciting bullfrog. It had belched at her before plopping into the water. Without thinking, she had reached for the bulbous creature and fell into the pond.

Even now she remembered the burn as water had

gushed through her airways. It had been her mother who'd yanked her to safety. Never mind the dripping mess of her pinafore or the pond scum coating her braids. Mother had held her close, crying and thanking Jesus for keeping her baby safe.

Amelia blinked and continued down the stairs. Perhaps her mother's French Huguenot heritage had contributed to the family religion. It was difficult to remember, but the impression that her parents had not lived by all the rules of polite society stayed with her.

That was a lineage she could be proud of. No matter what occurred, she'd not allow Ev to stifle her. In any way. She must contact Lord Ashwhite, spring Dukes from Newgate and then somehow make things right with… everyone.

"I can do it," she whispered. The life of her former servant was at stake, as well as Ashwhite's tenants and her own future. She would not give up so easily. She would not bow beneath the cleverly aimed barbs of her sister-in-law, despite the truth to them.

Chapter Fifteen

Spencer strode up to Eversham's house, a letter in his hand. His friend would see him. He knew that there were no sessions today and Ev wasn't at White's. Which meant he might be home.

As he knocked, he couldn't help but hope to see Lady Amelia. Granted, it was early in the morning and she'd still been at the soiree when he left. He'd slept well after she told him she'd still try to help him.

Though she'd seemed discomfited doing so.

He drew in a deep breath and, when the butler opened the door, gave him his calling card. He followed the butler to the parlor. The house was quiet. Perhaps he'd shown up too early, but he needed Ev to see this letter as soon as possible.

He paced the floor, skirting the fine rug. Mayhap Ev made faulty investments, but truthfully, he didn't look as though he hurt for money.

"You shouldn't be here."

Spencer pivoted. Ev stood in the doorway, hands planted on his hips. He looked like his sister just then, with his chin jutting mulishly and his lips pursed.

"Hear me out." Spencer held up his hands in surrender. "Has Lady Amelia spoken with you about Dudley and his scam?"

Ev squinted. "Dudley, you say?"

"You heard me, Ev. This is uncommon, to be sure, but it came to Amelia's—"

"Amelia? Since when are you using my sister's given name?"

"A slip of the tongue." Ashwhite grimaced. This wasn't going quite as he planned. "I know you're still angry about the other night, but I assure—"

"You don't know the half of it. That's my sister we're talking about, Ashwhite." Ev advanced forward, finger pointing and brow lowered. "You stay away from her."

Spencer eyed the man who'd been a close friend since university. Jaw tight, he didn't back away but held out the letter. "You may be interested in this. And while you're reconsidering your superior decision-making abilities, give a thought to this sister you claim to love so much. She is miserable."

He spun on his heel and stalked out of the room. He stopped in the hallway. Lady Amelia hovered near the front door, in a froufrou dress that did her no justice. Her expression was—he frowned—sad, perhaps. Or resigned.

"My lady." He bowed. "How do you do this fine morning?"

"Well enough, my lord. Would you care for a stroll through our gardens?" She picked up her chin and thrust it toward the door.

A not unsubtle hint. Evidently she had something of import to say and wished to tell him in private. Even though Ev remained in his study, she obviously feared his overhearing their conversation.

Being alone with her wasn't the best idea, though.

Last night had been…close, he thought ruefully. Very close indeed.

He was no stranger to moonlit kisses or enraptured ladies, but that was in his past, and he didn't intend to revisit such a place. Not for anyone.

He took her arm and escorted her outside. "I have an appointment at Newgate, my lady, and can spare no time for a tête-à-tête. Perhaps this evening or tomorrow?"

Her eyes brightened. "Excellent! That is exactly what I meant to speak of with you. Let us go now and rescue Dukes before he perishes." She took her arm from his fingers and shook it as though jiggling his touch from her sleeve.

"Wait a minute. You're not coming with." He frowned.

"'Tis only right. He doesn't know you." She winced. "I recant that statement. He does know you. As an irritating caller who wouldn't leave me alone. I think it best if I come to assure him all is well."

"So that he doesn't think I mean him ill?" Spencer asked drily.

"Precisely." She beamed him a smile so bright that despite the ugly dress she wore and her odd hairstyle, he found himself staring a little longer than he should. He marveled at how her eyes gave the impression of sparkling with merriment.

"Now let's leave before Ev stomps out here and demands I play nursemaid."

Perspiration tickled his neck. The sun was warming the day quickly. He pulled at his collar. "Have you told him about Dukes?"

"And add to his burdens?" She wrinkled her nose, a guilty look passing across her face. "In truth, I've done my best to avoid my brother today."

"Avoidance doesn't solve anything."

"Oh, don't lecture me." Her hand waved through the air in a flowing gesture. "I know perfectly well that procrastination is the key to failure. But in this case, do you think it right to load him with such dour information when he already has so much on his shoulders?"

"It would be wrong not to tell him."

Again that guilty look. It was in the way her eyes skittered away and her pretty lips twisted. "Very well." She turned, and he followed her into the house.

Surprisingly Ev took the news calmly and gave permission for his sister to go with Ashwhite. Perhaps he'd thought about Spencer's earlier words and sought to lessen his sister's entrapment. Or maybe he just didn't care because of the worry he held for his wife. Either way, soon enough Spencer found himself alone in an open carriage with a very satisfied-looking lady.

Off to rescue Dukes, though how he would manage it, he wasn't sure. But he found himself determined to do it not only for the old man's sake but also for Lady Amelia's.

Amelia fanned herself as she waited for Ashwhite to return with Dukes. On the way into London, they'd stopped by his house and exchanged the open carriage for a curricle, as a few clouds on the horizon hinted at a storm brewing. If she sat far enough inside, no one would know she'd ridden alone with a man.

The carriage didn't mask the stench emanating from the gruesome place. Odors marred the breeze that intermittently passed through the carriage. Though she longed to see Dukes and assure him all was well, by the time they'd reached the city, it had occurred to her that going inside might not be the best idea. Newgate's reputation created no end of speculation and worry. She feared

Dukes might no longer be alive, and it was that fear causing her to shift to and fro as she waited.

Waiting brought about other mental ignominies, as well. With her body forced into stillness, her mind frolicked about, revisiting all sorts of things and finally landing on the moment she wished to avoid most: the prior evening.

Last night on the bench, when her corset had been strung too tight and she'd imagined Lord Ashwhite might wish to kiss her.

Her! Of all creatures. A proudly on-the-shelf spinster/artist/bluestocking. She never could decide what she wished to be and felt all three suited her rather well. But while they suited her, those qualities had never attracted men. Well, not men like Lord Ashwhite. There was a certain tough masculinity to him, coupled with kindness, that she found hard to ignore.

Oh, fine. Impossible to ignore.

No, he had been distracted. She'd mistaken that look in his eyes last night. She must have. Why, what would she do with a kiss anyhow? She had no use for men or marriage. Look at how much trouble Ev had proved himself to be. Or rather she to him. She'd probably make a horrid wife.

But an excellent matchmaker.

She'd written such a dandy list of wives for Lord Ashwhite, too, and he hardly showed interest in the women he might spend the rest of his life with. It was enough to make any decent businesswoman have a serious case of the vapors.

Biting her lip, she looked at the nasty old prison, a blight upon London.

She wouldn't think of Ashwhite when she had so many other problems on her plate. Cousin Lydia, for one, who still insisted on marrying a second son when it was obvious she could find a better prospect.

One with a little more to his pocket and a lot more to his life expectancy.

Then there was Lady Eversham. This morning had proved a deeper problem than Amelia expected. It seemed a situation beyond remedy. Besides refusing to see her, Lady Eversham had given the housekeeper a list for Amelia. Different items to accomplish from letter writing to supervising the meal menu. She had been told to refrain from balancing the books, for which she was extremely grateful. The thought of looking at numbers in a ledger sent palpable waves of panic through her.

And had she been able to paint once?

No, not at all. The sketch she'd begun of Lord Ashwhite still sat in a closet. Amelia thought of the pout on Harriet's face this morning. A horrible part of her longed to capture the look in oils and show it to her.

Which solved nothing.

Certainly it couldn't bring back the lost babes.

She frowned, tapping her restless fingers on the seat. Ev knew about the financial scam now. She hoped that when she returned, he didn't ask her how she'd discovered the investment in the first place. Her twin had little patience for her investigative methods.

When the doors to the prison swung open, she perked up. Scooting to the edge of her seat, she peered out and saw Ashwhite and Dukes heading toward her. The poor man walked with a limp. His arthritis must be paining him.

Her heart constricted. Why had she let this happen to him? She should have double-checked his whereabouts. Made sure he was safe.

She hastened to the far side of the curricle as Lord

Ashwhite helped her former butler inside. Dukes's face was lined more deeply than when she'd last seen him, grooves ridged into his skin. But his eyes met hers and, though rheumy, they seemed to smile.

"My lady," he rasped.

She could not speak past the lump in her throat. She took his arm and brought him to her side, where he settled with a relieved exhalation. Lord Ashwhite sat across from them. She flashed him a grateful look, stifling the quick surge of feeling that swept through her at his answering nod.

The curricle started on its way, winding through factory smoke and litter, leaving the dankness of Newgate behind. She inhaled deeply once they'd reached a part of the road where sunlight cut through clouds and warmed her face. She found Dukes's hand and clasped it. He did not return the gesture, and to her surprise, she saw his eyes had closed.

He must have suffered in such a place.

She looked to Lord Ashwhite. "How did you do it?"

"Do what?"

"Get him out."

"You were right about the petty thievery. I paid his fines and dropped some names, and they were happy to release him. Seems things are a bit overcrowded lately."

A wonderful relief crashed over her, so intense her whole body seemed to sink into the seat as the weight of worry lifted from her shoulders. "I cannot thank you enough, my lord."

He waved an elegant hand. "Nonsense. You may thank me as much as you want."

"Very funny." She tried for a frown and failed. "Once we get home, I shall ensure Dukes gets a long rest, complete with full meals and a soft bed."

"We are not headed to Eversham's, though."

"What do you mean?" She craned her neck to the window and saw that, indeed, they were on their way out of London, but not toward Ev's estate. "Wherever are we going?"

"My mother's." The corners of Lord Ashwhite's eyes crinkled.

"Your mother's?" Flummoxed, Amelia could only stare.

"She unexpectedly returned from a trip to the Continent. I spoke with her this morning and discovered she's in need of a new butler at the dower house."

Amelia wet her lips before glancing at Dukes. His eyes remained closed, sleep temporarily softening the age of his face and giving him a peaceful look she hoped wouldn't be destroyed by this news.

"I assumed he'd be returning with me to Eversham's. With people who care for him," she said pointedly. "Once I find a cottage, I should have enough left to cover our living expenses." Some might think it very crass of her to discuss financial matters with Lord Ashwhite, but after everything that had happened, she couldn't deny she felt a certain trust with him.

"It is no business of mine, of course, but perhaps Dukes would like to make a little extra money until your cottage is ready."

"Yes, perhaps," she said hastily, though her insides felt as though they were plummeting to the wheels. Nothing, absolutely nothing, was happening how she wanted it to. She would just have to try harder. Pick up that sturdy spine she was known for and walk with it.

"You look quite forceful right now." Lord Ashwhite's teeth flashed.

"Do I? It is this list of duties I must accomplish. Nothing is going my way." At once she regretted the plaintive words. He'd mark her a whiner, no doubt.

"Why don't you share your list with me? Mayhap my male practicality can lend some insight." A mischievous grin furled the corners of his lips, and Amelia felt her own mouth twitch in reply.

"Very well," she said primly. "My most important job has been accomplished. Dukes is now safe, and I'll not let him out of my sight. Which is why he should come home with me."

"We'll ask him what he prefers when he wakes."

"Excellent idea." Of course Dukes would want to be with her. That heavy feeling that plagued her began dissipating. A bubble akin to satisfaction lightened her chest. Tapping her chin, she gave Lord Ashwhite a cocky look. "I must cancel next week's soiree due to Lady Eversham's illness. This leaves me with only the house party at Ashwhite to plan. Less mingling for you but more time to invite the perfect guests."

"I'm feeling an acute onset of the ague," Lord Ashwhite said drolly, but the corners of his eyes remained crinkled.

"Don't be silly. I need this income, and you need a wife. A cottage I can afford exists somewhere, but I need time to find it. Between my duties at home and helping at Newgate, I've found no time to search for a place to live. Let alone paint." She missed painting the most. A knot had formed in her stomach, and every day she didn't get time to release her emotions, the thing only grew larger. "Then there's Cousin Lydia. She is insisting on marrying this…this second son."

"Your voice is dripping with haughtiness."

"I am trying not to be snobbish, but really, Ashwhite. Cousin Lydia could do so much better."

"And when you say *better*, you mean more money and a title?"

"Yes. What do you think I mean?" Was he playing with her? Frowning, she picked at her dress, an ugly new thing she hated but wore because her wardrobe was slim at the moment.

"So these husbands you find for wives..."

"Are all good prospects. They must be titled and have a solid financial standing, and compatibility is necessary, as well."

"How do you determine compatibility?" His head tipped.

She had the uneasy feeling he disapproved of her somehow. She forced her chin up. "Mutual interests are the best indicator, but I also consider temperament and hobbies."

His brow arched.

"You are surprised, my lord?" she asked stiffly.

"Not really. Suppose this second son meets the other requirements and only lacks the title? Miss Stanley's prospect has a career, does he not?"

"A dangerous career. One that will leave Lydia a lonely and impoverished widow."

"Most likely she'd have more money than you."

Amelia wanted to wipe the smirk off his face. "This is not a laughing matter, Ashwhite."

Beside her, Dukes snuffled, his sleep temporarily interrupted by her strident tone. Deliberately she softened her voice. "Lydia does not know men the way I do. This man is taken with her looks, nothing more. I haven't had time to see if he's suitable or to ascertain his compatibility. She is in the mad rush of first love, and her heart will be broken."

"Is that what happened to you?"

"What?" Her brain fogged.

Ashwhite leaned forward, his green eyes intense and bright. "Your heart was broken, and you fear the same for Miss Stanley."

Amelia's mouth dried. She clenched her skirt. Unclenched it. "That is neither here nor there. We are speaking of my cousin's future."

"Nay, my lady, you are speaking of your past. He hurt you badly, I daresay. I'd like to punch the man in the mouth."

"Ashwhite," she gasped, her hand going to her lips.

"It's a horrible thing to trifle with a young woman's heart." He shook his head, and a piece of dark hair swung over his brow. "But you need to step back and be objective. Understand that your experience doesn't define everyone else's. Attempting to control Miss Stanley's heart will lead to nothing but pain between the two of you."

Amelia's chest hurt horribly. She wasn't quite sure why. "We made an agreement. Her family asked me to find her a husband, and if she chooses the wrong man, my reputation as a matchmaker will be harmed." Even though she wasn't being paid in this instance.

"That won't be an issue, since you've quit matchmaking."

"Only for a bit. Once I have my cottage, I might do a little on the side."

Ashwhite's eyes weren't twinkling anymore. "Lady Amelia, might I offer you advice?"

"You may." She waited for his response. Dared him with a steady gaze.

He took his time in answering. His eyes had sobered, his mouth relaxed as he took in her question. At last he leaned back, crossing his feet at the ankles and giving her a lopsided tilt of the lips. "I was not referring to my earlier words, but perhaps you would like to discuss the matter?"

Spencer could tell by the look on Lady Amelia's face that his response greatly displeased her. Or maybe it discomforted her. She arched her neck as though trying to look down at him. All stiff pride and wounded heart. He had the undeniable impulse to wrap her in a hug and protect her from whoever the cad had been who'd hurt her.

That was an inclination he'd ignore, though.

This lady amused him. He enjoyed watching her eyes widen and sparkle with excitement over the list of deeds she claimed to dread. It seemed to him she relished planning and controlling life. Though she missed her painting. There was no denying the sadness in her voice when she spoke of her art.

"God is..." Lady Amelia trailed off, looking past him with one of her vacant stares. The kind that told him she'd gone off in dreamland somewhere, forsaking her practical façade for a more gentle place. "I'm not quite certain who He is and what I'm supposed to do with the idea of Him."

An honest answer, though it pained him. "A Bible is a good way to get to know Him. That's how I learned."

She laughed. "A Bible? I don't know that I could read such a thing."

"It contains more adventure than your novels, and quite a few romances."

Her mouth did that cute little purse it did when she was intrigued by something. "You don't say? Like what?"

"A man who falls in love with one daughter and works out a deal to marry her, but then is tricked at the last moment into marrying her sister."

"Why…that is quite scandalous." Her eyes grew wide. "You're saying that story is in the Bible?"

"And many others."

"But what is the purpose? Surely God has more important things to tell us than stories of romances gone awry."

"Don't you see, my lady? God's relationship with us—with me and with you—it's a romance gone wrong."

"I believe in logic, but I must say that I also believe in romance. I shall admit you've intrigued me with all this talk of God and feelings." She glanced out the window as though searching for God in the sky.

The carriage made a turn and the rising sun splashed into the curricle, splaying against Lady Amelia's face and hair, throwing streaks of gold through her tresses and warming her cheeks to a becoming pink.

She faced him, making the sun glint against her spectacles.

"Believing in a personal God is difficult. If there is this deity, and if He cares for us, then why did my parents die? Why do children suffer in the streets from neglect and malnutrition? Mothers wasting away for lack of food and clean water. You're a marquis. I think…perhaps… that it is easier for you to believe in a God who cares."

His windpipe contracted at her words. He had to work to draw breath. Did she think he had never felt sorrow or suffering? "I've never experienced the pangs of starvation, but that doesn't mean I'm immune to pain."

"I am only suggesting that faith comes easier to those who've not had their beliefs crushed beneath the realities of life."

"You think I live in a bubble," he ground out. He knew he shouldn't be angry, yet a flame raced through his blood, bringing heat to his entire body. She thought very poorly of him indeed.

Her smile was tight. "This is a subject better discussed when we've had some food and laughter."

"Quite right." He gave her a curt nod, trying to get his thoughts together. Soon enough they'd stop for a quick meal at an inn on the way, and they should reach his mother's home by late afternoon. The thought of seeing her added to the tenseness in his shoulders.

He had no reason to be this upset. Lady Amelia's thoughts were valid, and if she thought ill of him, she had reason. Long before he'd gone to the Americas, he'd lived as though tomorrow didn't matter, as though he was accountable to no one. Yes, he'd followed certain rules of morality, and he preferred to think that for all his carousing, he'd been a good man who treated others decently.

Yet in his heart there had always been the knowledge of failure. And when he'd gone to the Americas and heard that preacher speak words that had aimed straight for his heart, life had become much clearer.

He had at one point been the spoiled son of a marquis. Could he blame her for believing him to be far removed from suffering?

He looked at the lady opposite him. Such a smart and funny woman. Too stubborn, but she didn't deserve his irritation.

"My lady," he said quietly. "Forgive me. My annoyance is not at you, merely at my own inability to articulate what I feel. You are right in that many ways, I grew up cosseted and protected."

She gave him a graceful nod, regal bearing in every line of her body. "There is nothing to forgive. My words were not meant to invalidate your experiences or to suggest that you have not felt pain."

Their gazes held, and strong emotion grasped him at the understanding in her eyes. Perhaps she did not think lowly of him, as he'd assumed. And why should it matter what she thought of him?

The answer was that it shouldn't.

Yet her opinion did matter, and he couldn't fathom why.

Chapter Sixteen

They had just left the inn when the carriage broke.

Perhaps *fell apart* was a better term, for one moment they sat drowsy and satiated with lunch and the next the floor gave way, the curricle lurched and Amelia went sprawling against the door. It cracked open and, unable to stop herself, she hurtled out onto the ground.

When she woke, it was to a throbbing head and an aching body. Sunlight abraded her eyelids. Instinctually she kept them closed. She slowly became aware of the hum of insects, cool dirt against her cheek and grass itching her elbows. Pain radiated through her back, arching up her spine and ending in a pulsating sensation at her brow.

She moaned, wishing for darkness again. She didn't know how long she lay there, riding the never-ending spasms of pain, but when she revived, it was to cooler temperatures. She cracked open an eye slowly and carefully. The entrance of light did not bring any more pain, and so she opened the other eye and looked around.

Clouds had moved across the sky, dark and heavy with rain. They stifled the sun and brought a blessed wind to scurry across her body. She didn't try to move. There was no need to bring additional throbbing to her brains.

She wet her lips, which felt dried and cracked. Water. The thirst overwhelmed her, pushing past any other need. For moments she was lost in darkness again. She woke to wetness and stuck her tongue out. Her body protested even such a minor movement, but her need for drink bypassed the pain.

When she'd eased the torture of thirst, she blinked and visually searched the vicinity. Nothing to see but grass and dirt. She couldn't locate the curricle.

Where was Dukes? Lord Ashwhite? Were they lying somewhere just out of reach? Were they hurt? She dared not entertain the thought of death.

She couldn't.

A shiver sneaked through her. The rain, which had been a blessing, pasted her clothes against her skin, cooling her body temperature. Hopefully this would pass soon, for despite her uncomfortable position, she did not relish the thought of lying in mud much longer. It squished beneath her cheek.

She dragged in a careful lungful of air. No pain. Gingerly she moved her toes. Then her legs. Could she roll onto her back? She was almost afraid to try, remembering her Aunt Louise, who had sprained her back when Amelia was a child.

Because she'd ignored the injury and walked to the doctor, her back was permanently affected, and afterward she'd often been bedridden.

Amelia weighed her options. It seemed she was quite alone in this situation. A sarcastic laugh escaped. The sound of it was lost beneath the soft patter of rainfall. How ironic, to die the same way her parents had. If God existed, and if He did indeed have a personality or humanlike nature as Lord Ashwhite believed, then this must be a colossal joke.

Poor Eversham. He'd be quite destroyed.

She frowned at the thought. Is this what God wanted? To destroy her family? No, she would not allow it. Locking her jaw, she inched onto her back. Though her muscles twinged with stiffness, no extreme pain accompanied the movement.

Finally she was flat on her back. Different parts of her body vibrated with pain, but nothing she couldn't handle.

At this new angle, she was better able to look around. The clouds above were thinning, she noted. She tried to push herself into a sitting position, but the moment her elbows dug into the ground, waves of fire undulated toward her scalp.

Uttering a groan, she lay back.

It seemed she must lie here until someone passed through or until Lord Ashwhite found her. Or Dukes. Surely they would wake up soon.

She stared at the sky. Was there really a God up there? Some great father figure who watched the people below with entertainment?

Lord Ashwhite had mentioned romance. Love. 'Twould be comforting to believe in a loving creator, but her heart rebelled at such thinking. If she believed God cared for her, then she might believe He cared for her parents. But when one cared for someone, one did not allow all that person held dear to be ripped away.

She did not, leastways.

Offering that deity who might or might not be watching her a grumpy harrumph, she looked to her right. To the stretch of trees that lined a jagged horizon, bereft of humanity.

Perhaps when their party did not show up, Lord Ashwhite's mother would come looking for them? That feeble hope waned as the minutes passed. Her optimism

dwindled with her energy. How long would she lie here?
Limbs numb with cold, mouth dry… She wanted to hold
on to a forceful attitude, but her stomach rumbled, and
her thoughts were turning to a darker place.

Was this how her parents had felt? Lying in wait for
help and never receiving it? She'd been told her father
died instantly. But her mother… A sharp prick gathered
in the corners of her eyes. They burned and she blinked
hard, but this didn't stop the tears from spilling onto her
cheeks.

The hotness of them seeped into her skin. And still
they didn't stop. They rolled down her face, gathering
force until she could no longer hold in her cries. Her body
strained beneath the force of her emotions.

It was this dreadful situation. Being reminded of so
many things. The gentleness of her mother's touch as she
dabbed perfume upon Amelia's wrists. Her father's low
rumble as he read aloud from the family Bible. Such old
memories, dusty and stored beneath an iron lid of control, but now that lid had rusted and the remembrances
tumbled out.

How could she have forgotten her parents' faith?
Turned her back on it in order to escape the sting of remembering? For the first time since her parents' accident, an unlikely urge to say a prayer for help prodded her
heart. *God help me*… She wanted to speak the words, to
allow them past her lips, but she remained silent within.

Because what if He did not help? What if she asked
and didn't receive?

She daren't be so vulnerable as to put her trust in an
unseen force.

And yet the strangest, most beguiling urge just to believe coiled inside.

As she sprawled upon the mud, looking a fright, no

doubt, a tendril of something new and untried had sprung within her. Amelia closed her eyes again, her limbs cold but her teeth not chattering, and let her body relax into the earth beneath her. She was exhausted. Every bone hurt.

When she slipped into sleep, it was deep and dreamless.

Spencer opened his eyes. Shivering, he rolled to his side and sat up. His body shrieked a protest, but his vision remained clear. One moment they'd been riding, and the next the carriage had lost control. Slowly he stood and took in the damage. The carriage lay on its side several meters away. The horses stood idly nipping at the spare blades of grass poking up from the road.

He didn't see the driver or Dukes.

He didn't see Lady Amelia.

Panic crowded his throat. He sprung forward, reaching the carriage in seconds. It was empty, as he'd known it would be. Turning, he scanned the side of the road. A boot rose above a small mound. He rushed to Dukes's side. The old man stared up at him.

"My lord," he rasped.

"Can you sit, Dukes?"

The old man nodded, and Spencer helped him rise to a sitting position. His shoulders felt feeble, but Spencer saw nothing out of place. He shrugged off his overcoat and draped it across Dukes's frame. "Though it's wet, perhaps it will give you some warmth. Stay here. I must find Lady Amelia."

Dukes nodded, but Spencer hardly registered the movement. Every muscle felt tight with apprehension. The English countryside stretched before him, muddied and ripe from the rain that must have passed while he was unconscious, but he saw no sign of Lady Amelia. He dashed to the other side of the road. Still nothing.

She could not have gone far. Fists clenched, he bounded in front of the carriage and scurried down a rutted area. His foot slipped in the mud, and he bumped the rest of the way down but barely felt it. For there was his lady, flat on her back, eyes closed and skin as pale as a waxen statuette.

For a moment he forgot how to breathe. His heart simply stopped.

She lay like a broken doll at the bottom of the hill.

And then feeling rushed through him again. One long, painful breath propelled him to trip over rocks and roots to get to her side. He took her hand. It was cold and limp. Her eyelashes were dark spikes against pasty cheeks.

In the sunlight that had chased away the earlier clouds, she looked unnatural. He put his ear to her mouth, his heart thumping terrible long beats in his chest. It was so loud he dared not breathe lest he miss the sound of her feeble breath.

Her exhalation basted his cheek, though, and he buried his face against her neck. It was the closest he'd ever been to this inspiring woman. She was alive. Her skin did not smell of mud, but of flowers and freshness, much like the lady herself. A brilliant orchid in an endless hothouse of white lilies. Once his pulse settled, he edged his arm beneath her neck.

He had to lift her carefully. If she'd wrenched her back in any way, he could make it worse. There were also his own bruises to be aware of. The lady was featherlight. He would not have guessed it when her stubbornness was as weighty as an anchor.

Tucking back the unanticipated humor, he scooped beneath her knees with his other arm. He stood and gingerly stepped up the hillside. Her head lolled into the crook of his arm. Her lips were too white. He didn't like it. He picked up the pace until he reached Dukes.

"I must take the horse."

Dukes nodded. "I know."

"My lord," a voice called from behind them. "Let me help."

Their driver limped toward them. Though mud covered a good portion of his body, he appeared relatively unharmed.

"Thank you," Spencer said. "Do we have a saddle?"

The driver nodded.

"And do you know where Ashwhite is?"

"Aye, my lord."

"Ride quickly, then, for the lady is in need of the physician."

Hours later, Spencer paced the bedroom, hands clenched and body sore. "When will she wake?"

The doctor shook his head, his eyes calm behind his spectacles. "When she is ready. There is nothing wrong with her besides bruises. I've given your mother instructions for her care."

His mother rose from her position on a settee situated near the expansive windows. The curtains were closed and candlelight flickered in the room, dropping shadows against her patrician features. She didn't look as though she'd aged a bit in the year since he'd seen her. "We will call you immediately should the need arise. Thank you, doctor."

The man nodded to them and left the room. Silence ensued. Spencer could not take his eyes from the prone figure on the bed. Both panic and anger clawed at his insides, and overriding that, a fear that she would never wake up. That he'd never again see that lifted chin or a challenge in her eyes.

His mother crossed the room and laid a hand on his arm. "You should sleep."

"Not until I know she's well."

Mother looked at Lady Amelia, a thoughtful expression easing onto her face. "Do you care for her?"

"She's the sister of a friend. You will like her."

"Perhaps. You cannot hold vigil in here alone, so I shall stay with you. Entertain you with my stories of adventure. I was almost kidnapped in Naples." A playful note entered his mother's voice, but Spencer could not find the energy even to smile.

He walked to the bed and sat down on the edge, very careful not to dislodge Lady Amelia's hand, which rested at her hip. Her fingers twitched, and then she let out a little sigh. His chest tightened as he lifted his gaze to her face.

Her lips moved, and then her eyelids fluttered. "Where...?"

Her eyes opened. Dark and questioning.

He wanted to take her hand, to cup it within his own, but his mother was watching and he did not want to deal with her questions. They had much to speak of, but not this...strangeness he felt toward Lady Amelia.

"You are in my mother's home, the dower house of Ashwhite. The doctor has seen you and pronounced you bruised but well." Then his throat closed. The pallor of her face alarmed him, for he'd never seen the formidable lady without her spark.

"Dukes?" she asked weakly.

"Hurt his leg, but other than that, fared the crash better than the both of us and is fast asleep in his room. The doctor left him some medicines."

"I'm glad. And you?"

"Very sore."

"Perhaps if your curricle had not cracked apart, we would not find ourselves in this predicament?" Though her voice was tired, he heard humor in her words.

"I don't think now is the time to complain," he said.

"Very well. I shall make a list once I'm up and about of all the ways in which you mishandled the situation." She smiled, and even though strain tightened her face, there was warmth in her eyes.

It didn't take long for her to fall back asleep.

"She has pluck." His mother's hand on his shoulder roused him from thinking about everything that had happened. He heard approval in her voice.

"Possibly too much," he said. Her pluck had gotten her in an uncomfortable position with her brother.

"Nonsense. There is never too much of such a quality."

Spencer grimaced. Maybe it would do to have his mother and Lady Amelia on friendly terms. Growing up, he'd never lacked in affection from his mother, but he recalled too many arguments between her and his father. Too many vases broken in the heat of battle.

All over his mother's "pluck." She had not wanted to settle as the wife of a marquis. She'd been bored by endless rounds of dinners and the straitjacket of the *haut ton*'s restrictions. As much as he loved her, he didn't have an abundance of happy memories involving her.

As a grown man, he could look back and see that it wasn't her fault. Not all of it. His father had separated Spencer from his mother. He'd taught him to do what he wanted, to feel no guilt.

But guilt remained. Until last year. God had forgiven him, and he felt that redemption with every pore in his body and every thought in his head. He gave his mother a considering look.

She was watching Lady Amelia, a crease at the corner of her lips. He ought to extend forgiveness to his mother. Had she felt the distance between them? He thought perhaps so. She'd sent letters to which he hadn't responded. On her various exploits, she'd always bought him a gift. Ever since he was a young lad, she'd given him presents.

Her way of an apology, he supposed, for leaving him in the care of nannies picked out by his father. He frowned. Bitterness was rooted deep. He didn't see how saying a simple "I forgive you" could erase three decades of hurt.

"You're deep in thought," his mother remarked. "I've never seen you care overly much for anyone besides your father."

The comment stung, though he doubted she'd meant it to. He shrugged, picking at the quilt. "I care for many things, but you were never around to know what those things were."

Despite his best intentions, bitterness coated the words and left a sour taste to his mouth. He stopped picking and glanced at her. Lines furrowed her forehead, adding a dimension of worry to her features. He wanted to kick himself. How could he be so crass? Was it her fault he'd grown up feeling unloved? Alone but for his governess of the year? They'd never lasted long. Due to either his shenanigans or his father's flirtations.

"That was uncalled for," his mother said quietly. She wore wounded feelings like a fur shawl. She was right.

Spencer stood, giving her an apologetic bow. "You're right and I apologize. The day has worn me out." He spared a look at the prone figure on the bed, gut twisting.

"She's going to be fine, son." His mother stood, also.

She approached and gave him a careful hug, which he barely returned. She smelled like rosewater. He remembered that scent well because as a child he looked forward to her trips home. When she visited, hugs became the norm. Unfortunately, her visits rarely lasted more than a few days.

He shook his head. Maudlin thoughts when he had so much more to worry about. He patted her back and stepped away. "Have you spoken to Father's attorney?"

"No. I haven't had a chance to do anything besides hire Dukes. Such a shame about this accident…" She returned to her seat, sinking down as though fatigued.

Spencer tucked back a groan. Of course she must be exhausted. "The accident should not have happened. There was no debris in the road, nothing to cause it. I'm having my man in the village inspect the carriage for wear and tear." Or something more malicious, though he would not worry his mother or Amelia about such a thing. The accident was too convenient after their investigation of Lord Dudley. Someone did not care for their meddling, and he was the first to come to mind. Amelia had told her brother, after all, and he himself had spoken with several people. Perhaps Lord Dudley was more intelligent than Spencer had assumed.

He shoved his hands through his hair and spun toward the door.

"Spencer," his mother said, following him into the hallway. "You are worried. Let us talk now, while we are here together."

"You never stay long, do you?" He regretted the barb the moment he issued it. By his mother's flinch, he could tell it had struck her.

"I don't know my plans at the moment, son, but I do wish you'd share whatever's burdening you."

He ground his teeth. He didn't want to talk about the curricle or the contents of the will, but he supposed she'd need to know as their futures depended on his decisions. "Very well." He faced her, noting the strain on her features. Why should she feel strain? She lived her life much as he had. Doing what she wanted, when she wanted, funds unlimited. No responsibilities except the ones she gave herself. He forced himself back to the chair, though it was the last place he wanted to be.

Only hours before, he'd felt new and fresh. Clean. Now unforgivingness and bitterness snaked through him, poisoning his every thought. It was being in contact with her. Remembering all the lonely nights. The days when he'd just wanted his mother, yet she'd been nowhere to be found.

"Your face is as stormy as a tornado." Mother's head tilted.

"I don't know how to say this, but everything you see here, this dower house, this bed… None of it belongs to me yet."

She waited patiently, her gaze not wavering.

"The stipulations of the will require that I marry within the next two months in order to inherit Ashwhite and the fortunes attached to it. Should I not find a wife by the required time, we will lose the estate to a cousin."

His mother didn't blink.

"No funds. Do you understand that? No more traveling. No more gifts."

"I understand perfectly well." She hesitated. Her fingers twitched against the satin of her dress. "There is something you must know, a reason I came home as soon as I received news of your arrival."

"Go on." He waited, his muscles trembling with sudden exhaustion. All he wanted to do was drag himself to bed and sleep for days.

"I know the requirements of your father's will. We developed them together."

Chapter Seventeen

His mother had known.

Spencer couldn't ignore this new information no matter how hard he tried. As he rode into the village to check on his carriage the next day, thoughts swirling through his head added to the aches of yesterday's accident.

She'd actually met with his father, and they'd agreed on something. It couldn't be.

Last night Mother's pronouncement had been so shocking that he'd left the dower house rather than hurt her with his bad-tempered words. And why it bothered him, he couldn't say, except that he'd chalked his father's silly edict up to one last hurrah in the "tell Spencer what to do" campaign. If his mother had agreed, though, did that mean he'd disappointed both of them? That they'd wanted more from him?

Granted, he'd been a bit wild. Rakish, though certainly not a despoiler of women. Yet knowing his parents wanted him married irritated him. Not because of what they wanted, but because of how he'd so obviously disappointed them.

A year ago it wouldn't have bothered him. He'd been

too busy playing with his friends. Even his service to the House of Lords had been halfhearted.

But now a heaviness that had nothing to do with the dreary day bent his shoulders. Yesterday's storm had returned, creating a black and growling morning. His horse cantered down the road to the village, seemingly unaware of the turbulent clouds above. Not that Spencer cared a fig about the weather.

Sleep had eluded him. He'd tossed and turned. When neither his mother nor Amelia had appeared at breakfast, he'd decided a ride into town might clear his head and give him some perspective. The rain-scented wind only served to heighten his turmoil.

He should be praying right now. Beseeching God for wisdom. Seeking guidance. An empty place had opened in his heart, though, and he hadn't the foggiest idea why. All his talk to Amelia about faith, and at this very moment he felt none.

It was an uncomfortable feeling, rather like the dreams in which one found oneself wearing only a nightshirt to a social gathering. Embarrassing and confusing.

"God help mine unbelief," he muttered, guiding his mount into the village. The well-kept huts and neatly trimmed trees stood testament to his estate's prosperity. He smiled at Mrs. Miller, who baked the best bread in the county, and chuckled when redheaded little Lucy waved excitedly in his direction.

He loved these people. He truly did. What did it matter that his mother agreed with his father about the marriage stipulation? Maybe she was concerned for the estate, as well. He wouldn't know until he spoke to her. Determined to put his hurt aside for now, he rode to the livery.

He was almost there when a feminine voice calling his name yanked him to reality.

Pulling the reins, he stopped his horse and prayed he hadn't really heard Lady Amelia.

"My lord," she said breathlessly, pulling up her mount next to his. "Where are you off to this fine morning?"

He eyed her as he scrambled for an answer. She looked peaked, to be sure, but also alive and well. A wisp of hair escaped from her riding hat to curl about her cheek. A slight bruise at the base of her cheekbone was the only evidence that she'd been thrown from a carriage yesterday.

"Must you frown like that?" She arched a brow. "Staying in bed proved unexciting, so I decided to explore a bit. Perhaps send a letter to my brother."

"We sent him news last night," he said flatly. "In the future, give your correspondence to our housemaid, and she will see that it goes out."

Lady Amelia should be in bed, resting. And yet, here she sat, wearing a bright purple riding habit no doubt borrowed from his mother. He didn't want her to hear his conversation with Jack about whether his carriage had been sabotaged. Frustration gnawed at him, overlapping with a giddy relief that she felt well enough to ride a horse all the way into the village.

"Sir, your horse? Mr. Jack said we be expecting you." The young man peered up at him, and Spencer found himself in a quandary. Take Lady Amelia with him and most likely alarm her sensibilities, or send her away and risk offending her? He didn't like these stakes.

"Would you take my horse?" Lady Amelia slipped off her mount with the man's assistance. A grimace fluttered across her features, but she landed safely on the ground.

Gritting his teeth, Spencer dismounted, as well. "You may take them both."

"Very good." Lady Amelia beamed up at him. "I suppose you're looking into why the curricle broke apart?"

"Why would you suppose that?" He walked toward Jack's shop. Lady Amelia shadowed him.

"Because it is altogether strange. I'd like to speak with the man fixing it."

Spencer gestured to a doorway. "After you, my lady."

"This is it?"

"My old friend is handy with many things, including fixing curricles." He followed Lady Amelia into the store, appreciating his friend's tidy place. The sweet smell of freshly cut lumber greeted him, mingling with the familiar odor of earth.

"You here, Jack?"

"In the back," a faint voice answered.

Spencer followed the sound to a door set at the rear of the store. Twisting the knob, he stepped into an outside workshop. Pieces of lumber littered the sparse grass. Jack bent over a rough-hewn table covered in oddly shaped tools. Fixing things had never been a gift of Spencer's. He held the highest esteem for those who worked with their hands.

"Ye here to pick up yer fancy rig?" The words floated over, muted by the position of Jack's body.

"Is it ready?"

"Aye, my lord. I parked her 'round the side of my store."

"None of that 'my lord' nonsense when we're alone, Jack."

His old friend straightened, his crooked smile showing off his missing teeth. "It's a mite silly calling someone whose face you've crushed 'my lord.'"

"Rightly so," Spencer agreed, trying to dodge the memory of that particular pugilistic round. "Let's just call a childhood full of dogs and mud holes reason enough to stay on first-name basis."

"As ye wish, Spencer."

He felt Lady Amelia's perusal, but she said nothing. "Jack, this is Lady Amelia Baxter."

"Pleased be, my lady." Jack inclined his head.

"You've a lovely shop," she said.

"Thank you, my lady."

"And what do I owe you?" asked Spencer. An itch between his shoulder blades warned him to leave before Lady Amelia was involved further. She had wandered to the other side of the room to inspect rocking chairs.

Jack waved his hand. "Not a farthing. I'm just glad ye and yer visitors weren't hurt." A sly look crossed his face, and he lowered his voice. "The young lady anyone particularly special?"

Amelia? She was special, but did Jack mean marriageable? No… Spencer wanted to shake his head, but the thought of marrying her took him by surprise. Certainly he'd thought of her in a serious way briefly. He'd pushed the matter aside, but now…she could be the answer to all his problems.

Or she could start more.

He dared not forget her dangerous exploits or bluestocking notions. Would she be content to live in a village like this? Surrounded by country?

"A family friend," he finally said. "Look, Jack, I've a question about that carriage of mine. Were you able to surmise the cause of the accident?"

"I did, my friend. Though I wasn't sure how to tell ye…" Jack's trailing-off words and averted eyes confirmed Spencer's suspicions.

"Tampered with. Am I correct?" His fingers flexed against his waistcoat as anger filled him.

"Aye, my lord. By people not trying to hide that they'd done so, either." Jack walked to another table at the side of the lawn. "Ye see this?" he asked, bringing up a large beam. "It be yer axle. And here's where it was cut almost completely through."

Spencer peered at the thin line running through the wood. This was more than tampering. This was a message.

"Someone wants you dead." Jack echoed what he was thinking.

"Who?" Lady Amelia demanded. She'd returned just in time to hear exactly what Spencer hadn't wanted her to hear. "I'm putting my runner on this immediately."

Not if he had anything to say about it. Spencer cleared his throat. "I insist on paying you, Jack. How much?"

"Nay." Grunting, Jack hefted the wood back into a pile of other mismatched pieces. A gold band encircled his fourth finger.

"Are you married?" The question sputtered out before Spencer could stop it.

"Over a year now. 'Twas the best decision I ever made. She's my love, my dearest friend."

"How very romantic." Lady Amelia sounded a quite chipper for someone who'd just escaped with her life intact.

"Good for you." Spencer clapped him on the back, but his insides felt queasy. Would he ever feel that way about someone? Did he want to? That required vulnerability, a trust he didn't know if he could muster.

"Get yerself a wife." Jack nodded firmly as though it were a done deal. "You'll be a happier man for it."

"Believe me," Lady Amelia asserted, "he shall have one within the fortnight."

"A runner is unnecessary."

Amelia peered up at the sky, considering Ashwhite's

words. They were riding home now. The clouds hung low, and wisps drifted toward the ground like searching anchors. Every so often a low rumble shook the air around them. Her body ached in too many places to count, but she was happy she'd set out this morning.

If not, she might never have discovered that someone had tried to kill them.

"While I appreciate your opinion, you must understand that Mr. Ladd has resources we cannot come by. He is utterly trustworthy."

"How did you guess about the carriage?" Ashwhite's voice carried dark and tight with tension. Almost as dangerous as the clouds overhead.

She eyed him carefully. "Surely you noticed the coincidence? We stop Lord Dudley in his criminalistic tracks, and suddenly your curricle, emblazoned with your crest, is breaking apart on the road. I certainly don't believe a marquis owns a faulty carriage. Even if you do, I feel better acquiring information on Lord Dudley and his whereabouts. Mr. Ladd has sources in places I dare not venture…" She trailed off, not liking the expression Lord Ashwhite wore. "Is there a problem, my lord?"

Was it her imagination, or did his jaw tighten?

"Put your man on it, then. I don't like you associating with Mr. Ladd, but your instincts are correct. The carriage was tampered with, and it's best to figure out who did it and why before any other *accidents* occur."

"Whatever do you mean, you do not like my associating with him? I hardly think it's your concern." Perhaps it was hunger or fatigue, but a distinct sense of annoyance was overtaking her.

"It's not for a woman of your station." He gave her a very deliberate look, as though trying to make her feel guilty.

Of all the underhanded things to do… Adjusting her spectacles, she looked down the length of her nose at him…though she had to lift her chin first. "I shall let you know when Mr. Ladd responds. I'll direct him to send the answer to my brother, since I'm sure I'll be to his estate by tomorrow evening."

"If you insist, madam." Lord Ashwhite's tone was cold.

He evidently didn't like her manner, but neither did she care for his. How dare he insinuate that she must answer to him, and worse, that her behavior was unladylike? Especially after the way he'd cared for her… Her insides warmed as she remembered his tender looks. It was like something from one of her novels.

The heroine in need of rescue. The dashing hero in the right place at altogether the right time. Unbidden, a sigh slipped from her lips.

Lord Ashwhite drew his horse close to hers. "Pray tell, have I vexed you with my words?"

"Balderdash," she said briskly, thankful he couldn't know her thoughts. There was no need for him to realize that she enjoyed a good romance as much in reality as in fiction. "I simply hope you understand that my activities are not up for debate. We shall get along fine once you accept that."

The dreadful oaf chuckled.

Evidently he thought her words funny. Irritated once more, she spurred her mount ahead. "If we are to beat these storm clouds, we must hurry."

"It's getting dark. Galloping is risky. Slow down. Settle for an even canter."

Of course, he was right. Gritting her teeth, she pulled back on the reins until her mare was neck to neck with his.

"When I find a wife, my situation will be fixed."

He sounded pensive. Amelia frowned.

"What I don't understand is why my parents created such a quandary."

"Your parents?" She dared a look at his fine profile.

"I know the responsibilities of running the estate. My father trained me, and I've taken over the duties at various times in the past years. So what is the use of a wife? The coffers are full. I looked at the books last night to double-check." He barked out a short laugh. The wind scooped it up and tossed it behind them, but the echo of his unhappiness remained. "It is just another way my father wanted to control me, and he's certainly had the last laugh."

"Do you truly believe that?" Troubled, Amelia guided her horse over a fallen log. She didn't remember the chunk of wood being there this morning.

"Yes." Ahead of her, Spencer ducked a low-hanging branch. His horse let out a nervous whinny at the clouds above. The air had thickened, cloying. Humidity blanketed Amelia, coaxing a sheen of sweat to her skin. Thunder clapped suddenly, startling her. Her mount pranced nervously, sidestepping another fallen branch.

What had been heat a moment ago swept away in a gust of cool air. The hairs on Amelia's arms lifted, and a tremor shuddered through her. Weather like this meant danger. She scanned the road ahead. Limbs littered it, strewn by an unruly wind. Treetops whipped against a charcoal-streaked sky. Their dissonant movements created a strange synchronicity.

All her concerns fled, replaced by the certainty that, halfway between home and town, they'd better find some cover. Her horse backed up, snorting unsteady breaths.

Beside her, Spencer's was equally discomfited.

"Shh," Amelia soothed. She patted her mare's flanks,

all the while searching for a low area, a dip in the land, somewhere to crouch before the clouds really did touch the ground. Because her horse kept up the nervous dance, she slid off.

"Good idea," Spencer shouted above the wind. He dismounted as well and brought his horse nearer. "No sense in getting thrown. Let the horses find their way home. We won't be able to hold them during a tornado."

He grabbed her reins.

"What…no." She reached for them but it was too late. As soon as the horses felt slack, they galloped off, tossing their heads, eyes bulging.

Amelia's skirts whipped against her skin with frightening velocity. Could they survive something like this? Fear pumped through her in waves, weakening her knees and tightening her vocal cords.

"There's a ditch here somewhere." Lord Ashwhite grabbed her hand. The steady warmth of his grip quieted her nerves. She followed him across the debris-strewn road. A windswept branch rammed into her shin.

Lord Ashwhite squeezed her hand as if apologizing, but kept going. As they reached the edge of the road, the wind moaned, a long, keening sound like a maiden in distress. The noise pierced Amelia's ears. Long grasses lashed against her skirts.

"Look!" Spencer pointed to his right.

A bruised cloud swayed against the sky, lengthening into a wispy curl that gathered strength and density. It caressed the horizon and then receded. The cloud dropped again. And stayed, turning the trademark funnel into a twister.

If there had been a hollow place in Amelia's faith, it was no more. She prayed as she dropped to her knees.

Chapter Eighteen

Spencer grumbled the entire way home. Mud clung to his clothes, heavy and smelling strongly of manure. His hair was plastered against his cheeks, which stung from multiple scratches he'd received while clutching a solid oak.

Sore and ornery, Spencer trudged up his driveway. The twister had missed them by the grace of God. They'd been scared witless, hiding in a hole near a tree with only roots to anchor them. Prayers had poured from his mouth. And God had saved him. His chest burned. Probably had a cracked rib or two. Wouldn't be the first time. When he reached the front door and rang, silence was his only answer.

"They all must still be in the cellar," said Lady Amelia.

"Yes," he answered, and his heart beat more quickly as he looked at her. She was both frightful and beautiful. Like a picture splashed with paint in all the right places. Despite the dirt on her face and the twigs in her hair, despite the scowl that matched his own, her hand had not left his the entire way home.

Little had been said as they walked. He supposed holding on to each other and a tree while the world blew away tended to do that to a person.

He glanced out across his property, wincing at the work to be done in the following days. He prayed his people were safe. Turning the latch, he gestured for Lady Amelia to enter.

She stopped in the entryway. She turned to him, eyes alight. "Do you smell that?"

The aroma of baking bread tickled his senses, sweet and heady and so thick his mouth watered. His stomach let out an answering growl.

He aimed for the kitchen, taking the servants' hallway because it was faster. Lady Amelia was quick on his heels. He pushed open the door and stopped. What greeted him was a mass of servants, maybe the entire household, gathered around a large plank table. His mother sat at the head, but when she heard his entry, her head whipped up.

Tears filled her eyes. "You're alive!"

"Of course I am." The words barely left his mouth, and she was upon him, her perfume familiar and comforting. "Did you miss me?"

"Cad." She drew back and lightly slapped his shoulder. Sniffling, she managed a smile. "We hadn't a clue where you were or what…oh." She brought her hand to her nose as their odor filtered through her joy.

"We found a hole to sit in." Grinning ruefully, he gave her one last hug. "Do you mind if we snag a bit of bread before cleaning up?"

"Certainly." His mother led them to the table where the servants ate. Now was no time for formality.

Lady Amelia sat down and buried her head in her arms. "That was a horrible experience," she said, voice muffled.

He agreed.

"My lady." Dukes came to their table, his face haggard. The man's suffering was in his eyes. He wrung a handkerchief round about in his hands.

"Dukes." She lifted her head, and Spencer's heart twisted at the pain on her face.

Her butler settled beside her, and they hugged. Spencer fiddled with his food. Perhaps he should get up and help his mother.

They parted, and Dukes touched his kerchief to the corner of his eyes. "I've wanted to tell you something for a long time, my lady. When your parents passed—"

She held up a hand. "No, Dukes, I don't wish to hear it."

The butler's eyes briefly met Spencer's. There was resoluteness in that rheumy gaze. "But I was to tell you something, and I never did. Your parents... They died peacefully," he said gently.

"Not my mother." A sob escaped Lady Amelia.

The sound rippled through Spencer, and his arms ached to hold her.

"They found her suffering. Bent and hardly able to breathe," she said.

"She felt no pain but the discomfort of shortened breath." The lines on Duke's forehead deepened. "How do you know these details?"

"I overheard the servants."

"She was able to speak, my lady. I was there, in the carriage behind them, when the accident occurred. I sat with your mother as we waited for the physician."

Beside him, Lady Amelia stiffened. "Why did you never tell me this?"

Dukes flinched. "I tried, my lady, but you would not bear the mention of your parents. As your Season came near, I thought it better to wait, and then as time passed, it seemed insignificant to mention any details. Although…"

"Although?"

"When I was with your mother, she prayed with me. That was the night my life changed." The gravelly quality of his voice deepened with conviction, and Lord Ashwhite's skin prickled. He knew of what Dukes spoke.

"What do you mean? My mother was talking to you before she died?"

Dukes reached over and took her hand. "Her parting words to me were for you and his lordship. She wanted you to be at peace. She asked me to watch over you."

Lady Amelia blinked, but a tear leaked through and rolled down her dirt-smudged cheek.

"If the accident hadn't happened, I wouldn't have the faith I have now." Dukes squeezed her hand. "Your mother told me to take care of you and your brother, but never to mourn her passing, because she went to a far better place than I could imagine…" A solitary tear slipped down his face. "I've never seen such peace, my lady."

Crushing her fingers against her dress, Lady Amelia appeared to struggle to speak. "My parents… They would be disappointed in me."

Spencer touched her shoulder. It was all the touch he would allow himself. She turned to him, eyelashes tipped with jeweled moisture. "They would be proud of your strength, your goodness and caring."

"'Tis the truth, my lady." Dukes smiled.

"Thank you, Ashwhite." She held his look, and in her eyes he saw comfort. Then she said to Dukes, "You've done your job. I have learned that faith is powerful and love more so."

"A beautiful lesson." His mother set two steaming bowls of soup and some bread in front of them. She sat across the table. "I've been on many trips, but never have I been stuck in a tornado. Was it terrifying?"

As Lady Amelia regaled them with details, Spencer glanced around the kitchen. Cook was humming and servants bustled around, relief evident in their features.

Clearly they were all happy to have survived the storm, but what would happen when he didn't marry in time to fulfill the clause in the will? The estate, the people, they would be in the hands of Lord Dudley.

Disquieted, he finished his soup and bread and prayed for wisdom.

The damage had been costly.

The next morning, Amelia stared out the library's window at the expansive estate. The sun peeked out from behind a billowy cloud as if hesitant to see the wreckage the tornado had wrought. Tree limbs were scattered across the broken countryside, their misshapen bodies testament to nature's fury. A tentative wind served only to dry the mud faster.

Yesterday had been spent recuperating and painting. She'd had much to think about. Two days of danger and she'd survived them both. Was there a reason? After a warm meal, she'd retired to her room where she'd enjoyed several chapters of the Bible.

Imagine that: she, a person of practicality, reading the Bible. Passages she never knew existed jumped out at her. Some flavored with poetic verses, others simple in their logic. And still others challenged her.

Give and you would receive more? If someone stole her cloak, she was to offer her coat, as well? A mind-boggling conundrum, and yet there was a truth to the words that struck at her heart. This morning she'd risen and felt different somehow. More alive and hopeful than ever before.

The servants had been given leave to check on family members or to repair their own homes. That left today as the day of cleaning. She felt useless here.

All available staff had been sent to various parts of the estate for cleanup. Though Amelia tried to help, Lady Ashwhite insisted she sit quietly at the house until her body aches subsided. Even Dukes stayed abed. The time in Newgate combined with the carriage accident must have taxed him sorely.

At half past eleven, perhaps it was time she herself rested. She'd been up since early morn, and her muscles quivered. The terror of surviving a tornado had stirred her desire to paint. Even now, she remembered the wind ripping through her hair, the whine of the tornado and the warmth of Lord Ashwhite as he made his body her shield.

Flushing at the memory, she dropped the curtain and turned to her canvas. A housemaid who enjoyed painting had thoughtfully lent her supplies. Her eye roved her painting. It was different from any she'd ever done. Rich with burned umber and cerulean blue, wild with no restraint.

Looking at it, an odd yearning filled her.

Ridiculous. She was not some youngish miss looking for the safety of a man's arms. She was, mostly, independent. And once she finagled her way out of her brother's household, she'd have her own little cottage in the country. She might miss the city life a bit, but no doubt she'd be just fine with Dukes and Sally. Perhaps a little kitten to round out the familial picture...

She picked up the turpentine with one hand and scooped up her brushes with the other. Arms full, she turned and almost ran into Lord Ashwhite. He stood directly behind her, an arrested expression on his face.

She pressed a brush-filled hand against her bodice, her heart fluttering beneath her fingertips. "My lord, I did not hear you enter."

"You slept well, Lady Amelia?" Stubble darkened his cheeks and enhanced the gem-like quality of his eyes.

"Very well indeed. Yesterday was an exhausting experience."

"That it was." He moved past her to look out the windows. "But our home stands, and our people are safe."

"'Tis providential we survived."

"I'm sure you're ready to return to your brother's estate."

"Not quite."

At her wry tone, Lord Ashwhite's eyes crinkled in a most becoming way. "That kind of attitude won't help solve your list of problems."

"I've already solved one, if I'm able to speak to your mother about my plans for you."

"Sounds ominous."

She ignored him. "Your mother invited me to her poetry reading this evening. It's a last-minute affair, which is why there's such a rush readying the house. I only hope to listen and learn, as I am not well versed in poetry."

"Novels are more your style, I presume?" Teasing layered his tone.

Amelia sniffed, a bit miffed he'd bring up something she kept very private. "Poetry has its place, and if anything, I shall be in the company of free-spirited thinkers."

Lord Ashwhite chuckled. He moved away from the window and stopped suddenly, staring at her painting. "You did this…" His voice faltered.

Feeling unsure, unsteady, she tightened her grip on

the turpentine. Its odor bit into her senses. "'Tis nothing but a storm of emotions."

"It's a masterpiece."

"Balderdash." But it was a feeble protest. What artist didn't long to hear such words and preen? "It's hasty, I know," she explained, disliking the sinking feeling in her stomach. Why should she care what he thought of her work? He was no artist, no connoisseur of fine art. When his hand reached out to the canvas, she stopped him. "Don't touch. The paint is still wet."

"Will you sell this?"

"And who would buy it?" Roving the canvas with a critical eye, she shook her head. The smell of the turpentine reminded her that it was time to clean up and get ready for tonight's activities.

"It's exquisite."

She paused. "What did you say?"

"The colors, the passion in the strokes… Look at those lines. It's as though you captured the storm in movement."

Amelia's fingers tightened around her paintbrushes, and she squeezed her arms tightly against her rib cage as if she could still the millions of emotions that had just been released by his words. "You tease me, my lord."

"No, not at all." He leaned forward to stare at her painting.

"It is an odd painting. Out of style with what is popular."

"You've used darkness and movement to create a work that stands out. It has depth." He rose suddenly, towering over her. "This should be in a gallery. Did you sign it?"

"I always do," she said, feeling her chin lift. "Thank you for the compliment, but even I know this is much too eclectic for the haut monde."

"Never say never, my lady." He flashed her that devastating smile, the one that made her knees feel quite weak. Drawing herself to her full height, she gave him a haughty look and spun on her heel.

"You know very well that I'll say what I please. If you don't mind, I must go speak to your mother about the house party for you. Invitations must go out immediately. Especially if we cancel next week's soiree at my brother's." Her last conversation with Harriet indicated that the soiree was canceled, but she would not send out notices until she was sure. "I've invited several eligible ladies as well as an assortment of colleagues."

From behind her, Spencer groaned.

"Do not dare complain to me," she ordered, marching toward an exit. She couldn't stay any longer in this room with him. One, he was too suave. And two…well, they were both alive. Her prayers had been answered. It was too much good to be true. If she stayed, she might say something she'd later regret. No room for regrets. Or for vulnerability.

Which was what she felt whenever he was around. Open and vulnerable to his words, his opinion… She cared too much what he thought. Somehow, some way, she must find the strength to relegate him to client status.

"Where are you going?" he asked, closer than she expected. The barest hint of breath brushed the back of her neck. She lengthened her stride.

"To find your mother and obtain blessing and perhaps a spot of help for your event." She hurried down the long hall, aware of Lord Ashwhite at her back. "I quite expect you to be engaged by the time my house party is over. If you find a young lady who you think will do, the next day is a perfect opportunity to take her out for a ride."

Her walk stopped abruptly when he grabbed her arm. Surprised, she allowed the gentle grip to continue.

"What if I don't want one of those women for a wife?" His eyes glittered dangerously.

Whatever had come over him? Carefully she extracted her arm from his clutch, unsure exactly why her stomach roiled at his tone.

"You haven't much of a choice," she pointed out, ignoring the strange stirrings of her heart. "All this—" she flung up her arm "—will be gone, squandered by your cousin, who no doubt will have the estate in ruins within six months. Is that what you want? I know 'tis not."

The way his brows narrowed sent a quiver through her. Surely anger did not possess him. But why did he glare at her so?

"Be calm, my lord." She placed a palm on his arm. "I shall have this straightened out in no time." His body heat seared her fingers through the thin cotton of his shirt. She'd overstepped boundaries and found she didn't care. The man needed comfort.

"Tonight is the poetry reading, however. Do you plan to attend?"

His grimace said all she needed to know.

"You might find that it would inspire you to greater depths of thought," she said.

"Or to abandon sensibility."

"Your mother is reading."

"I have no intention of hearing what she has to say." The hardness of his words cut the air between them. Their bite stung.

"What do you have against her?" Amelia asked carefully, knowing she trod stormy waters, yet unwilling to let the comment pass. She would do so much to have her own mother back.

For a minute she thought he might not respond. He turned his back to her, his broad shoulders a barrier to any connection. He'd have to unbend if he wanted a wife. No woman deserved a man who shut her out. Perhaps she asked too much of him, though. Obviously he carried wounds, and her questions only reopened them.

"I apologize. What is between your mother and you is none of my business."

"No, no, don't apologize." He drew in a deep breath. "I will be there tonight to hear my mother's poem." Swiveling around, he gave her a curt nod and walked away.

Chapter Nineteen

Another verse of this fluff and Spencer might punch himself in the head. He sat in an uncomfortable, stiff chair, ankles crossed, barely holding in his yawns. When they overcame him, he covertly covered his mouth by looking to the side. This movement also gave him a nice glimpse of Lady Amelia, who reclined primly on a couch with a pasty-faced gentleman who looked as though his skin never saw sunlight and a rotund matron who blushed every time he peeked at Lady Amelia.

Perhaps mischief still lingered in his redeemed soul, for when the matron caught him yawning/staring again, he gave her a slow wink. She immediately looked away, shifting her body in a way that jostled the others on the couch. Lady Amelia sent him a meaningful glare, suggesting she was not immune to his antics and highly disapproved.

And yet there was a certain tightness to her lips implying restrained laughter.

After a while he gave up teasing her and tried to concentrate on the speakers. He caught his eyes closing during a particularly long rendition of Chaucer. Some speakers shared a poem that had touched their hearts. Others shared original works.

At the moment he thought he could stand no more, his mother cleared her throat. Intrigued, he straightened in his seat. This woman who birthed him, who spent the bulk of his childhood traveling and championing causes beyond his ken, now wore an expression that strained the corners of her eyes. A shininess emanated from their depths, a trick of the candlelight, no doubt. But as she looked at him, an uncomfortable knot formed in his belly.

"'The Mother's Return,' by Dorothy Wordsworth." A tremble touched her lips.

As she began speaking, irritation rose within him. He tapped the arm of his chair, certain he'd have to leave before bitterness poured out of him and poisoned the atmosphere. The longer he saw his mother, the more he realized his inadequacy with forgiveness. Glancing at Lady Amelia, he noticed the troubled stare she directed toward him.

He grimaced and pushed himself out of his seat.

His mother's voice continued.

"We talked of change, of winter gone,
Of green leaves on the hawthorn spray,
Of birds that build their nests and sing,
And all 'since mother went away!'"

Striding to the door, he left that room and the emotion it evoked. "Since mother went away?" Had she ever come home to sit and speak of all that passed? He recalled not one single time she'd rested beneath a tree with him. Not a single lullaby.

But her perfume… He remembered it. Sweet-hued hugs. Easy and available. Never had she discouraged affection during her brief times at home. Drawing a large breath, he walked the hall to the kitchen, determined to get a treat out of Cook. At least she'd always been where he needed her to be.

He found her at the stove, stirring a large pot of something enticing to the nose. "Is that for me?" He peered over her shoulder, prompting a swat, which he promptly dodged.

"Ye never gets out of practice, do ye?" She belly laughed and made to swat at him again, eyes sparkling with merriment.

"Not with your cooking. Just a little taste?"

"Be off with ye. I've cookies in the bin, but mind ye leave a peck for later."

"You're the best." Before she could duck, he planted a kiss on the top of her cap and then swiveled away before her spoon could catch him. He crossed the kitchen, a large and spacious room with all the newest appliances, in search of cookies. Butter and rum always hit the right note, but sugar cookies satisfied a craving, as well.

Anything to rid his mouth of the tang of unforgiveness. The sin rotted inside him, a corpse he refused to shed even knowing it poisoned him. The morose thought discouraged him enough to frown into the cookie bin.

"Ah, Shrewsbury cakes, my favorite," he said.

A delicate hand crept beneath his line of vision and snagged one of the cookies. Sauciness in her smile, Lady Amelia bit a chunk from the cookie and raised her brows. "You might find that a nibble or two would ease those lines digging into your forehead."

"Might I?" he murmured, enjoying the way his heartbeat quadrupled with her nearness. At the present moment, 'twas hard to remember why she could not be a candidate for a wife. Full of surprises and yet logical, warmhearted, intelligent… Any man would want her.

"Suppose you tell me why you ran out of the salon like a frightened kitten?"

Oh, yes, nosy and blunt. Those adjectives explained her singlehood.

Irritation returning, he munched into his own cookie. If only the soft dough and rich chocolate bits melting in his mouth were anger melting away. "I was hungry." A truth, though only half so.

She finished her cookie and withdrew a hankie, which she patted around her lips. "I detect falsehood, Lord Ashwhite, and from what I've been reading, that is against the laws of God."

He immediately bristled. "And what do you know of these laws?"

"Your defensiveness means something. I know not what." Her head cocked to the side, eyes bright behind her spectacles. "Why don't we return to the salon in order to avoid hurting your mother's feelings, and later we can have a biblical discussion. I've discovered some interesting things to ask you about."

"No, my exposure to poetry is over. I've a few matters to take care of before leaving the estate tomorrow."

"Leaving?"

"Duties in London," he explained shortly. His fascination with her hair and quirky manners did not excuse her from prying into his personal affairs. She had trodden too close to a wound long ignored. He moved past her, intent on leaving the kitchen and the lady's inquisitive eyes, but at the door he stopped short.

His mother stood before him, regarding him in a sober fashion, her eyes sadder than he wished to see.

"I had hoped you'd forgiven me by now, Spencer."

Lungs tight, Spencer pressed past his mother. Forgive her? He knew he should, but he hadn't realized the extent of his anger toward her. Tonight the uncomfortable feeling had become obvious. Even eye contact grieved him. Tightness spread to his limbs as he strode down the hall. His muscles coiled and wound. What he would not give for a pugilistic round with someone.

To vent this frustration.

Not at his mother, but at himself. *God, help me. She asks too much.*

Footsteps sounded behind him. He hoped dearly she did not plan to chase him down. But apparently she did, for moments later, her hand touched his sleeve. He stopped near the salon door, loath to pull away and hurt her more yet unable to deny the palpable pain spearing through him.

How many times had he wanted his mother home?

Now he looked at her, nuances of himself carved upon her features. Vaguely he became aware of Lady Amelia a few feet away, carefully watching them. The cadence of a poem being read hummed softly around them, the words indistinguishable yet the tone full of pain.

How ironic.

"Son...I'm very sorry. I—I wish I could explain my choices, or defend them, but that time has passed and I can never get it back." His mother stepped toward him as if afraid he would bolt.

And perhaps he would. A hot pain clawed at his throat, urging him to move, to leave, to escape what forced him to look at himself more clearly than ever.

A former rake. Unwanted by his mother, manipulated by his father.

Redeemed by God.

That created tension within him. His mother took

another step. Pleading shone in her eyes. Her fingers clenched, and even from this distance he saw the whitened knuckles. How it cost her humbly to beg his forgiveness…yet the knowledge gave him no pleasure.

He glanced at Lady Amelia again. Her brow knit as she watched, and he was aware that his actions might speak louder to her than any word he'd ever uttered. Swallowing against the vise clamping his throat, he nodded tersely at his mother.

That seemed to encourage her, though her features remained tight. "I was afraid of you in so many ways. And my relationship with your father needed much…" She trailed off as if realizing that her own weaknesses did not alleviate the rejection he'd felt. "Please forgive me, Spencer. If you can."

"I will do my best." He delivered the words in a stiff manner, more cold than he intended, but he could not bring himself to utter falsity.

"That is all I ask." She reached for his hand, and he drew her into an embrace, inhaling her familiar scent. He met Lady Amelia's serious expression and saw approval. His shoulders loosened. Patting his mother's back, he withdrew.

A slow curve to her lips alleviated his guilt for being unable to offer her what she'd so kindly asked for. For now, this was what he could do. Hug her and pray for help.

As they turned to the study, a loud knock reverberated against the front door. The butler, a younger man whose name Spencer could not recall, bounded from out of nowhere and answered the door.

He escorted his mother to the salon, letting the butler take care of matters. They entered the salon quietly and as unobtrusively as possible, but he was aware of how Lady Amelia paused behind him in the doorway. He helped his mother to a chair. Questions lurked in her face, but he only patted her shoulder.

Where was Lady Amelia? She'd disappeared into the hall. He wasn't going to suffer poetry alone. He reached the hall in time to see Lady Amelia rushing out the front door.

He frowned. It was near dark. Surely she wouldn't go anywhere. Almost growling, he strode after her. Of course she would do something reckless. What was he thinking?

He lengthened his stride, clapping open the front door to scan the drive.

"Looking for someone?"

Lady Amelia's voice came from the right. He turned. Pelisse secured at her throat, she regarded him with an indefinable air. He could not tell her mood, which increased his irritability.

"You, actually. Going out this evening?"

"An emergency has arisen. The butler will give your mother my regards. I don't know when I'll be returning, but please let her know how thankful I've been for her hospitality."

Spencer forced a slow, ragged breath even though his pulse ratcheted through his body. "You're leaving the premises because…" He saw the way her body stiffened. Head up, chin pointing in his direction and her gaze sharper than a sword.

"I have business to attend to."

"This late?"

"Am I your prisoner, my lord?" Though her words were light, accusation weighted the syllables.

Mindful that he trod uncertain ground, he forced himself to relax. "Not at all. I only hope to assist you." And keep her from harm, his mind interjected.

"I shall accomplish this on my own, but I do appreciate your concern. Oh, look." She sent him what could only be called a relieved smile. "The carriage has arrived. Certainly I will see you soon." And with those last words, she scurried down the front stairs. The driver helped her into the curricle.

Nonsense. He'd not sit here wallowing in worry while she traipsed off into unknown dangers. He leaped down the stairs and pulled himself into the carriage in the nick of time. He caught the shocked look on Lady Amelia's face and couldn't resist giving her a long, slow grin.

His driver took the change of plans in good stride, setting off as soon as the curricle door closed. Spencer reclined in his seat, crossing his arms across his chest and regarding Lady Amelia with a determined stare. She avoided his eyes, choosing to instead pluck at some nonexistent impurity upon her coat.

Questions nudged his consciousness. He held them in, choosing instead to pin her with the kind of look he knew she hated. The type of look at that put her in a corner and forced her to ignore the problem or respond.

And she would respond. He had no doubt of that. Lady Amelia preferred attack over retreat. But to his surprise, despite several venomous glares, the lady chose silence over confession.

She truly wanted to strangle him.

Or at least wipe the beatific smirk from his lips.

Amelia ground her teeth, forcing herself to recite Wordsworth in her head and clasping her fingers so that they might not fly out and do exactly as her imagination suggested. Lord Ashwhite sprawled across from her, looking entirely too stubborn. As well he should. She'd made off with his mother's carriage and owed him an explanation. He'd hijacked her plans, thrusting himself into her life. She fixed a dark glower on him, hoping it might inspire him not to speak. How she wanted to tongue-lash him…but it was not her place.

Constant thoughts pelted her. Worries.

Everything was spiraling out of control. She didn't wish to return to her brother's, but she had nowhere to go. If she didn't find Ashwhite his wife, she couldn't get paid. And without money, any independence she'd hoped for would slip outside her grasp, forever relegating her to a poor relation or a governess.

Without meaning to, she sighed heavily.

"Fine." Lord Ashwhite's voice broke the rhythmic rattle of the carriage. "I concede defeat. How can I help?"

"There is nothing you can do." She alone was responsible for the ruination of her plans.

"Surely I can do *something*. I am, after all, a marquis." A smile carved his cheeks. Too charming, by half.

"A humble one, too, my lord."

"No need to be nasty, Lady Amelia. Share your burdens. I promise they will seem lighter." He wagged a finger. "Do not give me that look. I'm quite sure you'd discourage Miss Stanley from scrunching her features in such an impolite way."

Oh, what a pickle. She might as well confess. "My cousin is wayward and unmanageable, and now I must deal with a problem before it spirals out of control."

"And you need my carriage because?"

"We are on our way to Gretna Green."

Horror crossed his face. He still looked too handsome. It was his green eyes; they were her undoing. And such a silly thing, in the grand scheme of things, to be done in by a color not found on one's palette. What would he do if he ever saw the painting she'd created of him? It was stashed beneath her bed, and she prayed no one stumbled upon it.

"Do you mean…Scotland?" he asked.

"No one forced you to accompany me," she snapped. He acted as though this was her fault.

His fingers drummed against the seat. "So we are heading to an illegal wedding—"

"Not illegal. That's why people go there. In Scotland you can marry whenever you want. No waiting for banns to be read. Which reminds me, you have very little time left before you're out of an inheritance."

His brows narrowed. "You change the subject."

"Simply pointing out a quite inconvenient fact. Your worry over my actions is misplaced, especially with this deadline looming over your head." Satisfied she'd successfully rerouted him, she tapped her chin thoughtfully. "Those two young ladies… They are really worthy candidates. Why, either one would be happy to marry you, and 'tis certain they'd make warm and loving wives."

An image of Lord Ashwhite kissing one of the said ladies blasted into her mind. She shut her eyes, trying to squelch the picture, but that didn't stop a pang from striking her heart. Opening her eyes, she forced herself to keep a straight face while a sudden longing infiltrated her defenses and weakened her resolve.

No…no, she had to find him a wife. That was the goal. *Keep your eyes on the goal*, she reminded herself. Did she want a home to herself? Yes. Did she want Dukes and Sally with her? Yes. Did she want to paint and sell her work in galleries? Yes.

All that required money. Money she didn't have unless she found the irascible, charming lord in front of her a wife.

Lord Ashwhite appeared to be mulling over her statement. "Do you really believe they'd marry me?"

"But of course!" She gave him what she hoped was a compelling and believable stare, while everything within her resisted the thought of him with someone else. How had this happened? No, she couldn't feel this way.

Focus, Amelia, focus.

"Are you all right?" Lord Ashwhite leaned forward. "You look pale."

"Perhaps I need to rest," she offered. 'Twas true she felt a tad tired and overwhelmed. Maybe sad, too. After all, nothing in her life was moving as planned. She had been supposed to marry in her first Season. Make her family happy. Instead, she'd alienated her only brother, and now Lydia...

"We will talk of this later," Lord Ashwhite said. The setting sun shadowed the deep velvet cushions and intricate brocade inside the carriage. She hadn't felt much of a bump during the ride. This curricle was very, very in keeping with what a marquis should use.

Thankful for the reprieve, she stroked the soft fabric and wished life could be so smooth. They spent the next hours in tense silence.

He waited until night fell to question her again. It was a misty evening, the air cooler near the lowlands. It almost seemed the fog could seep in around the edges of the curricle door. Lady Amelia drew her shawl more carefully about her shoulders.

Her plan was plucky. Outlandish. But she prayed dearly it worked.

Lord Ashwhite heaved a deep, melodramatic sigh. "I tire of this silence, my lady. Confess your plans at once."

Wetting her lips, Amelia had trouble meeting his very astute gaze. With one word, he could turn this curricle around and go home. That was not to say she'd still be inside, but nevertheless…his vehicle, his staff and he had been very patient. Fun, even.

"Go ahead. Assuage my worries and tell me we're rescuing someone or doing an important duty for the king." The sarcasm in his voice was clear. He'd allowed her privacy for a time, but now he was impatient.

Steeling herself for his displeasure, she swallowed a very large, very deep breath.

"You have every right to know that…"

"Yes?"

"To put it simply, my lord, I must stop a marriage."

Chapter Twenty

"I knew it," Spencer said flatly. He wanted to barrage Lady Amelia with questions. He was unable to find any words to express the frustration barreling through him right now. She stared at him as though daring him to stop her. It almost appeared she leaned toward the door, ready to jump out at a moment's notice.

Her shawl, a deep orange that reminded him of a slow-burning sunset, bunched around her shoulders. The shade brought out the color in her cheeks and the soft rosiness of her lips.

He grimaced. He couldn't let her prettiness detract him from the matter at hand: namely, her obstinate refusal to stay out of other people's business.

Her shoulders hunched, and her fingers plucked at the fringed edges of her shawl. She took off her spectacles and rubbed them against the cloth.

"I take it you do not wish to boot me from this carriage?"

"I most definitely want to boot you from this carriage. I'd like to wring that pretty little neck of yours, as well." He crossed his arms.

"How very crass of you, my lord." Despite the prim tone, a blush stained her cheeks.

"Don't you think this is over the top? Racing to stop someone from marrying the man she loves. Leaving behind all your responsibilities... Why? So you can be right?"

"I am right. I know that I am."

"This is unwise, but as we are over halfway there, I won't interfere with your plans." Grudging words, but he realized he meant them. "The good Lord knows I've learned my lesson in trying to control others."

"What do you mean?"

"My father, for one." His fingers waltzed across the seat. Did he really want to go into this with Lady Amelia? Taking in her open expression, the interest she displayed, he realized he did. "From the time I was a young man, I tried my best to usurp him however I could. It became almost a game. He'd lay down a rule. I'd break it. When there were responsibilities to be had, I shirked them just to see the frustration on his face. So that he would know he didn't own me."

Lady Amelia's head cocked as though she was trying to understand him. "But you are so responsible and good... I cannot believe this of you."

He smirked though a hole had opened his chest. Now she'd know the truth of things. "This is why I think your determination to stop a wedding is ridiculous. People make their choices. There's no changing a person's will."

"I will simply point out the logic of things. Her entire reason for getting married was to protect her family. To provide for them. How shall that happen now? I'm sorry to hear about your father, but he sounds as though he was a difficult man."

His brow rose. She had the grace to look chagrined. Her nose scrunched.

"I do apologize, but I hope you understand my meaning. And your mother—why, she only longs to have a relationship with you, yet you push her away. She doesn't strike me as a woman who tells others what to do." She adjusted her spectacles. "As you know I do."

"You two are very much alike," he said. He'd rather take a nap than continue this conversation. But the lady proved to be a dog after a bone.

"How so?"

He shifted uncomfortably in his seat. Hours still to go, and now trapped in a discussion about his mother. "You're both bluestockings."

"I don't read poetry, and your mother is not political."

"You both strive for independence."

She regarded him in a quiet manner.

He'd bumbled his words. Charm might not smooth away the furrow on her brow. And that should not bother him, except that he cared for her good opinion. Sighing, he rested his head back against the seat. "My point is, you share similar qualities. And just because I don't want to have long conversations with her doesn't mean I push her away."

"Whatever you say, my lord." Her eyelids flickered.

Annoyed, Spencer tried to find something witty to say but failed. He couldn't explain how he'd felt as a child or the fact that his mother stirred unwanted emotions and memories. The walls of the coach closed in on him. Trapping him.

Just as marriage would do. He thought of the ladies he'd known, the women who were not quite ladies, and the eager expression they all wore in their endless search to ensnare a man. They wanted the ring on a finger, the home to boast about. The prize catch.

And then there'd be conversations like these, in which he was pressured to talk about things he did not wish to speak of.

Could he really marry and be stuck for the rest of his life with someone who might make him miserable? Feeling dizzy all of a sudden, he sucked in a deep breath. It was either be leg shackled or live without Ashwhite. Both options scared the wits out of him.

The carriage clipped along at a steady pace as he struggled to think of something to say. Lady Amelia beat him to it.

"Doesn't God want you to love your mother and treat her well? And I feel sure I read passages about forgiving others and not returning evil for evil."

His shoulders knotted. "I do love my mother."

Eyes wide, she leaned forward. "Watching the way you speak to her, I cannot tell that. And neither can she. What happened? Why do you hate her so?"

"I don't hate her," he muttered. "You can't possibly understand."

"Why?"

"Because your parents lived with you and took care of you. They showed you the meaning of love. Mine fought constantly and without remorse." The sound of breaking glass echoed through his consciousness. "When she was home, the household held its breath. But she was gone more often than not. She said she helped my father create this will ordering me to marry. I find it hard to believe."

"Did you ask her why they did it?"

"No," he growled.

"Of course you didn't." She steepled her fingers. "You

men never ask anything. Always assuming you already know the answers."

"That's an unfair accusation. I don't travel for days just to ruin a wedding, nor have I tried to stop true love based on nothing more than superficial reasoning."

"Superficial?" Her voice squeaked.

"That's right. Superficial. Hair colors and fortunes and who plays the piano... That has nothing to do with a good marriage. It doesn't guarantee love."

"You've deeply misunderstood me." Lady Amelia's eyes flashed. "How dare you compare what I do to superficiality? My success rate is impeccable because I weigh expectations and desires. I match them. You are being difficult and your head is in the clouds if you're looking for perfection. No woman can be such a thing."

"As can no man," he countered. The strike hit home, for her jaw set and she glared at him.

Well, good. What did she expect, that she could march into Gretna Green and tell her cousin to leave the man she loved? Obviously Lady Amelia understood nothing of love. A pang cut through him, right to his gut.

Too late he realized he wanted her to know love. Not only that, but he wanted her to feel love for him. Imperfections included. He studied her profile, proudly turned away from him. She would have to surrender more than her independence. She would need to let down her guard, and he wasn't sure she could do that. The lady built a cage around herself more sturdy than the walls of Newgate. And in all this time, he'd accomplished little to breach them.

A short time later, they reached the inn. Spencer hopped out of the curricle and then assisted Lady Amelia. She had little to say for herself, though the proud strength of her posture told him clearly that she would not change her mind about this futile mission.

He went to speak to his driver.

"Ben, sir." The driver doffed his hat and bowed.

"We shall be heading to Gretna Green, if you did not already know. Can you get a message sent immediately to my mother? Also, two dinners and two rooms. Thank you, Ben."

Spencer turned back to Lady Amelia, who surveyed the inn without a smile.

Let her stew. She'd chosen this madness, and taken his mother's carriage, of all things.

Though she hadn't had a choice, being confined to his estate. Nevertheless, the strangeness of it all was not lost on him. Nor did he anticipate his irritation ebbing. In fact, he did not know whether he'd get any sleep at all. Perturbed, he led the way into the inn.

Small and cozy, the inn with its warm atmosphere invited patrons to sit. Several scenic paintings graced the walls, and the tables appeared well kept. A few diners were scattered around the room. Lady Amelia said not a word.

It crossed his mind that she might leave during the middle of the night just to escape him, but he resisted the notion. If she did, what could he do to stop her? He wasn't here to stop her, merely to see to her safety. For reasons unbeknownst to him, the lady meant a great deal to him. He did not wish to examine why, or the strange constrictions in his chest when she was near.

After a hot meal, they trudged up the stairs. The barmaid, a friendly girl with big curls and bright eyes, gestured to the doors of two rooms.

"Clean and fresh, my lord. What else shall I bring to 'ee?"

"This is very good, thank you." He took the keys she offered. He nodded, and she curtsied before leaving him and Lady Amelia in the narrow hall. He had no bags, no spare change of clothes, but he'd noticed the lady had brought a small satchel. No doubt packed quickly by a servant whilst the carriage and horses were being readied.

He held out Lady Amelia's key. How he wished he knew her thoughts! She did not take the key immediately. Instead, her gaze lifted to his. Her eyes were dark behind her spectacles and he could not guess at her thoughts. She seemed frail in that second. Small and tired.

As though sensing his empathy, her chin nudged forward. She took the keys in one quick swipe. Turning her back to him, she pushed the keys into the lock. She fumbled with it, but it finally turned for her. She hurried into the room. The slam of the door punctuating the silence.

Spencer let himself into his own room, knowing it was ridiculous to stand guard outside her door. Knowing she did not want protection. Yet he wanted to provide it. He wanted to wipe that blank look from her face. He wanted to see her emotions.

He wanted…her.

Yes, he wanted Lady Amelia. Not just as a wife finder, but as a wife. Did he love her? What was love, anyhow? He knew he enjoyed being with her, that he missed her presence.

He crawled into the bed. Small, it nevertheless smelled clean. The mattress sank beneath his weight.

The lady reminded him of an onion.

No, a flower.

Yes, a soft, sweet-smelling flower with many layers of petals. Knowing his mind wandered strange territory, yet not caring, Lord Ashwhite fell asleep to the images of Lady Amelia and roses. They were atop her beautiful hair. She cast him a stunning smile, eyes bright for him, her dress lacy and white, as she ran up the aisle to greet him. He slipped the ring on her finger, kissing the paint stains as she giggled.

They lived happily ever after.

By the third day of travel, Amelia drooped with exhaustion. Last night's sleep had been horrendous. The daytime journey dragged in the most tiresome way. Ashwhite had little to say to her, and his silence proved more meddlesome to her sanity than she could have imagined.

Every so often, a cramp knotted in her calf. She rubbed at it to no avail. Her argument with Lord Ashwhite weighed heavily upon her. She'd done nothing but roll his words in her brain, examining them from every angle, wondering why they hurt her so. The peace she'd felt after praying had all but faded away, replaced with a sickening anxiety that she was doing the wrong thing.

How could that be so? Cousin Lydia deserved a financially stable and kind man. Someone to care for her and her family. Security was important. Lydia didn't understand the feeling of being adrift in the world, uncertain of your next moment. She and Lydia had shared many memorable times that included laughter and confidences. Surely her cousin would trust her enough to see reason.

Throwing a fortune away for a man… Amelia worried her lip. All this had happened beneath her very nose, and if it hadn't been for Mr. Ladd's investigations, she would have never known of Lydia's plans. Questions pounded Amelia's skull, and for the first time since leaving Ashwhite, uncertainty stirred within her.

It didn't help that Lord Ashwhite smelled good, which boggled the mind, as she felt bedraggled and uncomely. While she hadn't slept a wink for worry, he apparently had slept just fine. Even the clothing he'd procured at the last town fit him well.

With a huff, she crossed her arms and focused on the scenery outside her window. They'd gotten an early start. She'd wanted to leave him in the middle of the night, but despite her pique, she knew she couldn't do that. One, she knew the driver wouldn't take her anywhere. And two, she might take risks, but rarely were they foolhardy. To mount a horse in the black of night just because Lord Ashwhite had horned in on her rescue plans was the height of foolishness.

She'd said a prayer this morning. Asked God for patience. And to her surprise, she'd managed to bite her tongue for most of the day.

She ignored Lord Ashwhite's frowns in favor of staring out the window. Hours slipped by. They stopped for lunch and hardly spoke. She forced down mutton pie and overcooked vegetables, refusing to look at him. If only she wasn't dependent on his money or vehicle. If only he didn't seem so concerned.

If only he didn't touch the deep places within she'd forgotten existed…

When they finally reached Gretna Green, Amelia barely contained the urge to growl. As soon as she finished here, she'd go immediately home… No, she didn't have a home. Fine. She'd return to her brother's and demand they allow her a painting room. She'd hide in there and never husband hunt again. Quite obviously she had failed miserably at it. Who would hire her now?

Lord Ashwhite left the carriage and horses to be cared for while she huddled at the edge of the road. A fierce wind stirred the dust, swirling it around her skirt. Goose pimples danced upon her arms, and she shivered. Had they reached the town in time to stop the wedding?

She truly prayed so. *Please God, if You love Lydia, please keep her from making the biggest mistake of her life.* Her pleas felt empty, though. Where could her cousin be?

Lord Ashwhite strode toward her, his confidence strangely calming. The air of assurance he wore fit a marquis. The grim twist to his lips marred not his handsome face.

She set her expression to match his, pressing a palm to her belly to contain the apprehension fluttering through her. "Have you located them?"

"It doesn't appear they've arrived yet. You may have received your post from Ladd before they were able to leave London, so we are probably ahead of them." He pointed down the road. "I've been told weddings are easy and quick to perform. If we hurry, we may be able to talk to the blacksmith before his next ceremony."

They started off, Amelia stretching her legs to match Ashwhite's brisk stride.

They entered a dim storefront, and the odor of metal ground into her senses. So this was a smithy. She'd never visited one. She took note of the muted colors and darkness.

Surely the blacksmith must do his work in a lighter area.

"Is the blacksmith available?" Lord Ashwhite called out.

"Here," a voice returned from the back of the room.

Taking the lead, Lord Ashwhite rounded a large table that held a multitude of iron products. Grays and browns were the color of this place. And the dust… Her nose twitched. She scooted closer to Ashwhite and followed him into a brighter, much hotter room.

A man bent over a roughly hewn yet sturdy-looking

table. Behind him the stove crackled with heat. The flames licked upward, forever reaching.

The plot of her own life, she thought wryly. Ending up a spinster at her brother's house was not in the plans. Perhaps it might be best to look into governessing.

She certainly would not be getting married in order to improve her lot. Her bodice seemed to close tighter against her ribs. No, that might prove to be as disastrous as being beneath her brother's thumb. But if an employer fired her… The thought was too much. She straightened, wishing the perspiration upon her brow stemmed from the sultry room and not her own mangled emotions.

"Do you perform weddings?"

"Aye, sir, got one in just a bit." The blacksmith struck his project repeatedly, and the sound echoed through the room, ringing in Amelia's ears.

"We are looking for a particular bride, Miss Lydia Stanley. She might be coming in this evening or in the morning." She pushed a damp strand of hair behind her ear. "We wish to find where they're to be married at once. Can you help us?"

The blacksmith cocked his head, his eyes roving up and down. She tilted her head and looked at him over the rim of her spectacles. He guffawed, slapping large paws against his legs.

"People don't make appointments in Gretna Green. They just show up. Now, ye might check with the blacksmith down the road, but this week we be the only ones performing weddings. Ye haven't come to stop one, have ye? I won't have that in my shop."

Amelia plastered her hands on her hips. "Never fear. I'll see you still make your money."

"That be the truth, my lady?"

"You have my word. We will be staying at the inn. You might make a bit more should I arrive in time to halt the proceedings."

She could see his mind working over her words. It didn't take him long to come to a decision. "'Tis hard times, and a man must feed his family. I'll send some-one round to fetch ye if the need arises."

"Very well." She pivoted and left, aware that Ashwhite had not said much. As they meandered back into the open road, she asked, "You do not approve?"

"Not a bit." He reached out, his hand cupping her arm and stopping her in the middle of the road. Thunder rolled, and her skin prickled with the sensation of static in the air. Or perhaps it was the look in Ashwhite's eyes.

She could not tell if he was angry with her or some-thing entirely different. The darkening afternoon played with the angles of his face. A shiver coursed through her. Mouth dry, she wrenched her arm from his hand. "It is not for you to approve or disapprove. Lydia cannot marry this man. Her future will be in ruins."

"The only ruination I foresee is the kind that results from refusing to give in to one's heart."

Absurd. Why did she bother arguing with this man? She crossed her arms as another strong breeze brushed past her. "You don't understand."

"Enlighten me, then, for you say that money and sta-tus should not determine the qualifications for a happy marriage, yet those are the only things standing in the way of this one."

"Nay, there is more. They've barely known each other, and their marriage defeats the entire purpose of her search for a husband." A raindrop plopped against her cheek. She wiped it away.

Ashwhite's gaze searched hers. Another raindrop fell

between them, and another, until suddenly they were standing in a downpour. Thunder cracked above them, and Amelia jumped. Her clothes stuck against her skin. Her heart raced and her throat felt tight. Ashwhite made no move to get out of the storm, and though she would have liked to, there was something in that keen look of his that challenged her to stay. Despite the burn behind her lids, she would not back down.

"Do you not think a marriage based on love is more beneficial than one based on desperation?"

"That has nothing to do with what I said." She blinked against the deluge battering her vision. "I think he's carried her away. Made empty promises." She waved a hand. "Led her to believe things about himself that are not true merely because he is lonely and about to leave England for parts unknown. He has charmed away her senses." The last words stopped her cold, for she clearly remembered how it felt to be swept away. The heady exhilaration of thinking oneself wanted, only to discover how mistaken one was…

Ashwhite stepped forward, crowding her. He grabbed her shoulders and hauled her against him. Right there in the street for all to see. His fingers dug into her arms.

"What, pray tell, are you—"

His head lowered, and his lips absorbed the last of her words. For a moment she was too stunned to move. Or perhaps it was that her knees felt like custard. And then the full impact of his kiss slammed into her. How warm his lips were, how tender his embrace. Dizziness, pleasure, all enveloped her until she could no longer think.

Long-suppressed emotions overwhelmed her. Waves of feeling crashed over her, resonating through her soul like a thousand pinpricks of bliss. She pressed against

Spencer, feeling the tightness of his arms around her as though this was the most perfect embrace in the entire world. He smelled of clover, fresh and invigorating.

The rain fell around them.

She felt safe.

She might have stayed there forever had he not drawn back. Had he not given her the most crooked smile imaginable. Satisfaction practically glowed from his skin.

"I've been wanting to do that for quite some time."

"Wipe the smirk from your face, my lord. You may have just ruined my reputation." She worked hard to control the trembles ricocheting through her. They were from a chill. Merely that and nothing else.

He waved a hand, dismissing her concerns as though they were but flotsam. "Nonsense. No one saw a thing. They are all huddled cozy in their homes whilst we stand in the rain, kissing."

She shivered as anger flushed through her. What could she say? She was standing in a downpour, wishing he would kiss her again, and he acted as if nothing important had just happened. She wanted to slap him for his impertinence.

Mud sucked at her shoes as she spun away. She'd march right back to that inn and leave him here in the rain. As she started forward, he stopped her...again. The press of his fingers prodded her to face him.

"Kindly unhand me." A regal voice despite the rain wetting her cheeks and dripping from her chin. She lifted said chin, just to make sure he understood she meant exactly what she meant.

His hair clung in dark rivulets against his face. A searing energy coursed through her. Her heart throbbed against her rib cage in hard, quick knocks that belied the irritation engulfing her. Was he going to kiss her again? He certainly looked as though he would, and the worst thing was that she wanted him to.

Chapter Twenty-One

Spencer knew he'd made a big mistake.

As rain soaked his clothes and lightning rent the sky, regret pummeled at him. Lady Amelia appeared uncertain, and he'd never seen her look that way. Eyes wide, she backed up.

"Perhaps it's better that I see you in the morning." Thunder followed her words. She grimaced and looked around. "We shall search for Lydia then."

She flounced away, or maybe ran away, and he massaged his neck. What a horrid thing he'd just done, swept up in a tide of emotion, carried off by a need deeper than he could explain.

One kiss, and he'd pushed her from him. That had caused the distance he saw in her eyes. He was sure of it. And the kiss had told him only one thing: Lady Amelia was the woman he wanted to marry.

Groaning, he trudged after her to the inn. Warmth from a flickering fire greeted him. He gratefully took the cider a maidservant offered him and sat near the fireplace. Lady Amelia had no doubt retired to her room. Ruminating, perhaps, on her horrible client. He stared into the fire, cognizant of the owner's watchful eye. Tension radiated through his shoulders.

He'd misread Lady Amelia. Yes, she responded to his kiss… He sipped the cider slowly, remembering the way she'd melted into him as though only he mattered to her.

He wanted that, he realized. In a marriage. Passion and trust. His parents had had neither. All his errant pursuits before had been nothing more than a longing to fulfill his loneliness. Finding a deeper relationship with God had only shown him how deeply alone he'd been.

Should he pursue her?

Why not Lady Amelia, when he knew with certainty that his life would not be whole without her in it?

That settled, he drained the last of his cider and made his way up the narrow stairs to his room. Though the inn was small, it appeared clean and cozy. Tomorrow should be interesting. If events went well, if he could salvage what had happened tonight. Then he hoped for a more amenable outcome.

A prayer slipped past his lips as he fell asleep, and the feeling inside him blossomed into a hope he couldn't ignore.

The next morning, that blossom felt more like a thorn than a flower. He winced as he followed a very determined Lady Amelia. They'd visited a smithy and a parson with no success in locating Miss Stanley. Yesterday's storm had passed, and the sun rose across the misty Scottish lowlands in muted hues of gold.

Which only reminded Spencer of Lady Amelia's hair. Though only paces ahead of him, she strode without looking back at him. In fact, breakfast had been a strange affair. She'd rambled on about politics and the state of the prisons without ever once meeting his eyes.

Lengthening his stride, he caught up to her. Her hair, plaited becomingly, was just as beautiful as in his imagination. Before he could say anything—and he wasn't sure what he would say, only that something needed to be aired—she hurried forward into the smithy they'd visited yesterday.

Voices hushed as he rode Lady Amelia's wake. Several faces looked up from the front of the room, which had been decorated with ribbons. There stood a man he recognized as the blacksmith. Black cloth draped his shoulders.

Spencer frowned at the farce.

The other face he recognized belonged to none other than Miss Stanley. Even with her hair down, he recognized the bright blue eyes shining at him.

"Why, Amelia, whatever are you doing here?" The ingenuous question popped from the cousin's mouth and landed in the room like a tornado-hewn tree hitting the ground. No one made a sound.

Not the people next to Miss Stanley, including the fresh-faced young man who must be her groom, or Spencer. He watched Amelia carefully. She plucked a small white cloth from somewhere on her person—he knew not where these things were kept—and wiped at her fingers carefully.

"I'm sure it is a surprise." Her tone said the opposite. "However, I felt I must speak to you privately before allowing this to continue."

Allowing? He barely stifled his snort. Miss Stanley did not look amused. Her arms crossed.

"Whatever you have to say can be said in front of William."

In response, the young man put his arm around her.

Spencer raised a brow at the gesture. He could almost hear Lady Amelia's indignity.

"Are you sure of that?" she asked tightly.

He couldn't see her face as she stood in front of him, but the shape of her shoulders indicated anguish.

The blacksmith held up his hand. "Now, before we resort to fisticuffs, let it be known that there'll be no brawling in this shop. Take ye words out the door or there'll be no wedding today."

"We only mean to have a conversation, sir. I have come to point out reason to my cousin and her parents." Lady Amelia stepped forward.

So those were the extra people—Miss Lydia's parents. What an interesting situation, and yet Lady Amelia did not see her plans were doomed to fail. If Miss Stanley's parents were here, then they supported their daughter. Which led him to wonder...why the hasty marriage?

He leaned against a clear spot on the wall and waited, knowing this couldn't end well. He'd be there for Lady Amelia, though. The thought of her disappointment brought him no satisfaction, only a hollow pit in his stomach.

"We support Lydia," the older man, her father, stated. "Your presence isn't needed unless you can support her, too."

From this angle, Spencer caught the wince that crossed Lady Amelia's face. "I understand, and if I could but speak to Lydia for a moment..."

Miss Stanley waved a hand, elegance in her movements. "Go ahead, cousin. I know you shall not be able to rest until you state your case."

"I'm simply concerned. You've known this man for less than a month. Marrying him will not accomplish your goals or protect your family. I'm sure you feel great affection for him, but shouldn't you wait longer to get to know him? At least post the banns and don't rush into a decision that will forever affect your future." Lady Amelia twisted the cloth in her hands. It was the only sign of her distress.

"My dear Amelia, you worry overly much." Miss Stanley moved to stand in front of her cousin. She placed her hands on Lady Amelia's shoulders. "You have not failed in any way, but William has his orders to leave within the week, and we do not wish to be apart."

"Letters are often helpful during times of distance." Obstinacy coated her every word.

"They will not suffice. I feel peace and God's blessing in this relationship." Miss Stanley's smile warmed the room, and suddenly Spencer realized that this young lady was not just a pretty face. She held a genuine love for her suitor and was willing to give up comfort and family to be with him.

Though Lady Amelia spent the next ten minutes trying to change Miss Stanley's mind, nothing she said caused so much as a flicker of indecision to cross her cousin's brow. Her parents and the blacksmith waited patiently in the background. Finally, Lady Amelia's shoulders slumped. She stepped back, and it was all he could do to refrain from pulling her into a hug.

She took this too personally. She remained silent during the ceremony, and though she did not frown, he sensed the tension radiating from her. Afterward the family hugged, and Miss Stanley's mother was misty-eyed.

Spencer slipped outside to give them privacy.

Lady Amelia joined him shortly thereafter. "We may as well leave."

"Already?"

She stared out across the street. "I have no need to stay here. Lydia is happy with her family and her groom."

Unsure how to respond, Spencer walked with her back to the inn. They collected their meager supplies and then walked to the stable to get his carriage and horses. The entire way, he rehearsed what he should say on the long journey home. How sorry he was to have taken advantage of the moment…but how much he enjoyed kissing her.

No, that wouldn't do.

Absent-mindedly, he paid the stable owners. The driver sat at the ready, and he climbed into the carriage after Lady Amelia. She huddled in a corner. It would be a warm ride home, though that didn't explain the sweat dribbling down his neck.

Never had he felt so nervous. As the carriage moved out of the little town and back toward England, he struggled for the right words to say. Lady Amelia sat across from him, looking out the window, hands folded neatly in her lap. The picture of primness and propriety.

Why did his heart beat faster every time he saw her? It could be only one thing, the thing he'd avoided most of his life.

Yet he had to marry…and he could not imagine a life without this plucky, beautiful lady.

"I don't understand."

Lady Amelia's somber words interrupted his thoughts. He met her gaze, heart sinking at the confusion written plainly across her face. While he pondered marriage plans, she was thinking about something else. He searched for words, but before he could come up with something sensitive and sweet, her foot began a tap against the floor.

"She isn't being rational, and her parents support her

decision. A choice made on something less than logic. I just don't understand it."

"Why do you read novels?"

"What?"

"Those stories of ladies in distress and highwaymen who rescue them. It's for the redemption, right? You enjoy a tale of justice and good ultimately winning."

She made a face. "I suppose that is one way to put it, though I do enjoy the intrigue, as well."

"Perhaps your cousin sees the same in this husband of hers." Spencer rubbed at his neck. How could he put this? "Perhaps she longs for the companionship of one she likes being with, one with whom she can share many adventures and affection. He seems a simple and happy fellow."

"And she is so bright." A heavy sigh erupted. "Any young man could satisfy those feelings, and one with a future to boot. I feel as though I've failed, Ashwhite. Dismally."

In the confines of the carriage, he wanted to put his arms around her and kiss away the sadness in her eyes. But he'd made a mess of things earlier, and that might send her running for good. Hands clasped, he leaned forward.

"You did not fail. You heard what Miss Stanley said. She feels God's peace. She loves that man, and who are we to get between them? Instead, honor her wishes. Relinquish the control you long for and let her go." He paused, blood pumping wildly through him. "I propose a different kind of adventure. I am still in need of a wife, with only a month and a half left until I lose my family's estate."

She reached out and patted his shoulder. "Two parties are planned for you. They should suffice." She tilted her head. "What adventure are you speaking of?"

This was the moment. The thrill of the unknown raced through him, challenging him. And yet in his heart he knew this was right. No perfect moment, but the right moment. Not every problem was solved. There was still Lord Dudley to deal with after all. But for now, in this second, all his worries faded beneath an inescapable knowledge: he loved this lady.

"Lady Amelia." He took her hand from his shoulder and cupped it in his palms. "Will you do the honor of marrying me?"

Amelia's heartbeat was a caged bird in her throat. A hot sweat flushed beneath her clothes, and her breath grew thin. Carefully she removed her hand from Lord Ashwhite's grip and looked away from the intensity of his gaze.

Marriage? Surely he jested. He must be teasing. Why ever would he want to marry her? To try to change her? To mold her into something she never longed to be?

Wetting her lips, she drew up the courage she suddenly lacked to meet his stare. "This is sudden, my lord. Your wish to save your estate is admirable, but I believe your perception has been skewed."

Something uncertain flickered across his brow. She longed to smooth the worry away, but that would only encourage this nonsense. Her stomach hurt.

"Many things have been crooked in my life, but my head is finally straight." He regarded her soberly from his seat. "'Tis true I'd keep Ashwhite, and you'd have financial independence."

"You propose a marriage of convenience," she said carefully.

"No, I want a family."

The thought of kissing Ashwhite again sent flutters

to her belly, followed by the pang of something worse. Fear. A huge and looming presence that made her head spin. She blinked, willing the dizziness to pass.

"Lady Amelia, in the course of the past weeks, I have seen a young woman who is kind and generous. You are everything I'd want in a wife, and I find myself…" He paused, his lips unmoving. There was a question in his eyes, a precipice he desired to fling himself from.

Though a novice in the ways of romance, Amelia knew what he wanted to say. The emotion shone out of him. She tried for a deep breath, anything to take this throat-clutching fear from her, but her rib cage refused to expand. Toes curling, she whispered, "Don't say it."

"It needs to be said." Lord Ashwhite shifted as though he would come sit beside her.

Every nerve in her body was on edge. Her emotions ricocheted. Never had she felt so uncertain, so deliriously uncertain.

He didn't move, though, perhaps sensing her turmoil. "Lady Amelia, I am in love with you."

She shut her eyes, wanting to block him out. Needing to ignore the confidence in his eyes. If only he pleaded like a lost puppy, or demanded. She could resist those forms of manipulation. But his statement asked for nothing in return. It was a declaration that made her want to run away.

This reminded her of another time, another place.

Opening her eyes, she gave him a tight smile. "Those are words I've heard before."

He could not look more taken aback. "You have?"

"Yes, I was engaged once. It wasn't made public and Ev ran him off when—" She couldn't continue. The hurt was no longer a jagged, open wound, but the scar was tender. What would Lord Ashwhite think of her?

"When what?" His tone was soft.

She swallowed and stiffened her shoulders. "When I found him kissing a maid." She waved a hand, attempting to brush off any sympathy. "Oh, I know that this is common in the *haut ton*. I'm aware that wives are to look in a different direction or perhaps even find their own *amour*, but I could not put up with such a thing. I had thought he loved—" Again her voice broke, and this time she could not keep her eyes from stinging. Blinking, she stared at her fingers, which unmindfully clenched and unclenched. Clenched and unclenched.

Lord Ashwhite must look at her with distaste, or perhaps pity. She did not want either. She rushed on, "He was a rake in his heart, though every other part of him was respectable. When I stumbled upon them, he dismissed her and then had the audacity to tell me he loved me and she meant nothing to him." She shrugged, though it cost effort. Every muscle in her body ached from reigning in her emotions. "He continued to insist on his love, day after day, but it became clear by his actions that his version of love was not healthy for me."

"And what is your version of love?"

Her version? Dumbfounded, Amelia tore her gaze from her fingers and met the piercing challenge in his stare. Before she could answer, the carriage slowed and a man's shout could be heard.

"Whatever is going on?" She looked out the window and gawked at her brother riding fast alongside the carriage.

Unfortunately the carriage veered too much to the side and jolted. Hard.

Her hands flew up to brace herself. Lord Ashwhite was rousted from his seat. Unable to stop himself, he collided with her, breaking her hold and slamming her backward. Oxygen rushed from her being in one painful exhalation.

Lord Ashwhite slumped over her, his heaviness a weight crushing her lungs. She tapped his shoulder, which jutted near her chin. No response. She struggled to draw a deep breath, but her lungs protested. Healing aches from the previous carriage accident revived in her muscles. They cramped and the pain made her hiss.

She had to find a way to move him. His prone form suggested he'd hit his head. Trying not to panic or give in to the faintness edging her vision, she pushed at his body. Suddenly the door to the carriage flew open.

An unrelenting burst of sunlight speared into the carriage. Squinting, she brought her hand to her brow. A form stepped in front of the light.

"I knew it," Ev shrieked. There was no other word for the high-pitched sound of his voice. He lunged forward and she reared back, but he reached only for Ashwhite.

Grasping his clothes, Eversham hauled Ashwhite out of the carriage.

Chapter Twenty-Two

Immediately, air rushed into Amelia's cramping lungs. She struggled to a sitting position, ignoring the pains shooting through her body. Crawling forward, she pushed open the carriage door.

Eversham stood beside the road, anger twisting his facial expression. His hands were knotted at his sides. Ashwhite swayed in front of him.

"Ev, stop it!" She barreled out of the carriage. Her feet hit the ground hard, but she regained her balance and bolted forward. "Stop it, I said."

She reached Ev just as his fist connected with Ashwhite's cheekbone. The thud of impact sent a sickening sensation to curl her stomach. She yanked at Ev's arm, the cloth of his shirt fisting in her fingers. "Whatever are you trying to accomplish?"

Not waiting for his answer, she knelt beside Ashwhite, whose groan of pain spiked sympathy pangs in her heart. He pushed to a sitting position with her help. Two separate streams of blood trailed his face. One from the gash on his forehead, which accounted for his unconsciousness in the carriage, and the other from his nose.

Amelia shot the filthiest glare she could muster at

Eversham while she dragged her hankie from her reticule. "I shall be gentle," she murmured. She pressed the cloth to the gash, hoping to stem the flow.

This also gave her time to cool her temper. At the moment she wanted nothing more than to tackle her twin and grind his face in the dirt, just as she'd done when they were children. Gritting her teeth, she dabbed Ashwhite's wound.

She would not think of anything else right now. Not the closeness of their hearts or the words he'd uttered in the carriage. Just the remembrance made her heart hurt.

Behind her, Ev gasped for air. He'd evidently fatigued himself attempting to fight. Too much time behind a desk, no doubt. She pressed her lips together. Well, it must be done. She must confront him in the heat of the day. Thankfully no one else traveled the road today.

The Scottish lowlands rose in splendor around her but offered little in the way of shade. The scent of flowers and blood intermingled to provide an odd dissonance. Her gaze roved her surroundings, taking in the varied colors. Sap green for the land, and a mix of Prussian blue with ultramarine for the sky. She wanted to memorize this for a future painting.

Ashwhite stirred. She became aware of her knee resting near his thigh. He watched her in his way that seemed to suggest he understood things about herself that she wanted to remain secret.

She squared her shoulders. Fiddle-faddle. All of it. She must get herself together and gain control of the situation. She brought the handkerchief down and pressed it into Ashwhite's hand.

"Wipe your nose." Brushing off her skirt, she stood to face her wayward and extremely irritating brother. He had not regained himself, evidenced by the high color in his face and the huffing noises he still made.

She raised her brow at him. "Do you plan to assault Ashwhite further, or are we finished with the theatrics?"

He started to speak, but she lifted her hand.

"I'll not hear it, John. This is beyond the pale. Why, grabbing an unconscious man and beating him... I would not believe you capable of such a thing had I not seen it with my own eyes. Do you care to explain yourself? Here, in this hot and unrelenting Scottish sun? As you chose to stop our carriage in a most aggressive manner, thereby causing poor Ash—"

"I'm not poor," he grumbled behind her, though she noted he had not moved from his position.

"As I was saying—" she lifted her nose a bit higher for emphasis "—you've caused Ash to suffer a concussion. Not only is my dress ruined by perspiration and dirt, but also I am in pain and quite miffed with you." She put her hands on her hips. "I want an answer, and it had most certainly better be suitable, for I've had enough of your bullying tactics."

She felt it, too, a hard knot of determination in her belly, steel in her spine. Why, a lady could take only so much ear pulling until she fought back, and this was definitely the time to give a piece of her mind. What did it matter anyhow? She'd lost everything.

The thought brought a lump to her throat.

Eversham sputtered, clearly at a loss for words. As well he should be. Her anger at him had not abated. It had merely coalesced into a seething resentment that curled up inside, waiting to be unleashed.

Perhaps she should not be this angry. Perhaps it was not pleasing to God. She didn't know, and she wasn't sure how to make the anger leave, anyhow.

Ashwhite stood slowly, his pained movements increasing her ire. He glanced at Ev before moving to Amelia's side.

"Have you finished speaking, my dear?" The quiet intimacy of his words startled her.

"I did not give you leave to call me that," she said beneath her breath.

Eversham scowled, arms crossing and feet planting apart. She knew that look. He wanted to hit Ashwhite.

"You've got him all upset, and now he wants to clock me again," said Ashwhite. She heard a laugh in his voice but did not dare look at him for fear her heart would melt into a helpless puddle at his expensively shod feet.

"He arrived this way." She shifted away. How had he recovered so quickly? "I have everything under control."

"You always like to think that."

Her nose wrinkled at Ashwhite's ridiculous words.

"Would you two quit bickering? Amelia, get over here. We are going home." Her brother's tone made her want to pummel him.

"Not until I know what's going on."

"I'll tell you what's going on." Eversham pointed a finger at Ashwhite. "My so-called friend is a rake who has demeaned my sister in the lowest fashion."

"Nonsense. Whatever are you talking about?"

"I came to his estate to get you. When I heard you were in an accident… That is beyond the point. I found out that you two were in his carriage, heading to Gretna Green. Really, Ash? You couldn't even propose properly? You knew I'd say no, too, didn't you." It wasn't a question. Eversham's arms folded. "And so here I am, but too late to stop you, I suppose."

His look moved to her, and an unexpected fear

took root in her stomach at his expression. He almost appeared…sad. Why?

"I warned you," said Ev. "I warned you to leave her alone, but you ignored me. You've sullied her reputation, and so help me, if you break her heart—"

"You are ahead of yourself, brother." She laughed a hollow laugh. "Ashwhite and I are not married."

Eversham's face slacked.

"That's right." Her lips trembled, and all the fortitude she'd felt earlier fled beneath an excruciating wave of failure. It engulfed her as the enormity of her actions and how they'd affected her family slammed into her. Suddenly weary, body aching, she nodded. "Your sister has done it again."

"What Amelia means to say—" Ashwhite's arm slipped around her waist, a bulwark she didn't pull away from "—is that we left in a hurry to see your cousin Lydia marry."

Eversham gaped. "Lydia? But your note said you two were headed to Gretna Green." Though he saw Ashwhite's arm about Amelia, which was highly inappropriate, he said nothing.

"I apologize," Ashwhite said. "We received the news of the marriage and hastily left with little thought to the consequences. It seems your cousin has fallen in love with a military man who leaves this week for parts unknown. She longs to go with him and so, with her family's blessing, they decided to marry quickly."

"Is this true?" Ev posed the question to her.

She nodded, knowing she should step away from Ashwhite's support but unwilling to. Who knew when she'd ever feel this comfort again? And why had he come to her defense so brilliantly? All for love?

If only her brain would shut down. What she needed now was to paint, to escape, not to overthink.

"Your sister is exhausted. Shall we continue our journey?"

A grim expression crossed Ev's face. "You may leave, but Amelia will be going with me."

"Still doubt my honor?" Ashwhite's chuckle was dry.

"I know you are honorable, but you are not a man content with one woman for the rest of your life, and that is the kind of man my sister deserves."

Amelia blinked. Was there something she didn't know? Though lassitude still draped her spirits, a tiny tendril of fear unfurled within her.

"I told you I'd changed."

A hint of a smile tugged at Eversham's cheeks. "God changed you. It is what you claim, and perhaps it's true, but I'd rather not let my sister be your experiment."

"I am no man's experiment," she said before she could stop herself. "And God can change a person. Furthermore, I shall decide what I deserve, not you."

"Is our friendship done, then?" Ashwhite asked her brother quietly. A muscle flickered in his jaw. "I did not know you thought so low of me."

Amelia winced at the pain in his voice, yet that small fear was blossoming within her, her brother's words a fertilizer that brought forth fruit. She moved forward, realizing that Ashwhite's arm had hugged her for the longest time, and that she'd been comfortable in his embrace. Safe, even.

But not now, because her brother's accusations rang in her ears. "Why don't you want me to marry Ashwhite?" she asked him. She dared not look at Ash behind her as she inched forward, closer to the man who had both protected her and betrayed her.

Ev's jaw firmed in a signature look.

She pointed her finger at him. "You talk of what I deserve? A forthright answer on why a good man would get such words from you—I deserve that, Ev, and you know so."

His eyes flickered past her. She turned. Ashwhite dragged his fingers through his hair, rumpling it. The look of despair on his face brought her fears to full bloom.

"What did you do?" she whispered. Her mind raced, envisioning his winning smile, his charming personality. She'd never met him before this year. Never seen him at Almack's or soirees. Not even balls. Yet he'd been an eligible son of a marquis...

He raised his eyes to meet hers, and in their depths she saw a truth she hadn't expected.

"You might have called me a rake once upon a time, my lady."

Her jaw dropped. She snapped it closed as a thousand tiny explosions sparked within. "I don't believe it."

His smile was self-deprecating. He shrugged and his lips curled. "Perhaps once a rake, always a rake, eh, Ev? Probably good he stopped me now before I ruined your life. After all, infatuation fades and then insufferable boredom sets in. You wouldn't have been happy with me, Lady Amelia."

She could not speak past the pain billowing up inside her. This made no sense. At no time had she sensed anything disingenuous in the man before her. Nothing to give her pause... Her mind stuttered. The first time she'd met him, that woman... The pieces clicked, and she remembered why his *lady friend* had appeared familiar.

She was an actress.

He kept company with actresses! It appalled her, though not for their profession, but for the reasons he would get slapped by one. What had he done? Who had he been?

Who was he now? The way he stood, languid and defiant, more handsome than anyone she'd ever seen, spoke of a past she knew nothing of. A past she could not begin to fathom.

Her heart split within her chest. She used resolve to pull herself together, to regard him calmly when she wanted to scream with frustration and confusion.

"Thank you for the use of your carriage, Lord Ashwhite." She patted at an invisible spot of dirt on her skirt, gathering her composure. There was but one way to exit this situation.

With breeding and excellent manners.

"Take care and good day."

The ride to Ashwhite was torturously slow. Finally Spencer arrived. He entered the house. Though the floor glowed with polish and fresh flowers had been set out, he had never felt more lonely or disgusted with himself. Had Ev spent the entire ride home regaling Amelia with tales of Spencer's past decadence, inebriation and gambling? That had been his life for too many years. And there were worse things he was sure Ev would not sully a lady's ears with. How he bitterly regretted those years! Trying to prove himself capable of making his own choices. Foolish with his money, time and affections.

He trudged to his room, not bothering to see Cook or nip a few cookies.

His stomach would not tolerate anything tonight. Not food, leastwise. The temptation to head to the nearest pub prickled through him, growing in intensity.

He'd almost made it to his room when his mother called his name. Reluctantly he turned around. She came up the stairs, concern etched across her brow. "Where is Lady Amelia?"

"She went home."

"Oh." His mother's hand went to her throat. "I had thought, or hoped…"

"That we'd run off to marry?"

The look on her face confirmed his suspicion. He'd never felt worse. Sourness coated his stomach. "Nay, the lady refused my offer of marriage." He dug deep for the carefree, mocking smile he'd worn during his youth. It came back naturally, and he flashed it at his mother. "It seems that the combination of my rakish ways and her lack of affection toward me will conspire to cause us to lose Ashwhite. That and the ridiculous stipulation you and your husband put together." To call such a man *Father* went against all that felt right at this moment.

No, nothing felt right.

Maybe never again.

He bowed to the waist, feeling the mockery twisting through him in poisonous vines, choking any semblance of morality he might have discovered this past year. Despite the Spirit's nudging, despite his intention to go to bed, some other part of him prodded him back down the stairs, past the shocked expression on his mother's face. One thing might comfort him tonight, and it would be exactly what everyone expected from him.

Exactly what he really was.

Chapter Twenty-Three

Amelia finished her final letter to the patrons of the Prison Reform Society and put it on her stack of teetering mail. Between writing invitations, preparing for the upcoming soiree and dodging her brother and sister-in-law, she was exhausted.

She tried to avoid that ever-present memory as well, though it came to her in her dreams.

Lord Ashwhite and the way he'd said he was in love with her... Would a rake sound so sincere? She tried to remember Lord Markham, but his memory had faded so that she could not even recall the sound of his voice, let alone the color of his eyes. She seemed to think he'd sounded honest, but what had she known? They'd danced a trifle of dances. Their carriage rides had been chaperoned, and all had been proper.

Lord Ashwhite had never pretended to be anything other than himself.

Shoving her chair back, she shook her head. No, she refused to think of him. The entire trip home had been silence between her and Ev. She'd felt his regard, his questions, but they knew each other well enough to know that no civil words could be passed. As soon as they arrived home, he'd been called to London for his duties in the House of Lords, leaving her with Harriet this past week.

Thankfully her sister-in-law still hid in her bedchamber.

Amelia winced at the unkind thought. She stood, swiped the letters from the desk and proceeded to leave the study. Today marked one more day of political shenanigans, albeit from the countryside. After delivering the letters to a servant to be mailed later, she went up the stairs.

She paused outside Harriet's room. Dinnertime was a quiet affair. She brought a book to the table, and her sister-in-law often took her meals in her room. Perhaps she should invite her to lunch today? Offer the proverbial olive branch, propose a truce?

Her heart quailed within. She did not wish to bear the brunt of Harriet's anger and pain. She could not imagine how it felt to lose a child. As she read the Bible, she'd been realizing how beneficial it could be to show someone a bit of kindness. Particularly those whom she'd like to hit over the head with a book.

She paused to enjoy the mental image and then swiped it from her mind.

She had not been there for Harriet in the past, but times had changed, and slowly so was she. She knocked on the door.

"Yes?" came the plaintive answer.

Amelia wrinkled her nose. Now or never, she supposed.

"It's Amelia. May I come in?"

The silence that followed spoke quite loudly, but she waited anyhow. If she planned to make amends, then she'd have to be pushy.

And Lady Amelia Baxley had never worried about

being pushy. When the silence stretched to a ridiculous amount of time, she knocked a second time.

"Harriet, may I enter?"

"Come in." Definitely a more querulous tone this time.

Amelia set her chin and opened the door. Light filled the room. Harriet sat in a rocker near the window, a pile of colorful squares at her feet and a needle in her hand. She kept busy. That was a good sign. Amelia came closer. Pretty squares. Soft pastels.

"Good morning, my lady. You are making a quilt?"

Harriet's bright blue eyes lifted from her lap. The dark circles were gone, and her skin held a healthy pink glow. Not knowing where to sit or what to do with her hands, Amelia stood near the window and peered outside. The summer sun made the grass look like a verdant ocean.

"Would you care to go for a horse ride?" she asked.

"No, it is better for me to stay here. I'm not feeling well."

"Still?" Amelia frowned. "I would think you'd be almost recovered…but forgive me. I know nothing of these things." *Foolish tongue.*

"Amelia, I've been meaning to speak with you about something."

That sounded unpleasant. Amelia braced herself. "Yes?"

"The things I said about you causing my miscarriages were…" Harriet looked down at the blanket in her lap. "I'm ashamed to say they were cruel words and unbefitting of a lady of my station. You did not deserve such accusations. Ev shall be apologizing to you, as well."

Amelia did not know how to respond. Humbled and contrite, she knelt before her sister and placed her hands upon hers. "No, you were deeply hurt, and my actions have been thoughtless. I did not want to live beneath the rule of another and did not consider how my lifestyle might affect you."

"But that is just it. You did not affect me."

Amelia met Harriet's dewy gaze, and her heart twisted. "There is no more need of apologies. I forgive you and will do my utmost to cause our family shame no longer."

Though Harriet managed a wan smile, her eyes glistened. "I confess I do not understand your desire to dirty yourself with oils or to write inflammatory letters. This business of yours, that I do understand. Every woman deserves a man like my husband."

"Many years ago I wrote a scathing letter about your father." Amelia paused, searching her sister-in-law's face. "Though I cannot regret my opinions of his actions, I am deeply sorry for hurting you in the process."

Harriet inclined her head, the visual forgiveness easing the vise in Amelia's chest.

"So it's true that you love my brother?"

"He is an amazing man. I know that I am not an easy woman. I have expectations and perhaps am too needy, but he genuinely likes me. I make him laugh, and I can't say that I've ever accomplished such a thing with anyone else."

Amelia kept a straight face. Ev laughed with her? It was incomprehensible, but then again, what did she know? Ashwhite had turned out to be an accomplished rake, and she'd not once suspected his true nature.

Harriet let out a blissful sigh that sounded a little too much like Lydia's for comfort. "A man who can be trusted to do what's right is worth his weight in gold. One who will protect you and is kind… But I suppose you know about these traits, as you find husbands for women like me?"

Amelia nodded. Perhaps those traits should be higher on her checklist.

"I want you to hold that soiree for Ashwhite. While you were gone, I took the liberty of arranging for an orchestra and setting a menu."

Now Amelia felt like crying. She blinked hard. "Why would you do such a thing?"

"Ashwhite is a good man. When he returned from the Americas, I saw the change in him." Harriet blushed. "Shame on me for withholding something that could bring him further happiness."

"My lady...I am speechless." Could it be true? Could Ashwhite truly be the man she believed him to be? Her sister-in-law had no reason to say otherwise.

"I'm tiring, Lady Amelia, but there is one more thing you should know before you go. Ev and I are expecting." Harriet broke into a grin.

Amelia straightened, shock rippling through her. "Why, that's wonderful! But how? I mean, the miscarriage?"

"The doctor was mistaken. When he visited the next day, he detected a faint heartbeat but waited to tell me until he was sure. Now it is certain."

"I am so very happy for you," said Amelia. She leaned forward and embraced Harriet.

Her sister returned the hug. "I didn't expect love with Ev," she said into Amelia's hair, "but it found me nevertheless. Should love find you, do not turn it away."

"I've had quite enough."

Ashwhite's mother barged up to him, interrupting his stint with a hammer and nail. He paused in the common labor to take in her flushed cheeks. "With what?"

"With you. With this." Her hands arced through the

air. "Whatever are you about fixing fences when you've a woman to win back to your side?"

"She's better off without me." Ashwhite placed the nail in the board and, in one strong swoop, drove it an inch closer to home.

"Says who?" His mother poked him in the leg.

He smashed the nail again.

"Quit visiting the pub every night. You're not a rake anymore, and I read those letters you sent your father."

Spencer bolted up. "You what?"

"That's right." Her face paled a bit, but she didn't back down. "He gave them to me to read, and that is how we decided you were ready for a wife."

He didn't know how to answer. He could be angry, but all his anger had been expelled within the past few days, replaced by a morose certainty that the one woman he wanted might be forever outside his reach. And perhaps she was better off that way.

"Son, go to Lady Amelia. Isn't your soiree tomorrow evening?"

"It is."

"Then, go. If she will not have you, we might lose Ashwhite, but I still have my unentailed property."

"We will keep Ashwhite. I will see to it." And he prayed God helped him love another the way he did Amelia.

"You're a good son, Spencer. I'm very proud of you." His mother hugged him then. Chest constricting, he returned the embrace. She might not have been what he needed as a child, but she was what he needed now.

"I haven't been to the pubs every night," he found himself confessing. Though the temptation to seek solace in old, empty ways had been strong, he'd had the strength to continue on the path God put him on.

She pulled away, relief clearly marking her features. "Where have you been?"

"Riding. Getting rid of energy. Praying."

"And has God answered you?" The concern in her eyes roused a deep love that swelled in his chest. He knew that look. The one she'd worn when he'd fallen from a tree as a brash ten-year-old. The time fever had raged through him and she'd happened to be home. Funny how bitterness wiped good memories from a heart. They rushed to him now. He remembered her touch upon his brow. She'd stayed with him in his room, refusing to leave until the fever had broken.

"Not yet," he said.

"He will, one way or the other." She put her hand against his cheek. "Follow His leading."

Spencer nodded. "Thank you, Mother. For everything."

The following hours were busy. Seeing his mother, their talk, had actually brought him a certain level of peace that in turn had inspired a rush of ideas. First he dug through the library until he located Lady Amelia's painting. It belonged in a London gallery, and he intended to see it put there. He gave a servant instructions on where to deliver it, and when his bags were packed, he, too, left Ashwhite.

He had a ball to attend and a lady to woo.

There was no time to waste.

Yes, there were other ladies he could marry, but he'd rather try again with Lady Amelia. She hadn't actually told him no. She'd been shocked, thinking of a past love. If she held his mistakes against him, if that was her reason for refusal, then he'd not bother her again.

But if she was merely afraid, then he could soothe her. These past few days had taught him that he wasn't the man he used to be, no matter what Ev or anyone else thought. He'd gone to the pub the first night but turned around.

It wasn't where he'd wanted to be, and the only lady he wanted to hold wore a pair of spectacles she used like a weapon.

His time in London was fruitful. He dealt with Lord Dudley, whom the constable had jailed with multiple charges. His cousin would have a hard time, but Spencer left knowing all would turn out well.

He had to rush to make it to his own soiree. It was surprisingly packed. A crush.

He pushed past people, searching Ev's ballroom for Lady Amelia.

There. In a frothy confection of creams and blues and some kind of green. The hair piled high on her head revealed her slender neck and strong bone structure. For a moment he admired the view. The proud set to her shoulders and the line of her profile. Such a perfect nose for an impossibly, amazingly imperfect woman.

He tapped her shoulder after an arduous trek through the crowded room. She pivoted, delight etched across her face. Behind her spectacles, her eyes sparkled.

"Isn't the turnout fabulous? You will have your pick, my lord." That fan of hers was out, waving wildly. Did he detect jealousy in her tone?

"You have done a noteworthy job, worth a hundred more than what I'm paying you." He searched her face, but she was blank to him, offering nothing but a canvas of what she wanted him to see.

All the determination that had buoyed him for the past day and a half faltered. Dare he face another rejection? As he took in the dogged jut to her jaw and the gentle curve of her lips, both testimonies to the personality beneath the skin, he knew he dared.

A prize was worth the challenge, and never had he worked so hard to regain a woman.

"And whom do you suggest I choose?" he asked mildly, hiding his feelings for now. After all, he was more skilled than she in this game of flirtation, and though he loved her, he must be smart about things. He did not wish for his heart to be completely smashed.

"Do you have the list I gave you?"

"I discarded it." He winked at her.

She flushed. "My lord, that is not appropriate given the setting."

"But you see, I do highly inappropriate things. As a former rake, it's in my nature."

"Pish posh." She tapped his arm with her fan, her color high. "That is ridiculous. I would never find a wife for a rake."

"And yet you work for me."

"First, my lord, you must understand that I do not work for you. Second, you are a former rake. There's quite a difference, you see."

Weight he didn't realize he carried lifted from his shoulders. Without it, his smile loosened. "I believe there is a difference, and I'm relieved you know so."

Music for a quadrille started. He leaned over and peeked at her dance card, inhaling a delicious whiff of her perfume. She jerked away, brow raised.

"If you want a dance, simply ask, though I must warn you that I have an atrocious habit of stepping on feet."

Spencer laughed. "That is an outright falsehood. But I shall take you up on the offer and prove you wrong." Though he enjoyed the repartee, he wanted to steer her closer to talk of marriage. This delightful lady was the one he wanted to be with.

Forever.

As they danced, Lady Amelia said, "A bird told me there is a mysterious painting hanging in an upscale London gallery. It is signed AB."

True surprise shot through him. News spread fast. Unless the little bird was his mother. He wouldn't put it past her.

"I've also heard Lord Dudley is in custody. A shameful thing he did, cheating honest people of their money."

They twirled again. He counted down for the end of the dance. He had a plan, and her flirtatious ways, while beguiling and adorable, did nothing to further his goals. He wanted to sit her down, demand she admit her love, suggest they marry and then kiss.

Yes, he most definitely wanted to kiss her.

The quadrille was torturous, but it finally ended, and he had her to himself. *Almost.* A man came up to inquire about her dance card, but before she could answer, Spencer snarled and tugged her toward the punch table.

"How about a bit of drink?" he asked.

She pulled away. "How about a bit of manners? You were quite rude to that young man. He will think you gave him a cut."

Chagrined, Spencer nodded. His desires were making him impatient. "I'll fix things later."

"Very good." She joined him at the table. "I have more to tell you. God and I have been talking."

He almost choked on his punch.

"Don't look so alarmed. I don't actually hear a voice. I just feel that peace you mentioned. Surrendering truly does bring about a wonderful freedom. I would have never known that if you hadn't told me." The teasing note left her voice. She took the glass he handed her and swallowed her punch in one long gulp.

Probably the most unladylike thing he'd seen her do.

Oh, wait. He was sure he'd seen her do the same when she'd dressed up like a man. Biting back his smile, he steered her toward chairs set against the wall. "I'm happy something I said made an impression."

"Indeed it did. In fact—" she drew a deep breath and stopped walking, halting him "—I have a solution for you."

"A solution?"

"To your current dilemma."

"Ah, my wife dilemma."

"Yes, that." There was pink in her cheeks again.

Perplexed, he sipped his punch and scanned the ballroom. Many danced, but he caught curious stares averted at the last moment. "I have a solution, too, but you go first."

"During our time apart, it occurred to me that I have been going about things all wrong. Putting logic before emotion, ruling out the necessity of feelings. It has become clear they work best hand in hand."

His attention centered on her face as what she was saying began to sink in. "That sounds pragmatic."

"Yes, well, I do try. And my solution is…" She licked her lips, and he saw nerves in her movements, but in her eyes he saw something far different.

Did he dare hope?

"Your solution is?" he prompted her.

"It involves a bit of finagling, but I believe two levelheaded people can handle such a thing. Eventually, leastwise."

"I am still waiting to hear this solution, my lady." If

she didn't say it soon, he'd haul her up and kiss her in front of the entire room.

Her fan waved, and he stopped it in one movement. Her eyes widened.

"Confess it now, before I tell you my solution and ruin everything," he warned.

"Considering our mutual compatibility, our friendship and your time constraint, I believe it your best interest to marry me."

"And is there anything else you wish to say?" His arms ached. One more moment, one more sentence and then a kiss to seal the deal.

"How did you know?" Her eyes glittered, and this time he realized it was with unshed tears. "I love you dearly, you pushy, insufferable—"

He did not let her finish. He pulled her against him and planted his lips on hers. She was as sweet as he'd expected, as alive and beautiful as he didn't deserve.

But God had given him more than he believed he could have, and hers was a love he'd not lose.

She returned the kiss, her arms encircling him. Her temerity might cause a scandal were it not for the imminent announcement of their engagement. She knew the rules well enough, he supposed. Well enough to break them, which he had to admit held an irresistible draw.

For now, there were only the two of them, their melding hearts and the God who'd brought them together.

Epilogue

Amelia smiled down at the infant cradled in her arms. Little Johnny turned three months today. His cousin, Roger, toddled over to Harriet, who sat at the desk balancing the books.

Johnny made the sweetest mewling noise Amelia had ever heard and she sighed.

"I never would have taken you for a sighing mama," Harriet remarked, her head bent over the ledgers.

"I adore children." Amelia grinned as Roger put his pudgy hands on Harriet's skirts and yanked with all his might. Of course she did not move. He plopped on the floor, his face turning a deep shade of red as he primed his vocal chords.

"Oh, no, not again." Harriet shoved up from her chair and plucked him from the floor, but it was too late. Her determined son had not reached his goal and he must let the entire world know so.

"Here, read him the post. He enjoys a good story." Amelia handed Harriet the letters from the table beside her chair. Ev's wife had not yet had a chance to sort the mail, as Roger kept her quite busy throughout the day.

Unlike little Johnny, who insisted on sleeping throughout the day and squalling throughout the night.

"I am so happy you decided to visit today," Harriet said, settling into a chair opposite Amelia. The rustle of paper caught Roger's attention and he stopped his dreadfully adorable cries.

"Mama?" he questioned as his fingers sought to rip the papers from his mother's hands. Poor Harriet looked a sight as she wrestled the letters away from him.

"There is a letter for you…" Harriet's brow lifted.

"Why ever would it come here?" How very odd. Amelia shifted in her seat. "Perhaps it is from Lydia? I do worry how she is faring so far away."

"India, is it?"

"Yes, her husband is with the East India Company." Footsteps sounded, followed by the entrance of Ev and Spencer. While her brother went to his wife and rescued her from their wiggling son, Spencer planted a soft kiss on her lips. He lingered.

Contentment spread through Amelia. How had she thought she could live without this?

"How is our dumpling this fine morning?" Spencer's eyes glittered with amusement.

"You know very well that he is sleeping, as is his wont. Don't forget—" she beamed him an innocent smile "—tonight is your turn to rock him to sleep."

"Amelia?" Harriet's voice interrupted them. She held up a letter. "It is from Rutherford Ladd on Bow Street."

"Oh!" Amelia pressed her lips together. She hadn't quite gotten around to discussing this little matter with Spencer. She avoided looking at him.

"Do read it aloud, Harriet. I'm awash in curiosity." Spencer's dry voice nudged a bit of a smile to Amelia's face.

Surely he would understand, once she explained.

Harriet's nose wrinkled. "It looks to be a report of some sort. Very tedious to read, indeed."

"Indeed," murmured Spencer.

Amelia felt his eyes on her, boring a neat hole right into the fabric of her conscience.

"Very well," she said stiffly. "I happen to know of a young lady with a horrible limp. She's a diamond of the first water, agreeable in every way, but she is unable to dance. Remember the young woman who plays the pianoforte as though she had been born to it? She is Lady Hazelthorn's daughter. Her mother kindly asked me for advice, as this is the girl's first Season."

Harriet gasped. "You are not thinking… Surely not. Eversham, what do you have to say to her?"

He laughed and held his hands in the air. "My sister is Ash's problem now, my dear."

"I daresay I am no one's problem, and well you know it." Amelia smiled down at Johnny, who remained sleeping. "We've plenty of time to talk about this. Let us enjoy the rest of our afternoon in peace."

"We certainly shall." Spencer crouched down and ran one finger down their baby's cheek. "Up to your old ways, are you?" His gaze slid up to hers, and she felt an enormous heat emblazon her cheeks.

"It is only to help someone, darling." Her voice caught at the intensity in his eyes. How did he still manage to disarm her with only a look? Even after a year of marriage, she felt incapable of intentionally displeasing him. "I will not be involved, if you wish it."

The words pained her to say, for she did truly believe she'd found the perfect match for Lady Hazelthorn's daughter, but her family came first.

Ash smiled crookedly, his heart in his eyes. She could

not but respond with a smile, which she knew must look quite mushy.

Behind Ashwhite, Harriet rolled her eyes.

He leaned forward and gave Amelia another heart-stirring kiss. Then he pressed his cheek against hers and said against her ear, "My sweet, indomitable Amelia… what say you to a bit of an investigation?"

* * * * *

Dear Reader,

Thank you so much for taking the time to read Amelia and Spencer's story. I truly enjoyed writing this book and wish I had a bit of Amelia's pluck and Spencer's charm. They are characters who will stay long with me. Not only did they live in my imagination, but they accompanied me through one of the darkest times in my life. As I wrote their pain, their redemption and finally their healing, I also experienced my own.

Please forgive any factual errors I may have made. I adore Regency romances, but I am still learning my way around the many details of that era.

I really love connecting with readers and writers. Please feel free to contact me through email, jessica_nelson7590@yahoo.com, or on my website, www.jessicanelson.net.

I can be found on Facebook and Twitter, talking books and plotting romances.

Happy reading!

Jessica Nelson

COMING NEXT MONTH FROM
Love Inspired® Historical

Available October 6, 2015

A DADDY FOR CHRISTMAS
Christmas in Eden Valley
by Linda Ford
Chivalry demands cowboy Blue Lyons help any woman in need, so he offers widow Clara Weston—and her daughters—shelter and food when they have nowhere to go. And whether he wants it or not, Clara and her daughters are soon chipping away at his guarded heart.

A WESTERN CHRISTMAS
by Renee Ryan & Louise M. Gouge
In two brand-new novellas, Christmas comes to the West and brings with it the chance for love, both old and new.

HER COWBOY DEPUTY
Wyoming Legacy
by Lacy Williams
Injured and far from home, sheriff's deputy Matt White finds love in the most unexpected of places with a former childhood friend.

FAMILY IN THE MAKING
Matchmaking Babies
by Jo Ann Brown
Arthur, Lord Trelawney, needs lessons in caring for children, so he decides to practice with the rescued orphans sheltering at his family estate. A practical idea...until he meets their lovely nurse, Maris Oliver.

LIHCNM0915

REQUEST YOUR FREE BOOKS!

2 FREE INSPIRATIONAL NOVELS
PLUS 2 FREE MYSTERY GIFTS

Love Inspired HISTORICAL

YES! Please send me 2 FREE Love Inspired® Historical novels and my 2 FREE mystery gifts (gifts are worth about $10). After receiving them, if I don't wish to receive any more books, I can return the shipping statement marked "cancel." If I don't cancel, I will receive 4 brand-new novels every month and be billed just $4.99 per book in the U.S. or $5.49 per book in Canada. That's a saving of at least 17% off the cover price. It's quite a bargain! Shipping and handling is just 50¢ per book in the U.S. and 75¢ per book in Canada.* I understand that accepting the 2 free books and gifts places me under no obligation to buy anything. I can always return a shipment and cancel at any time. Even if I never buy another book, the two free books and gifts are mine to keep forever.

102/302 IDN GH6Z

Name	(PLEASE PRINT)	

Address		Apt. #

City	State/Prov.	Zip/Postal Code

Signature (if under 18, a parent or guardian must sign)

Mail to the **Reader Service:**
IN U.S.A.: P.O. Box 1867, Buffalo, NY 14240-1867
IN CANADA: P.O. Box 609, Fort Erie, Ontario L2A 5X3

Want to try two free books from another series?
Call 1-800-873-8635 or visit www.ReaderService.com.

* Terms and prices subject to change without notice. Prices do not include applicable taxes. Sales tax applicable in N.Y. Canadian residents will be charged applicable taxes. Offer not valid in Quebec. This offer is limited to one order per household. Not valid for current subscribers to Love Inspired Historical books. All orders subject to credit approval. Credit or debit balances in a customer's account(s) may be offset by any other outstanding balance owed by or to the customer. Please allow 4 to 6 weeks for delivery. Offer available while quantities last.

Your Privacy—The Reader Service is committed to protecting your privacy. Our Privacy Policy is available online at www.ReaderService.com or upon request from the Reader Service.

We make a portion of our mailing list available to reputable third parties that offer products we believe may interest you. If you prefer that we not exchange your name with third parties, or if you wish to clarify or modify your communication preferences, please visit us at www.ReaderService.com/consumerschoice or write to us at Reader Service Preference Service, P.O. Box 9062, Buffalo, NY 14240-9062. Include your complete name and address.

LIH15

"You're living here with the children," Zack said. *"Alone?"*

"This is our home." Lizzie faced him, a petite woman whose auburn hair suddenly appeared as if streaked with various shades of reds under the autumn sun. Her vivid green eyes and young, innocent face made her seem vulnerable, but she must be a strong woman if she could manage all seven of his nieces and nephews—and stand defiantly before him as she was now without backing down. He felt a glimmer of admiration for her.

"*Koom.* We're about to have our midday meal. Join us. You must have come a long way." She bit her lip as she briefly met his gaze.

Zack still couldn't believe that Abraham was dead. His older brother had been only thirty-five years old. "What happened to my *brooder*?"

Lizzie went pale. "He fell," she said in a choked voice, "from the barn loft." He saw her hands clutch at the hem of her apron. "He broke his neck and died instantly."

Zack felt shaken by the mental image. "I'm sorry. I know it's hard." He, too, felt the loss. It hurt to realize that he'd never see Abraham again.

LIEXP0915R

"He was a *goot* man." She didn't look at him when she bent to pick up her basket, then straightened. "Are you coming in?" she asked as she finally met his gaze.

He nodded and then followed her as she started toward the house. He was surprised to see her uneven gait as she walked ahead of him, as if she'd injured her leg and limped because of the pain. "Lizzie, are *ya* hurt?" he asked compassionately.

She halted, then faced him with her chin tilted high, her eyes less than warm. "I'm not hurt," she said crisply. "I'm a cripple." And with that, she turned away and continued toward the house, leaving him to follow her.

Zack studied her back with mixed feelings. Concern. Worry. Uneasiness. He frowned as he watched her struggle to open the door. He stopped himself from helping, sensing that she wouldn't be pleased. Could a crippled, young nineteen-year-old woman raise a passel of *kinner* alone?

Don't miss
THE AMISH MOTHER by Rebecca Kertz,
available October 2015 wherever
Love Inspired® books and ebooks are sold.

SPECIAL EXCERPT FROM

Love Inspired HISTORICAL

Chivalry demands cowboy Blue Lyons help any woman in need, so he offers widow Clara Weston—and her daughters—shelter and food when they have nowhere to go. And whether he wants it or not, Clara and her daughters are soon chipping away at his guarded heart.

Read on for a sneak preview of
A DADDY FOR CHRISTMAS,
available in October 2015 from Love Inspired Historical!

Clara turned, squatted and swept Libby into her arms. "What would I do without my sweet girls?" She signaled Eleanor to join them and hugged them both.

Blue turned away to hide the pain that must surely envelop his face even as it claimed every corner of his heart. That joy had been stolen from him, leaving him an empty shell of a man.

The girls left their mother's arms and Libby caught his hand. "Mr. Blue, did you see how full we got your buckets?" She dragged him to the doorway where they'd left the pails. Each one was packed hard with snow. "Didn't we do good?"

"You did indeed."

She looked up at him with blue expectant eyes.

What did she want?

"Did we earn a hug?" she asked.

His insides froze then slowly melted with the warmth of her trust. He bent over and hugged her then reached for

Eleanor who came readily to let him wrap his arm about her and pull her close.

Over the top of the girls' heads Clara's gaze pinned him back. She didn't need to say a word for him to hear her warning loud and clear. *Be careful with my children's affections.*

He had every intention of being careful. Not only with their affections but his own. That meant he must stop the talk and memories of his family. Must mind his own business when it came to questions about Clara's activities.

She could follow whatever course of action she chose.

So long as it didn't put her or the girls in danger, a little voice insisted. But he couldn't imagine she would ever do that.

He had no say in any of her choices whether or not they were risky. And that's just the way he wanted it.

Don't miss
A DADDY FOR CHRISTMAS
by Linda Ford,
available October 2015 wherever
Love Inspired® Historical books and ebooks are sold.